SAVING THE GAME

CHICAGO RED TAILS
BOOK 5

SUSAN RENEE

Saving the GAME

Cover art by Jack'd Up Book Covers

Editing by Brandi Zelenka, Notes in the Margin

Proofreading by Sarah Pilcher

Reader Team: Kristan Anderson, Stephani Brown, Jenn Hager, Jennifer Wilson

Formatting by Douglas M. Huston

❀ Created with Vellum

To Matt E. for being that guy who jumps down the Urban Dictionary rabbit hole and learns some of the most random and gross NSFW definitions that make me laugh hard enough to even consider including them in a book.

Also, to @anniemiles33 (tiktok) for coming up with the very first sentence of this book! Love your inspiration!

1

QUINTON

"Dude, my love for you is like diarrhea," Hawken professes to Dex as he shoves a few more fries into his mouth to keep from laughing. "I just can't hold it in."

Clearing my throat, I pull Hawken's plate of fries away from him, grinning when he scowls at me as I slide the plate toward Dex. "Dexter I'm pretty sure your bromance boyfriend just said his love for you is shit."

Laughing, Dex grabs a few fries from Hawken's shared plate and tosses them in his mouth. "Trust me, I think I'm beginning to believe him. Chose my sister over me and everything."

"She's a lot prettier than you, and what can I say?" Hawken shrugs. "She sucks my dick better than you do, man."

Dex frowns and throws one of his fries on the table. "Fuck. And I watched tutorials for hours and everything."

Zeke nudges Hawken's arm, chuckling. "He means porn, bro. He watched porn for hours."

"Listen Dex, I've got this all figured out," I tell him with confidence. Lifting the hem of my shirt, I hold it out for him. "Feel my shirt. Do you feel that?"

Dex reaches out and rubs the fabric between his fingers. "Yeah."

"That's boyfriend material right there, man." I wink at him. "Fuck Hawken. There's a new bromance in town." Instead of the French fries Hawken's been gnawing on, I pass Dex my plate of pretzel bites and beer cheese.

The guys laugh as Dex rubs his chin pretending to consider my proposal.

"I do enjoy a good cheese," he says. "And if the next round is on you, I might just have to take you up on the offer, Quinton. Be a good boy and I might even let you grab my ass occasionally."

I sigh like a lovesick teenager. "Be still my heart. Of course, the next round is on me." I stand from our booth. "Be right back."

I head to the bar and order Dex and I another round, saying hello to a few of the mingling fans from out of town who aren't used to seeing the team hang out in a public bar. Pringle's has been good to us for years so most of the regulars know this tends to be our hangout spot. Occasionally though, we get a few newcomers who are shocked to see us here. We're just grateful we have a safe place to hang out and be ourselves once in a while and the management does a fantastic job of helping foster that kind of environment for us.

Cathy, the bartender, hands me my drinks and I thank her, turning to walk back to our booth when someone catches my attention.

"Yes. Quinton, Mom. His name is Quinton Shay."

My head turns toward the female voice when I hear my name. A woman seated at the bar is talking on her cell phone. She's facing away from me so I can't see her face, but hearing my name always makes me take notice. My parents weren't going for normal when they picked my name. They couldn't just settle on Sean, Mike, or Jeff. Nope. They had to decide on a unique name that always had me standing near the back of the line in elementary school. Quinton is not a name you hear often these days.

"What do you mean what does he do? He's a famous hockey player. I told you that."

That's right babe. Just another famous hockey player.

"Oh yeah. He's a super great guy. Total dreamboat. The whole package," she says. My brows peak in response as I stand behind her eavesdropping.

Well, well, well. Dreamboat huh? Maybe I'm gettin' lucky tonight.

"I mean, his schedule is really busy, you know? With games and his charity work and all, so I don't get to see him every day but we've been together for about six months now."

My expression changes from amusement to shock and then right back to amusement.

Who the heck is this girl?

"Dinner?" she squeaks. "Umm, yeah. He might be able to do that."

I tilt my head, watching her from behind with morbid curiosity. She brings a palm to her forehead and sighs. "I'll ask him but with short notice and all, you know...he might not be able to make it."

Wow.

This girl's got balls.

There's got to be a story here and I kind of want to know it.

For shits and giggles of course.

Noticing she's drinking the same thing I'm holding in my hand I linger a bit to listen to the end of her conversation, ignoring Dex's request for another beer.

"Alright. I'll see him in the morning but uh, I'll text him tonight and see if he can make it...yeah. Okay. Bye, Mom."

She lays her phone down on the bar, takes a deep breath, and then drains the rest of the drink in front of her. I know I could walk away from this. By all means I *should* walk away from this. Maybe it's just my lightened mood because of our upcoming All-star break or maybe I'm straight up stunned by this woman's audacity because last time I checked, I'm not only very single, but I also haven't been on an actual date in years. Whatever this is, I'm intrigued.

If the guys were to hear what just happened, they'd be egging me on to hit on the girl and have myself a fun night. Confidence is attractive in a woman and she surely has that, but something seems off the more I watch her. She's not joking with a friend. She's not texting someone else. Not talking to anyone else, so what gives?

Why the lie?

She finally turns and when I see her face I know I've seen her somewhere before. She's dressed in a pair of tight black pants. Maybe they're leggings, I can't tell, and an oversized sweatshirt that hangs off her shoulder. Her black bra strap is on display. Her chestnut brown hair is tied up in a messy bun, but it's the bandana bow that's making me scroll through my mental rolodex because I know I've seen this woman before.

I don't know what makes me to do it. Maybe sheer dumb curiosity but here I am sliding one of my beers in front of her.

No turning back now.

"So, we're meeting the parents, I hear?"

Her jaw hangs open when I lower myself into the seat next to her and she realizes who I am.

"Oh, my God!" She gives herself a face palm, a goofy smile on her face as she shakes her head. "I totally deserve this, don't I? This is what happens to people like me."

I take a sip of my beer and smile back at her. "People like you? Do you mean women who phone a friend or in your case, a parent, and lie to them about dating hockey players?"

"Shit. You heard all that?"

I laugh this time. "Kind of hard to miss when I was standing just a couple feet away."

"Oh fuuuudge." She brings her hands up to her blushing cheeks. "I am SOOO so sorry. God, you probably think I'm the biggest psycho." Her eyes grow into huge saucers. "I swear I'm not a stalker or anything."

"It's fine. Really," I tell her, mesmerized by her mossy green eyes. "Forgive me, but I feel like I know you from somewhere and I can't for the life of me figure out where. What's your name?"

She takes a sip of the beer I gave her. Part of me wants to chastise her for accepting an open drink from a guy. I might be a famous hockey player but we're not all fine,

5

upstanding men. "Oh. I'm Kinsley Kendrick. I took pictures at Hawken and Rory's wedding in the arena. Maybe you saw me there?"

"Yes!" I sit up taller, pointing my finger at her. "That's it. I remember now." She wore that pretty blue dress. "Sorry I didn't recognize you in casual clothing."

She slouches, slightly rolling her eyes. "Ugh, yeah, sorry. I don't usually dress up anymore unless I absolutely have to."

"Anymore?"

"My parents," she starts with an annoyed nod. "That's who I was talking to on the phone."

"Uh oh." I grin. "This doesn't sound good."

"If I tell you I grew up in L.A. where several celebrity families were our neighbors, does that give you any indication?"

"Ah, so you're a socialite." She narrows her eyes. "Ooor your parents are...or were?"

"In all honesty, I think my parents would scoff at the word socialite. They prefer words with a little more finesse."

I pass her a smirk. "So spoiled little rich girl doesn't describe you?"

She snorts and I smile because for whatever reason I think her little snort is cute. "Not hardly. I mean, if my parents had anything to say about it, I would be back in L.A. helping them run their empire and taking over when they retire, but their life is so far from what I want. That's why I moved here. Far away from them."

"Oh?"

"I've seen enough of that lifestyle to never want to be a part of it ever again."

"Why do you say that?"

She huffs out a light laugh. "Because the perfectly poised rich life just isn't for me. I'm more of a hot mess and happy kind of girl."

Interesting.

It's not every day you see someone who comes from money and does not want the life money can afford. Something about her demeanor draws me in though. Like she has layers I want to peel back one at a time as I get to know her.

"So, you were talking to your parents. Does that mean you're flying home to see them or something?"

"No." She shakes her head with a cringe. "They're in town for a few days on business and they want to meet my rich boyfriend. Because far be it for me to date a normal guy who has a normal job and makes an honest, normal wage." Realizing what she just said, she squeezes her eyes closed and cringes again. "Oh shit. I just put my foot in my mouth. I'm sorry, I didn't mean to say that you don't—"

"I totally get it," I reassure her. "Professional hockey isn't exactly on the list of normal jobs with a normal wage."

"Right, but it sure as hell made my mom happy to hear I'm not an embarrassment to the family and found a celebrity athlete to date instead of a local plumber, though I'm not positive she believes me. Not that I care at all. I'll tell her anything to keep her off my back so I can live my life in peace."

"So can I ask you something then?"

"Sure. I mean, I've pretty much laid my entire life story

out for you when you never really asked, haven't I?" She smiles. "Ask away."

"Why me?"

"What?"

"Why did you tell your parents you were dating me specifically."

"Uh..." She bites her lip to hide her nervous smile. "Because you're single aaand not at all hard to look at." She winces. "Aaaand you were the first person to come to my mind probably because I saw your post-game interview on T.V."

She's cute when she blushes.

"Well, that's as good a reason as any, and thanks for the compliment."

"No, I should be thanking you," she says as she smooths a hand down my arm. Her simple touch causes me to suddenly think about what it would feel like to have her hands all over me. Or really anyone's hands for that matter. Except for Dex. Not his hands. "For not getting someone to kick me out of this bar the minute you heard me tell my parents I'm dating you. According to my parents I'm a hot mess of one bad decision after another which is evident in the fact I just pulled a lie out of my ass to save myself from their wrath. I really am sorry and don't worry about a thing. I'll be telling them tomorrow that you caught a bug and can't make dinner."

I can't believe I'm doing this. "Or you could tell them I'm available."

She cocks her head. "I'm sorry?"

What the fuck am I doing?

"You said your mom probably doesn't believe you, so

why not shove her disbelief in her face? It just so happens, I'm free."

"Wait," she says, leaning back on her stool. "Are you seriously offering to be super petty with me to stick it to my parents to get them off my back?"

I laugh. "What if I told you my name was Quinton Petty Shay?"

Her eyes narrow. "Is it?"

"Not at all." I shake my head. "But this sounds like an opportunity too fun to pass up. If you're going to lie to them about us being in a relationship, go big or go home, right?"

"You're serious?"

"One hundred percent. I have the day off tomorrow. If you're in, I'm in. I could use a reason to have a little fun."

She considers it for a moment, an adorable smirk lighting up her face. I notice the cute dimple in her right cheek when she smiles. She really is quite pretty.

"Can we make up some crazy shit about how we met?"

"I wouldn't have it any other way," I tell her with a gentle laugh.

"Oh, my God, I can't believe I'm about to take you up on this kind of offer."

"Going once...going twice..."

"I'm in!" She laughs, taking another drink of her beer. "I'm so fucking in."

"Perfect. Let me give you my number and then you can text me the details."

"Okay. It'll probably be super upscale if that's okay. My parents would never step foot in a place like this."

Typing my number into her contact list, I smile. "Don't

worry. I'll wear a designer suit." I stand and she follows, offering me her hand.

"It was really nice meeting you, Quinton Petty Shay."

I wrap her hand in mine, her skin soft and warm. I find myself not wanting to let go, but if I don't walk away, I may do something we'll both really regret tomorrow. "The pleasure was all mine, Kinsley."

She sees herself out and I head back to where the guys are seated, laughing about who knows what and who cares.

"Dude, where's my beer?" Dex asks when I lower my near empty glass to the table.

"Our bromance is over before it started Dexter. I'm giving all my fake love to someone else."

"Fake love? What are you talking about?"

"Does this have anything to do with Kinsley?" Hawken asks. "I saw you talking to her."

"Yeah." I nod, sliding into the booth. "It does. She told her parents she was dating me."

The shocked expressions looking back at me make me laugh. "She was lying, obviously. She just wanted her parents off her back so I offered to fuck with them with her because why the hell not?"

Zeke chuckles. "So, you're going to pretend to be her boyfriend?"

"Yup."

"Oh, fuck. This ought to be good."

2

KINSLEY

"Shut up, you did not." Meredith places her hot coffee mug in front of her and waits for me to swallow my bite. This cinnamon roll might be one of the best things to ever enter my mouth and I am here for it. It's God's gift to carb loaders like me. As one of my best friends since middle school, Meredith and I have treasured our weekly Sunday morning face-time calls. We may not live in the same state anymore but we're committed to staying in touch. When I knew she would be calling this morning, I walked to one of my favorite cafes around the corner, set up my iPad, and here we are.

"Mere, I don't know what the hell came over me last night, but yeah, I totally did."

"And your parents believed you?"

"They didn't say they didn't." I shrug. "But then again, Mom doesn't usually come out and say she doesn't believe me. I'm sure she's assuming I'll make up some excuse not to meet with them or that I'll bring someone other than

Quinton in his place. She seems to be able to see right through me most of the time."

Meredith grins like the Cheshire Cat. "Well won't they be surprised then when the two of you show up?"

"You think?"

She scoffs out a laugh. "Uh, yeah. When was the last time you introduced them to someone you were dating?"

"Probably two years ago when I was dating he-who-shall-not-be-named."

She leans closer to her phone camera as if she's closer to me. "And you are never going back to that life. He doesn't deserve you. You're so much better off now."

"I agree. He was a total asshat." Memories of my ex-boyfriend Seth float through my mind. He was the perfect guy in the eyes of my parents but if I had to hear one more sideways comment about my looks or lack thereof, *Dateline* would've had a new story to tell about how I tried to get away with murder.

Meredith kicks back in her chair. Her favorite blue chair that I know sits in the corner of her office. "And look at you now, babe. You've landed yourself a pro hockey player."

"Well, not really."

She shrugs. "Hey, you never know, right? The universe is fickle like that. Have you texted him yet?"

"No." I shake my head, cringing. "I'm kind of afraid he won't remember who I am. What if he was a little buzzed last night? Or what if he met some other woman after I left and he took her home and made sweet love to her and now they're getting married and having three and half kids, two dogs, a cat, and a guinea pig?"

"That's oddly specific." Meredith giggles with narrowed eyes.

"The universe is fickle. You said it yourself."

"How about you just do it now?"

"Do what?"

"Text the hockey player."

"You really think I should? Now? What if he's still sleeping?"

"Then he'll answer you when he's awake. It's not like it's the ass crack of dawn. It's ten o'clock."

"Okay, I'll do it." I pull my phone from my pocket and stare at his number. "What do I say?"

"Pancakes or French toast."

"What?"

"Ask him if he prefers pancakes or French toast."

"Why would I ask him that?"

Meredith cocks her head. "Would you rather your first communication be asking him for a dick pic? Or whether he wears boxers or briefs?"

I stare into my iPad meeting her gaze and laugh when we both nod and say, "Boxer briefs" at the same time.

"Okay, okay, here goes nothing."

ME

Dear Mr. Quinton Petty Shay. Do you prefer pancakes or French toast?

ME

Oh. This is Kinsley Kendrick by the way. I'm sorry I should've led with that.

SUSAN RENEE

> ME

If you don't remember me just send me something like the donut emoji and I promise I'll leave you alone.

> ME

Or if you do remember me but maybe you decided last night was one wrong decision after another and you don't think you can be my fake boyfriend tonight because you're a busy rich hockey player and I'm…well, I'm me, that's totally cool too.

> ME

Maybe send me a boot emoji. You know, like you're giving me the boot.

> ME

That's not a sexual thing right? The boot? I don't think it is. But if it is and now you're offended, I sincerely apologize. Pretend I didn't say anything. Just send whatever emoji you want.

> ME

Or none at all. That's fine too. I shouldn't be telling you what to do. You're your own person and you make your own decisions.

"Uhh, how many texts are you sending him? Or are you recounting everything you two discussed last night?"

"Shit!" I raise my head, my eyes large round saucers. "I didn't recount anything." Glancing back down at my phone, I ask, "Do you think I should write him again? What if he doesn't remember our conversation?"

"Relax, Kins. I'm sure he'll remember."

14

It's not ten seconds before my phone is dinging with an incoming text and a smile grows across my face.

QUINTON

Actually, I prefer waffles.

QUINTON

QUINTON

QUINTON

QUINTON

QUINTON

QUINTON

QUINTON

I feel like those emojis don't get the credit or use they deserve.

ME

I totally feel you there. Who uses the yellow sponge emoji anyway?

QUINTON

Exactly. Also, remember you? How could I forget about the girl who told her parents we were in a committed relationship? Fairly sure that was a first for me and that makes you unforgettable.

ME

Hmmm not sure if that's a compliment or not so I'll just pat myself on the back and tell my cat he should be proud.

QUINTON

You have a cat?

ME

Yep. He'll be so excited to meet you. Uh, that is assuming he actually does meet you one day I mean. I wasn't implying anything or…you know. Maybe pretend I didn't say that.

QUINTON

So, your pussy is male?

ME

He is. Yes. And I guess while we're on the subject, my pussy is also hairless.

QUINTON

wags brows A hairless pussy huh?

ME

Yep. His name is Nutsack.

QUINTON

spits out drink Nutsack???

ME

😏 Have you ever seen a hairless cat before?

QUINTON

Can't say that I have.

ME

Picture a relatively hairless nutsack and that's my cat.

QUINTON

LOL! Well now I must meet him. My life can't be complete until I've met Nutsack the hairless cat.

ME

I can make that happen. It's the least I can do for what you're willing to do for me.

QUINTON

Right. So, I need to know two things before tonight.

ME

Oh. Okay. Shoot.

QUINTON

What's your favorite color and where do you live?

ME

Umm orange. And I'm in the loft on the corner of Sixteenth and Williams.

QUINTON

Perfect. And what time shall I pick you up?

ME

Dinner is at seven sooo...

QUINTON

I'll see you between six and six-thirty?

ME

Alright. Uh, in case I forget to say so, though I'm sure I'll be saying it about a thousand times tonight, thank you for this.

QUINTON

No thanks needed. Looking forward to it.
👍

I pocket my phone as my best friend looks on with curiosity from her California home. "Well?"

"I think we're going to get along just fine."

"Is he picking you up?"

"Yep."

"And you're meeting early to get your stories straight?"

I shake my head, sitting back in my chair and ripping off another piece of my cinnamon roll. "Nah. We both feel confident that we can pull this off. He seems to have a good enough sense of humor, so it should be a fun evening making up random shit about our relationship and if sitting through this dinner results in my mother finally leaving me alone, either because she thinks I'm in a serious relationship or she thinks I'm bat shit crazy, it will be worth every lie we tell."

"Then I wish you all the luck in the world."

3

QUINTON

"Thanks again, gentlemen," Rory says as she dishes us all bowls of chili. It's her way of thanking us for helping move her stuff into Hawken's place. "There's plenty more where this came from so eat up. Garlic bread is on the stove."

Rory told us she would be more than happy to hire movers, but Dex was adamant about helping out and pretty much voluntold us we had to be here. Not that I would ever say no. This team is like family. There isn't much we don't do together and I would bend over backwards to help any one of them. Especially Rory because it almost always comes with her cooking as a thank you.

"This is delicious, Rory," I tell her, scooping another heaping spoonful into my mouth. The warmth of her homemade chili hits the spot today.

"Thank you. I'm glad you like it." She turns to the ladies—her three very pregnant friends—and offers them each a second helping.

Carissa shakes her head. "I couldn't eat another bite if I tried."

"No kidding," Charlee laughs, patting her baby bump. "If I eat another bowl, I'll be sitting up with heartburn all night."

"Good! More for me!" Tatum pushes herself out of her chair and waddles to the kitchen for another ladle of the good stuff. "And baby likes chili so maybe Dex is right and it's a boy this time."

I guess a team that plays together and hangs together also fucks together. Not in a weird orgy kind of way but clearly last season was filled with celebrations. Last summer three of the four ladies with us on vacation in Key West found out they were pregnant all at the same time and they're all due within a week or two of each other. What are the odds?

"You know, if you all start popping out those babies at the same time, Coach is going to have a coronary." I lick the end of my spoon and then point it at each of them with my best parent face. "And it better not be during the Anaheim game because they're kicking ass this year and I made a little bet with Oliver Magallan over who's going to win."

Zeke claps me on the shoulder. "Don't worry man. I'll be there no matter what."

"Me too," Hawken promises. "We'll blow 'em off the ice."

"Hey, I'll just be happy if I don't have to deliver my own kid again," Dex explains, looking helplessly at Tatum. He kisses her temple. "You know I love you, babe, but I think I still have PTSD from that experience."

Deadpanned, Tatum replies, "Yes. Because you were

the one whose body decided to expel a demon on her bathroom floor with zero epidural."

Dex considers Tate's words and then nods. "Now that you mention it, it would save us a hefty hospital bill if we just had a redo of Summer's birth. I caught one, I can catch the next one too."

Tate flips him off, much to our amusement.

Standing, I take my empty bowl to the kitchen and rinse it out in the sink. "Thanks again for the chili, Rory. I need to get going."

"Where do you think you're going, Asshat?" Dex asks.

Zeke leans over and loudly whispers, "He has a date."

"Oh yeah! Totally forgot about that. You still owe me a beer by the way."

"Fuck off, Dexter." I laugh and make kissy lips in his direction.

Hawken makes up a bowl of chili for Rory and serves her at the table. "So, you're really doing this, huh?"

"Yeah. Sure. Why not? Might be fun."

"Might be?" Colby asks with a chuckle. "You're literally going to lie to this girl's parents about dating her."

"Yeah." I shrug. "What harm can it do? They'll get off her back and we'll have a good laugh."

Milo and Charlee look at each other, playful smirks on their faces as they say in tandem, "Fake relationship trope!"

"What?"

Charlee laughs. "Fake relationship trope. It's a classic romance book trope. See it all the time in the books I edit."

"What do you mean?"

"I mean two people make an arrangement pretending to be together," she says, using quote fingers. "Only somewhere along the line they actually fall in love and there's nothing fake about it anymore."

"Oooh let me guess," I scoff. "You think that's going to happen to me and Kinsley?"

"It's not a popular romance trope for nothin,' my man." Milo tries to hold in his cheesy smirk but he's not doing a particularly good job.

"Yeah? And when was the last time you saw me actively dating someone?"

"Uh, not since Lexi and I don't think any of us have forgotten how that turned out."

"But that's why this will be different," Charlee explains. "You'll fall for her. Just wait."

With a roll of my eyes, I head for the door. "Whatever you say weirdos. I think you might read too many books."

Charlee gasps. "You take that back! There is no such thing as too many books!"

Laughing, I shake my head and wave before I walk out the door to prepare for my very fake, not at all real, date. "Later gators."

I pull up in front of Kinsley's apartment and press the button by her door alerting her that I'm here. There are bumps and thuds and crashing sounds coming from upstairs making me wonder what on earth could be going on up there, and then there's the familiar click of the intercom before Kinsley's voice shouts, "Come on up, door's open!" Before she releases the button to the speaker I hear her shout, "Nutsack! Don't you dare!"

Yeah that's something you don't hear someone say every day.

Oh man.

This ought to be good.

Climbing the stairs to her apartment, the bumping and crashing sounds crescendo. I knock on the door before turning the knob, peeking my head inside.

"Hello? Kinsley?"

"NUTSACK NO! YOU GIVE THAT BACK!"

Kinsley clearly doesn't hear me come in as she's hastily running after the hairless rodent-like creature that just darted across the other side of the room...wearing clothes.

Her hairless cat wears clothes?

Do hairless cats get cold?

Is that why?

This is weird, right?

I've never seen a cat wearing clothes.

The feline jumps onto a nearby shelf, knocking off several rolled posters, a cup of paint brushes, and some white Christmas lights, and then leaps onto the back of Kinsley's couch. Kinsley comes from around the corner chasing after Nutsack who is now making a beeline to where I'm standing at the door.

"NUTSACK! THOSE ARE MY—"

As if the floor is a slingshot, the cat bounces off his hind legs and flies right into my chest, his nails digging into my suit. He's hanging on me for dear life and has the audacity to meow at me like I got in his damn way.

"Panties." A frazzled Kinsley gasps, coming to an

abrupt halt in front of me. She's dressed in a fluffy orange robe, her makeup half done, unless eye shadow on only one eye is a thing these days, and her curly brown hair appears a bit unruly. I wrap my hands around Nutsack the cat and pry his sharpened claws from my suit realizing he isn't wearing clothes per se.

"Oh God." Kinsley palms her forehead. "Quinton, I'm so sorry. He fell asleep in my clean laundry basket and I must've scared him awake because he leapt out of the basket entwined with my..." She gestures to the purple satin wrapped around his body and tries to catch her breath. "Panties."

Watching her cheeks flush and her ears redden right before my eyes, I can tell she's embarrassed so I try to play it off like it's no big deal.

For anyone keeping track, yes, her hairless pussy did indeed attach itself to my chest wearing her satin purple panties.

Yeah, that's definitely never happened before.

Holding the cat out in front of me I give her an understanding smile. "And here I thought Nutsack was just a snazzy dresser."

As if he understood my every word, the cat looks up at me and meows again.

"Nice to meet you too, Nutsack."

Kinsley takes a big breath and releases a light laugh as I hand her four-legged friend back to her.

"Thanks. Uh..." She quickly works to remove her panties from the cat's body before he jumps down and scampers across the floor. "Sorry about that, but uh, you know, welcome." She passes me a nervous smile and then runs a hand through her hair. "I'm sorry, I seem to be running a tad late. Please, come in. Make yourself at home. I'll just be a minute."

She turns and scurries to the other side of the loft as I take in the space.

"You live here?" I ask her.

"Yep."

The top floor of this building is one large open studio. One side of the space holds a bed, an old dresser, a full-length mirror, and a few potted plants, while the rest of the room is taken up by an array of art and photography supplies. Two easels stand side by side, each holding a different sized canvas. A collection of other assorted sizes leans against the wall behind her easels. Three different professional looking cameras with more lenses than I could ever know what to do with sit on a table to the right of the door along with a laptop and a pair of headphones. To my immediate left is cabinetry that takes up the entire west wall of the studio except for the large basin sink in the middle that currently holds a jar of paint brushes, two bowls, two spoons, and four random plastic tumblers.

I step further inside, taking note of the artwork hanging on her walls. Collections of outdoor photographs along one wall, and portraits of random body parts along another.

Whoa.

Yeah, let's take a closer look at those.

The curve of a woman's hips with the hint of lace decorating her skin, a pair of legs in black fishnet stockings leading down to red heels, a woman's chest clad in a deep purple corset.

I wonder if all these portraits are of Kinsley.

If they are...fuuuuuck me.

"Be right there!" Kinsley calls out from what I can only assume is the bathroom around the corner.

"Take your time."

A pair of knitting needles or maybe it's crochet, stick out of a light brown ball of yarn on the couch. I only recognize what they are because Dex has several sitting around his house. Next to the yarn is a box filled with what looks like crocheted rocks, each one with two black eyes and holding white signs. I pick one up and hold it in my hand just in time for Kinsley to come around the corner.

"Positive potatoes."

"Huh?"

I turn my head and she's standing before me, elegantly dressed in a black wrap dress that hits just above her knee. Her hair subdued and tied back with a black bow. She looks beautiful. Like the day I met her at Hawken and Rory's wedding.

"They're positive potatoes," she says again. "I like to make them in my down time and hand them out to people I meet or sometimes to friends who could use a little pick-me-up."

I turn the small, yarned potato in my hand and read the small sign it's holding that says, *I may be a tiny potato but I believe in you. Go do your thing.*

So, it's not enough anymore to simply compliment someone. Kinsley goes out of her way to make tiny potatoes for people to let them know she cares. The sentiment makes me smile. In the past twenty-ish hours, I've learned that Kinsley Kendrick lied to her parents about her relationship status, she comes from money but doesn't want it, her parents don't approve of her life choices, she lives in a studio space with a hairless cat aptly named Nutsack, and crochets positive potatoes for random strangers and friends.

"And the portraits?" I ask, gesturing to the pictures on the wall I was just ogling.

She glances at the hangings and then smiles. "Oh, those. I'm a boudoir photographer."

"A boudoir photographer."

"Mhmm. That's my main job, actually. I photograph women, and some men, in lingerie or sometimes nude. Whatever they're comfortable with."

"Aaaand you do this because they want those pictures? Or do you sell them illegally?"

She laughs. "No, I don't sell anything but my services right now. And yes, the people who come to me want to have the boudoir experience."

"I'm sorry, I've never heard of such a thing."

"Well, I'm happy to tell you all about it, but we better get going or my mother will do nothing but complain about us being late."

"Right. Dinner. Yeah," I say, forgetting all about the reason I'm here in the first place. We have a job to do tonight and that's convince Kinsley's parents that we're a serious couple madly in love. Learning more about the portraits on her wall and the positive potatoes in a box and Nutsack the hairless cat will have to wait.

Following her to the door, I help her slip into her coat and escort her to my car. "Your chariot awaits."

She climbs in and reaches for her seatbelt, clicking it across her lap.

"So how old are you, Quinton?" she asks as I pull out onto the road.

"Thirty-three. You?"

"Twenty-eight."

Twenty-eight?

Fuck...that's a five-year difference.

She huffs out a soft giggle. "I guess that makes you my sugar daddy, huh?"

Suddenly feeling hot I tug at the collar of my shirt.

Five years.

That's not that bad, right?

It's not like I could be her dad.

So, she was thirteen when I graduated high school.

Eighteen when I made it to the NHL.

That's no big deal.

Could be worse.

Right?

Right?

Fuck.

4

KINSLEY

Quinton puts the address of *Cuisine*, one of the more famous upscale restaurants in town, into his GPS and pulls out onto the road.

"So, uh, is there anything about you I should absolutely know before we get into things tonight? Like, did I miss a birthday recently or umm, what's your middle name?"

"Right," I murmur. "We have to go there."

Quinton steals a glance in my direction. "Go where? Do we need to stop somewhere first?"

"No, no, no." I shake my head. "Sorry, no. I just meant..."

Ugh.

Here it goes.

"Okay, so let's just rip off this band aid. My full name is Kinsley Ida Nippy Kendrick," I rattle off quickly.

His brows pinch but he continues to watch the road. "Uh, I didn't quite catch that. Can you say it again? Maybe a little slower this time?"

Sighing, I repeat myself. "Kinsley. Ida. Nippy. Kendrick."

"Nippy?"

I nod with a roll of my eye. "Yep. I know. Outstanding choice of name, right?"

He's trying not to laugh. I can hear it in his voice. "Is it, uh, like a family name or something?"

"Something like that. My mom wanted Kinsley Ida but my super perfect spoiled brat of a sister had this favorite stuffed teddy bear she named Nippy and insisted on her baby sister having that name too, so..." I sigh lifting my arms in a defeated shrug. "My mom conceded and Kennedy got what Kennedy wanted. So now my initials spell—"

"KINK."

"Yeeep," I drawl.

"Wow. That's..." He shakes his head and thank God he doesn't finish his sentence.

"You can imagine all the shit I had to put up with as a young kid in middle school. *Kinky Kinsley* or *Kinsley the Kink* or *Hey Kinsley what's your kink?* Total embarrassment as an eleven-year-old you know? So anyway, that's me. Now, this is where you tell me your middle name is something like Squirt or Flaccid or maybe something really cool, like Fartknocker."

He finally chuckles but gives me a sympathetic cringe. "I'm sorry to tell you this, but my middle name is Alan."

"Quinton Alan Shay?" I huff. "That's so...boring."

"It is," he agrees with a laugh. "That's me. In the grand scheme of things, I'm pretty boring."

"I'm certain that's not true."

His eyes narrow but he keeps his gaze on the road. "How can you be so sure?"

"Well first, you play professional hockey. That in and of itself is far from boring."

"I guess."

Turning in my seat, I take in his profile. Strong jaw, bulging arms if the tightness of his dress shirt has anything to say about it. Well-trimmed beard that's more than a five o'clock shadow but not lumberjack long. He appears to be someone who puts thought and effort into how he looks.

And how he smells because oh my God! If it wouldn't be ridiculously inappropriate to lick him right now, I would ride the whole way to dinner with my tongue on his neck.

"So, what do you do when you're not playing hockey?"

He huffs out a light chuckle. "You mean when I'm not practicing hockey, going over hockey plays, working out, or doing something for our social media manager?"

"Carissa?" I gush. "Oh, my gosh I love her so much! She was so fun to work with at that wedding event. I still tell people all about it. I mean, as if they didn't read about it in every magazine there is. Also yes, I meant, what do you do when you're not doing your job...which, obviously, is all things hockey?"

"Uh..." He stares mindlessly at the road for a bit, tapping his fingers on the steering wheel. "I guess when I'm not working in some capacity or another, I'm trying to relax as best I can. I don't really have...a thing, for lack of a better word."

"You don't go to the drive-in or take long walks at the park or go to the movies?"

He shakes his head. "Not really."

"Concerts? Art events? Something with some culture?"

"Nope."

"So, you just sit at home and stare at the wall or what?"

He cringes this time with a slight laugh. "Man, I probably look abhorrent right now. Should I turn the car around and take you home?"

"What? No!"

"I'm just kidding." He winks. "I hang out with the guys a lot."

"Your teammates?"

"Yeah. They're like family to me so usually we're together more than we're apart."

"And what do you do when you're hanging with them?"

He smirks. "Wouldn't you like to know?"

My eyes grow huge at his inference. "Well, now I would, yeah!"

Quinton laughs. "I promise it's not that exciting. Usually, we're sitting around at someone's house watching hockey with a beer in our hands. Sometimes we play video games or even board games when the spouses and girlfriends are around."

"Well, that sounds like fun!"

"It is. I mean, we all get along great. So, I guess what I'm saying is I'm boring when it's just me."

I wave my hand dismissing his self-deprecation. "Nah. Don't you worry one bit. By the end of this night, you'll be Quinton Alan Shay, the most non-boring pro hockey player I could have ever met."

I turn my body back around to face the front of the car,

smoothing out my dress. Quinton steals several glances my way, a humored smile on his face.

"I don't know exactly what that means, Kinsley, but something tells me I'm going to enjoy this dinner with you and your family very much."

"As long as you have your sense of humor with you, I promise this will be a fun evening for us both."

"So, you're not worried about being with your parents then?"

"Hell no. She'll pretend to care about some things and then jab me with her passive insults telling me how great my sister is doing yadda, yadda, yadda like she always does."

"That doesn't sound good at all."

"Yeah well, she'll also be drinking so I can make up whatever shit I want to about my life and she won't remember a damn thing I tell her."

"Hence the supposed serious relationship with me."

I can feel my cheeks heat at his comment. "Yeah. Exactly."

Quinton pulls over in front of *Cuisine* and then hops out, walking around the car to open my door for me. He takes my hand and gives his keys to the valet who hands him a ticket with a polite nod.

"Shall we, Kinky?"

I snort in laughter and squeeze his warm, strong hand. "We shall. Let's do this."

As far as introductions go, Mom and Dad were as welcoming to Quinton as I knew they would be given his social status and bank account standing. My parents are nothing if not snobs for the rich and famous. If it makes them money, they want it. If it's worth money, they own it and if not, they buy it. If it's none of those things, they have zero interest.

Hence me and my life.

They've snubbed their noses at little old me for years after I finally ended things with Seth and told my family I was moving to Chicago to focus on my art.

"Art?" They would say with a roll of their eyes as if Picasso and Monet slid out of the birthing canal with paint brushes in their hands. *"Nobody buys new art, Kinsley. It's not worth anything."*

Yep. If I had a penny for every time I heard that line over the years, I could move to France and build a studio right next to the Louvre. Tonight though, my parents are playing their game of woo-Kinsley's-boyfriend-because-he's-rich-like-them. I have no doubt they both assumed I would show up empty handed with my usual excuses, so the joke is on them because Quinton Alan Shay and Kinsley Ida Nippy Kendrick showed up to play.

"So, tell me Quinton, how did you meet our beautiful Kinsley?" Yeah, my mom just called me beautiful, but only because of who I brought to dinner with me.

"It's a funny story actually," he answers as he picks up his drink and takes a sip while giving me some side-eye. I take that as my cue to jump in so I giggle a little and nod.

"Funny indeed," I say. "I hit Quinton with my car."

My mom gasps as she clutches the nonexistent pearls around her neck. "Kinsley!"

"It's fine Mom. I didn't hit him that hard. I wasn't speeding. But if you saw a full-grown man in a pink sparkly tutu fluttering down a back road late at night singing show-tunes, you would've freaked out and lost control of your car for a second too."

Quinton nearly spits out his drink.

"Dear Lord, Kinsley," my dad chastises. "Tell me you didn't offer to sleep with this poor guy to get out of getting sued."

"It wasn't like that at all, Mr. Kendrick," Quinton answers for me with a shake of his head. "It was all my fault. I'm the one who had been drinking a little too much that night. I made a silly bet with a few teammates over another game we were watching together and obviously, I lost."

Dad's brows pinch together. "That's quite the punishment. A monetary bet would've been much less...embarrassing."

"Meh. None of us want each other's money. That's no fun. The guys had a good laugh watching me fulfill my punishment. Those are memories we'll remember and laugh over for years to come."

Swoon!

See parents? Money isn't everything.

"Anyway, I didn't even notice her driving by in all my diva princess glory and I accidentally stepped out in front of her."

"Mercy!" Mom cries. "Thank goodness you were okay."

"Oh yeah, I was fine." Quinton puts his arm around my shoulders and pulls me into him, his hand smoothing up and down my arm. "Kinsley was nice enough to give me a ride back to the house where I was staying. She was an angel that night," he says before planting a kiss on the side of my head.

Double swoon!

"Yep. And he wouldn't get out of my car until I gave him my number and then that entire night he was texting me random emojis that nobody ever uses. I wondered if maybe he had a concussion. It was weird for sure, but also, I thought it was endearing and cute."

"Who doesn't love a good left arrow emoji or the fleur de lis or the—"

"Yellow sponge," I giggle, finishing his thought for him.

"Exactly." Quinton glances back at my mom. "I asked Kinsley out after that more to thank her for not taking pictures that night and selling them to the tabloids, but also, she intrigued me."

"I even made him that cheesecake with the coconut I made a couple of years ago that everyone loved. Remember, that summer party with the Swintons? Who knew coconut was Quinton's favorite? He ate the whole thing!"

That earns me a wink and a smile from my fake Hottie McHotpants. "It was delicious and I was smitten. Kinsley's...different from other women I've dated before."

"Oh, she's different alright," Mom mumbles, stealing a glance at my father who scoffs out a chuckle. "Maybe a little bit of your motivation for the ultimate success and your obvious competitive drive will rub off on our daughter." Mom leans in and whispers, "She's had her head in the clouds a bit lately if you haven't noticed."

"Mom..."

Here it comes.

She waves her hand dismissively. "I'm just saying."

Quinton stiffens beside me, his arm still snug around my shoulder. "Actually, I find what Kinsley does fascinating. She's really finding her place in this huge city. Her fun-loving personality is what attracted me to her the most. Everyone I know just wants to be in the same space as her. If you ask me, we need more people like her to keep us rooted in our humanity, you know?"

"Mmm." Clearly, Mom doesn't seem impressed. "Yes, Kinsley definitely digs her feet in when it comes to what she wants verses what she needs. You call them roots, Quinton, but I see them more like...tree trunks. Insanely stubborn and without a purpose. Her kind of art for one thing. I've told her a million times there's no money in modern art by artists with no name for themselves, but here she is, living in this huge city, insisting she be allowed to chase a dream."

"It's not a dream, Mother. It's my—"

Our food is delivered to the table before I can finish my thoughts. Averting my eyes to my lap, I tell myself the faster I eat, the faster we can get out of this hell and then I can thank Quinton for his kindness and be on my way. If I'm lucky, I can still get in a good hour of painting and then cuddle with Nutsack for the rest of the night.

"Did your sister tell you she's being presented with an award?"

For what, Mom? Most expensive tits?

"Nope. But I'm sure you're going to tell me."

"It's the annual Cheryl Stevens Woman of the Year award for all her philanthropy with those inner-city children."

Of course, she's being awarded for sending a random charity a big fat check when she never sets foot anywhere to actually be of help or service to others. That's exactly Kennedy.

"Wow." I fork a piece of steak from my plate and stick it in my mouth before I can say what I want to say instead of what I should say. After chewing a few times, I finally nod. "I'll have to congratulate her."

"So, Quinton," my father starts while chewing his filet mignon a few moments later. "Any interest in the luxury hospitality business?"

"Hotel real estate, you mean?" Quinton asks.

"Indeed. Great opportunities for investment, you know."

Inwardly I roll my eyes. *Like Quinton doesn't know how to manage his money, Dad.*

Quinton dabs the corner of his mouth with his napkin. "Actually, yes. I'm a silent investor in my twin sister's hotel resort in Hawaii."

What?

He has a twin sister?

I didn't know this!

But I have to act like I've known all along.

"Are you really?" Oh, now Mom is interested. Of course, what's not to love about investments and real estate? Is this what all rich people talk about? "One we might know of?"

Like they know every resort in the world.

Okay, they might know all of them in California or maybe the New England coast but let's not go overboard.

"It's a small family-owned resort called Kamana Wanalaya. Was in my brother-in-law's pseudo family for years and when they wanted to retire, he and my sister were getting married and decided to move out there and take over the resort. They've been doing a wonderful job with renovations. I'm excited to get out there during the off season to see the place."

"That's wonderful!" Mom exclaims. "Isn't that wonderful dear?"

Dad nods. "Yes, well, it seems we have something in common now Quinton. Deborah and I purchased the Silver Pines Luxury Resort in Breckinridge and we've added a world class spa and we just hired a five-star Michelin chef for the new restaurant. Our grand opening is at the end of the month..."

Nooo no, no, no...

He can't...

Shit.

He's not going to—

"And there will be many noteworthy people in attendance to help us celebrate. We would love to have you both join us in our—"

"Oh guys, remember, it's the middle of hockey season." My nerves begin to flutter through my stomach at the thought of spending an entire weekend with my parents. Or making Quinton have to fulfill this fake agreement any longer than tonight. "Quinton has a busy game schedule. He'll hardly have ti—"

"I'd love to come. Thank you for the invitation Mr. and Mrs. Kendrick."

What the fuck?

Does he hear himself right now?

"Oh please, dear, it's Deborah. Deborah and Steve."

"Right. Steve, Deborah. Thank you. I think some time at your resort sounds wonderful and just so happens, since I'm not participating in this year's All-Star game, I'll have a few days off."

What is he doing?

"It's settled then." Dad nods with a smile. We'll host you in one of our luxury cabins."

I would rather lick shit from an ice-cream cone.

"Great!" I give them a well-plastered smile and pass a swift kick to Quinton under the table. He merely chuckles in response. "Can't wait."

We spend the next few moments in silence enjoying our meals before my dad starts talking hockey with Quinton. Then Mom cuts in with questions about his charity work, once again leaving me out of any kind of conversation. I get it. Quinton's the new guy for them. They want to know all the things. And I know now not to expect much from my family when I'm the black sheep who decided to take the road less traveled. It was my choice not to go into the family business. It was my decision not to spend my adult life rubbing shoulders with the rich and famous, always wearing a fake smile and pretending my life is perfect.

Still, it would be nice to at least be acknowledged at the table.

"What the hell was that?" I unbutton my coat once back in Quinton's car, the need to free myself from any kind of confinement growing stronger by the minute.

"What? You don't think it went well?"

Fanning my face, I give Quinton an apologetic smile. "I mean...I guess it could've gone worse, but you do remember accepting my father's invitation to join them in Breckenridge, right?"

"Yeah...about that."

"Don't worry. I can get you out of it with no problem. I'll just tell them that y—"

"No." He cuts me off with a shake of his head as he pushes his hand through his hair. "Don't tell them anything."

He pulls the car out onto the street joining the regular flow of the evening traffic and all I can do is stare.

At him.

At the road.

At him again.

"I don't understand. You really don't need to go. They'll totally understand if you—"

"I do need to go."

"Why?"

"Because I need your help."

5

QUINTON

"**Y**ou need *my* help?"

I don't know what I'm doing. I think I feel a bit like a fish out of water and I'm only saying that because, well, I have no idea what the hell it feels like to actually be a fish out of water but I'm assuming it's a bit like this. The feeling of having the air sucked out of you when you realize you're no longer swimming comfortably and so you're flipping your fins as fast as you can trying to catch that breath you know you need to survive. It's out there somewhere, you just can't reach it.

Like I said...a fish out of water.

That's what I thought of the moment the Kendricks started talking about their new resort and inviting me to attend their grand opening.

Panic.

Not because I was being asked to come. It was more because they were talking about charities and celebrities and being a part of that whole world. It dawned on me as I was chatting that in a couple of months I'll be attending a charity event for the organization I work with and the very last thing I want to do is show up there alone looking like a pathetic lonely sap when *she'll* be there with another man showing off her wedding rings.

"Yes, I need your help."

Kinsley blinks a few times before nodding. "Okay. What does it have to do with Silver Pines Resort?"

"It doesn't," I answer. "Not really anyway. This is more like...a tit for tat kind of thing."

She turns in her seat to face me a bit. "Tit for tat, huh?"

"Yeah."

"Alright. I'm all ears."

Gripping the steering wheel, I take a deep breath and release it heavily. "Okay, so you know how you asked me to pose as your boyfriend because you had already told your parents we were a thing?"

"Yeah."

"Maybe you could do the same thing for me."

Kinsley's eyes grow huge and her mouth opens wide. "Oh, my God. Quinton Shay, did you tell someone we were dating too?"

"What? No!" I shake my head. "It's not like that."

"Oh. Okay."

"Remember at dinner I was telling your parents I work very closely with this charity for kids called G.A.M.E.?"

"Yeah. Growing...umm, I'm sorry I can't quite remember what GAME stands for."

"Growing Athletically Mindful Enthusiasts. It's an organization that collaborates with community and school sports programs. They do a lot of coach training and leadership training with kids and adults. Even parents too. Their focus is on team-sports play and teaching others how team sports can help develop a young athlete's positive mental health."

"Right! Yeah. That's seriously cool. What a great asset to any sports community."

"Yeah. It is. And it's been great working with them for the last five years or so. Anyway, their annual fundraising event is in the early spring toward the end of our season and you know..." I shrug.

Kinsley shakes her head. "Nope. I don't know. Don't have a clue."

Ugh. She's going to make me say it.

"This used to be something my ex and I did together for a couple of years. I got her involved with the organization and she kind of ran with it. Now she's everywhere they are."

"Aaah. I get it. So, this ex is going to be there."

"Undoubtedly."

"What's her name?"

"Lexi. Lexi Stock."

Kinsley's mouth hangs open. "You mean Lexi Stock from the women's soccer team?"

"Yeah."

"Whoa! You two dated?"

"Yeah. For a couple of years."

"And you want to make her major jealous? Is that why you want me to go with you?"

"Ye-wait...no. I mean I couldn't care less about making her jealous. She's already moved on and married some other douche who I'm sure has way more celebrity to his name than me."

"Is that why you broke up?" she asks.

"Huh?"

"Did she ditch you for a quote-unquote bigger celebrity?"

Pangs of anger shoot through my chest at the memory of Lexi leaving me.

That night on the red carpet.

My arms around the woman I loved.

Until she walked straight out of them into the embrace of another man.

Talk about humiliation.

"Something like that. Look, I'll do it if I must, but I would rather not go to this kind of event alone so...you know. I'll go to Silver Pines with you if you'll be my date for G.A.M.E. night."

She touches my arm tenderly. "Of course, I'll go with you, Quinton. I can be a doting girlfriend. I'll even rave about you in the women's restroom and tell everyone how skilled you are in the bedroom." She winks. "I'll have them all wanting a piece of you by the end of the night."

A faint smile spreads across my face. "You don't have to do that. I'm perfectly fine having a fake girlfriend for the night with no unnecessary drama. Plus, with the other celebrities that will be there, I hardly doubt anyone will care about me."

Kinsley scoffs a laugh. "If you want to believe, that you go on ahead, but have you ever been a woman in a women's restroom when celebrities are around?"

"Uuuh no."

"Then trust me. They'll all be talking about your dick size before they're even finished reapplying their lipstick."

"Good God, can women think of nothing else to talk about in a bathroom?"

Kinsley narrows her eyes as she studies me. "Umm, no. No, we cannot. And are you seriously telling me you guys don't talk shit in the locker room?"

Her question makes me laugh because fuck, we've had some doozies when it comes to personal conversations in the locker room.

Like the scratches on Hawken's back from Rory.

Whose ass reigns supreme among the team.

Milo and his cock rings.

Dexter and...well, just about anyone he ever fucked before Tatum came along.

Colby and his Lucky Charms fight with Carissa.

Colby's brother and his Mardi Gras shenanigans.

"Touché. I suppose you have a point. So, is that a yes to extending our arrangement?"

"It's a yes, Mr. Shay. You have a deal. I'll be happy to pose as your super sexy and loving girlfriend and promise to be at your disposal the whole time."

"Super sexy, huh?"

She snorts in the most unsexy way but it makes me laugh because she's nothing if she's not cute. "I mean, hello! You're putting me up against Lexi Stock! She's like... gorgeous and...ridiculously athletic, but don't you worry. I'm totally up for this. I just hope this event is an evening gig because it's going to take me all day to get myself ready to knock that bombshell out of the park."

Why Kinsley thinks so little of herself is beyond me, though I expect her mother has made quite a condescending impression on her if what I observed tonight has anything to do with it.

"First of all, Kinsley, you're a beautiful person inside and out. I know this already and I've barely spent more than five total hours in your presence. Secondly, and trust me when I tell you this, Lexi Stock is not the goddess the media makes her out to be. I know that firsthand."

"Oh yeah?"

"Yeah."

"Are you saying she farts in her sleep and has cellulite like the rest of us?"

I try not to chuckle but dammit, it's hard to tell if she's being serious or if she's joking with me. "She absolutely farts in her sleep. She also has horrible morning breath, and she can't say the word breakfast."

Kinsley giggles. "What? What do you mean she can't say breakfast?"

I shake my head, smirking. "She can't pronounce it correctly. She says 'breftist' every single time."

"No, she does not."

Holding up my right hand I laugh. "Swear to God."

"You are too funny!"

"I'm just saying, comparison is the thief of joy. You seem to be someone with a lot of joy and a joyful personality is attractive so don't sell yourself short."

"That's extremely sweet of you, Quinton. Thank you. And for what it's worth, thank you very much for tonight. You did great. I'm sorry my parents were a bit..."

She doesn't finish her sentence so I finish it for her. "Passive aggressive but mostly aggressive?"

She turns her head to look out her window so I can't see her face. "Mhmm."

Uh oh. That didn't sound like a happy response.

It bothers her more than she lets on.

Silence fills the space like an elephant in the room before I finally ask what's been on my mind all evening. "Is it always like that with them? For you, I mean?"

"More often than not," she sighs.

"Have they actually seen your work before? They must know how talented you are."

"They have no idea that I'm a boudoir photographer. They know I paint and dabble in other kinds of photography but the boudoir photography is what I'm most passionate about right now."

"And why is that? What makes it special to you?"

She shrugs. "Mm. I have my reasons."

When she says no more I know it's a sensitive subject she's not comfortable talking about with me. At least not yet, so naturally I'm intrigued. I don't see Kinsley Kendrick as someone who takes sexy pictures of people for her own sensual pleasure. There has to be more to it and for some reason, I'm really interested to know.

"Have you always been seen as the outcast? To your parents?"

"Umm, well, there was this stretch of about six months back when my younger brother was a teenager that he was on the shit list because he got caught with drugs which of course made the family look bad. That didn't go over well for him, but Mom and Dad sent him away and when he came back he went right into the family business. Now they think he turns piss into gold."

"Wow. A modern-day Rumpelstiltskin, huh?"

She laughs quietly. "Yeah. Exactly. So, once he was all straightened out things were good until I broke up with the guy I was with. My parents weren't happy about it and were even more upset when I told them I was moving here to live on my own."

"They don't approve of you having your own life?"

"They don't approve of me not doing what they do. Or living the way they live."

"That seems all sorts of fucked up."

"Tell me about it. So much for just wanting your kids to be happy, you know?"

"Are you? Happy I mean?"

She's quiet for another few seconds before she answers, "I'm not unhappy. We all have goals, right? We all have aspects of our lives we wish were a little better than they are but that's what makes life exciting. If we all had whatever we wanted the way we wanted it all the time, there would never be growth. Nothing would ever change or move forward. We would be stagnant."

"I guess you're right. I've never thought about it like that before."

"Right? I mean if your team won the cup every single year, you guys would have nothing to push for. At some point you have to not win it so you can work hard to win it again."

"Hey now. Let's not go that far, alright?" I say with a laugh. "We like having that beautiful cup in our possession."

"I'm no negative Nellie, Quinton, but you might want to prepare yourself." She touches my thigh and fuck me,

49

SUSAN RENEE

my body reacts with a quick zap to my chest and I don't hate it.

What the hell?

"What goes up must eventually come back down. That's just science."

"Fuck science," I laugh again. "That cup stays right here in Chicago."

She smiles and pretends to type a note into her phone. "Okay, okay. Fuck...science. I'll be sure to put that on my next positive potato."

She slides her phone into her coat pocket and beams at me as I pull up to her studio. Something about her smile catches me off guard. Maybe it's that this one isn't forced like it was throughout dinner. Maybe it's that this isn't a nervous I-hope-this-goes-alright kind of smile. It's pure honest to goodness and comfortable happiness coming from her and it makes me smile right back at her.

It also makes me want to give her more to smile about.

"I had fun tonight, Kinsley."

Her smile fades and for a moment I wonder what I said wrong. "Listen, I feel like I owe you a huge, no, gargantuan apology for bringing you into my hot mess of a life. You seem like a great guy and I just...ugh." She brings a hand to her forehead. "I involved you in my stupid lie and—"

"Hey." I pull her hand down from her face and see the true sincerity in her eyes. "You didn't make me do anything. I didn't have to talk to you that night at the bar. I *wanted* to. You intrigued me and hey, it turns out you're helping me as much as I'm helping you. No harm, no foul."

"Really?"

"Yeah, really. It was good for me to get out of my own

50

head and not have to think about hockey for a night, so thank you for that. I needed the laughs and dinner was great."

She takes a deep breath, exhaling as she nods. "Okay. Yeah. I had fun tonight too. Parental passive aggressiveness but mostly aggressiveness not included."

"Don't worry about them. I'll be on my A-game next time now that I've spent some time with them. Can I walk you up?"

She shakes her head quickly and then opens her car door. "Oh no. That's not necessary. Besides, who knows what kind of new havoc Nutsack has gotten himself into while we've been away."

"Just promise me if he's wearing a bra this time, you'll take a picture and send it to me."

She snorts in laughter, which makes me chuckle all over again. She's cute when she laughs like that and I get a kick out of bringing it out of her. Her mossy green eyes sparkle back at me, her cheeks pulled back with her smile.

"Right. I cross my heart. Good night, Quinton."

"Good night, Kinsley."

She closes the passenger side door and I roll down the window as I watch her walk toward her front door.

"Oh, hey Kinsley?"

She turns quickly. "Yeah?"

"I'm allergic to coconut."

Her head tilts. "What?"

"The cheesecake you told your parents you made me," I remind her. "It was delicious, I'm sure, but you should probably know I'm allergic."

She gives me a sympathetic look. "To coconut?"

"To coconut." I nod. "Just thought you should know."

She cringes but agrees. "Wise thinking." She taps on her temple with one finger. "I'll store that knowledge away for safe keeping. Good night."

"Night Kinsley."

I wait to make sure she gets inside safely before pulling back out onto the road toward home. Parts of the night replay through my mind. My first meet and greet with Nutsack, our many laughs throughout the night, her unease around her parents, making her smile one last time before she left. Overall, not such a bad night. The traffic light ahead of me turns red and as I stop to wait I lean my head back on the headrest and take a deep breath murmuring to myself the only thought in my mind.

"She's pretty."

6

QUINTON

"You're shittin' me." Zeke laughs as he blocks one of my shots. I give him the cheesiest grin and move out of the way for Milo to take his shot next. "Promise I'm not, man. She for real calls him Nutsack."

Zeke laughs so damn hard his foot slips and he falls on his ass. "That's the funniest thing I've ever heard. She has a pussy named Nutsack?"

"Rascally little bugger too," I tell him as I reach out a hand to help him up. "Flew right across the room coming right at me wearing a pair of her purple panties."

"Holy shit." Dex slides to a halt. "You got a look at her panties on your very first fake date?" He pats my back. "Well done, Shay. I wasn't sure you had it in you."

"I saw her panties, yeah, but they weren't on her."

Hawken wags his brow. "Even better, bro!"

"That's not what I mean, asshat! It was just her... Nutsack was playing in her clean laundry."

SUSAN RENEE

"Oh, God! Stop! Stop!" Milo grabs his side, bending over in laughter. "I can't breathe."

Colby grabs his chin between his thumb and forefinger. "Sooo your girl has a nutsack? That's new info."

"Ugh. No. Sorry, this is all coming out wrong."

"Yeah it is," Zeke says, blocking a few more shots. "We get it though, I think. But did the night go as planned? Did you blow her parents out of the water for her? What's her name again?"

"Kinsley. And yeah, I think I did. They even invited us to the grand opening of their new ski resort in Breck-inridge."

"Us?" Dex asks. "Define Us."

"Kinsley and me."

Hawken sweeps up the remaining pucks into a pile on the ice. "Wait...I thought this was all fake."

"It is."

His brows peak. "Oh. So, you said no to Breckinridge?"

"No, I said yes to Breckinridge."

"What the fuck for?"

"Yeah," Dex says. "How long is this ruse supposed to last?"

I give them a halfhearted shrug. "I don't know. She's fun to hang around so I figured what the hell. Let's go to their resort. Plus, then she can come with me to the G.A.M.E. Night Gala."

"Oooh, I see now," Zeke claims. "Tit for tat."

"Yeah."

"Because Lexi will be at the gala."

Even the mention of her name makes my stomach lurch. Not because I still have feelings for her. I don't. At

54

all. But there was a time when I thought I really loved her and when she left me it was devastating. I swore I wouldn't put myself through that kind of romantic bullshit again.

"Exactly."

"Alright then." Milo nods. "Bring her to game night on Sunday."

"What? Why?"

"You said she was fun to hang around, so why not?"

"Because Kinsley and I aren't a thing and our game nights are just for...you know, family."

"Charlee wasn't family the first time," he argues. "We barely knew her but you all accepted her presence just fine."

"Tate too." Dex nods. "You guys didn't bat an eye."

I shake my head. "Nah. I don't think I'll invite her. She's probably busy anyway."

"Right." Zeke winks. "Busy keeping her nutsack warm."

"Hey!" We all turn to the sound of Coach Denovah's voice. "Enough with the tea party over there, gentlemen. Let's get back in focus or you can hand tomorrow's win over to Phoenix before you ever take the goddamn ice!"

I wasn't lying when I told Kinsley I'm a rather boring person. On a stretch of away games, life seems busy and exciting traveling from city to city, hanging out in hotel bars, laughing for all hours of the night. But when we're at home, it can sometimes be a whole other story. Sure, we

have our nights off where we'll hang out together but now
that so many of the guys have settled down, sometimes they
want a quiet night at home with their women. I don't blame
them. As professional hockey players we spend a lot of our
time around people. Even I appreciate some alone time
once in a while.

Tonight though, it's been a boring night, which means
I'm lying in bed earlier than usual semi-watching the Griz-
zlies play the River Frogs but also flipping through social
media on my phone. I don't know what makes me do it
other than sheer curiosity, but I search Kinsley's name and
grin when a picture of her and Nutsack show up with her
profile. Most of the pictures she's posted are random things
nobody else would ever post. A close up of an acorn
followed by a chipmunk with two acorns in its mouth.
Then there's a park bench, I'm guessing in Lincoln Park,
with several pigeons sharing a piece of bread, a picture of
the sunset over the lake, snowflakes flying near a streetlight,
and then a picture of Nutsack wearing an ugly Christmas
sweater.

That one makes me laugh.

I tap the like button on her picture of Nutsack and then
immediately wonder if that was an okay decision.

Is she going to read into that?

Maybe I should unlike it.

But if she's already seen it, she'll know I unliked it.

I'll look like a jerk if I unlike it now.

*But if she sees it, she'll know I was creeping through her
profile.*

Does that make me look stalker-like?

I didn't even follow her yet.

Should I follow her?

Will the public get the wrong impression if I follow her?

Surely not. I've followed other women before...right?

Am I being creepy?

My chest feels tight and I almost break out into a sweat agonizing over what I should do when my phone dings in my hand.

KINSLEY

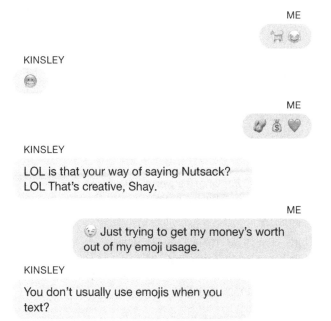

"Fuck." I huff out a laugh.

She saw me.

Or maybe she didn't and it's just a coincidence.

Nah. Fuck it. She's on to me.

Just write back asshole.

ME

KINSLEY

ME

KINSLEY

LOL is that your way of saying Nutsack?
LOL That's creative, Shay.

ME

Just trying to get my money's worth out of my emoji usage.

KINSLEY

You don't usually use emojis when you text?

ME

Rarely. And when I do it's either a thumbs
up or heart to my sister or the middle
finger emoji to the guys on the team.

KINSLEY

Oh yeah, then we definitely need to
broaden your emoji vocabulary. It'll take
practice. I hope you're up for the
challenge.

ME

I promise to give it my best shot.

KINSLEY

Sooo you creeping my social media or
what?

ME

I was bored.

KINSLEY

Oh, so I'm just something you think about
when you're bored? Thanks...I think.

ME

I didn't mean it like that. I'm Sorry!

KINSLEY

😊 No worries. I'm only teasing.

ME

For what it's worth, I liked your pictures.
You have a creative eye.

KINSLEY

It's what I love. There's beauty all around
us in our world. Sometimes we just
struggle to see it because we're too busy
focusing on the negative.

ME

I suppose you're right about that. Do you do anything with these photos you take? Publish them?

KINSLEY

If it's the right picture at the right time, sure. Some are just for my own happiness. Some I take as inspiration for painting.

ME

So, photography and painting and crocheting positive potatoes? What don't you do?

KINSLEY

LOL pretty much anything else. Art is fun for me. I like having fun.

ME

Umm, do you like playing games?

KINSLEY

Like Monopoly? Or like beer pong?

ME

LOL both, I guess. But I was thinking about board games? Card games? Group games? That sort of thing.

KINSLEY

Yeah sure! Why do you ask?

ME

The guys on the team get together every now and then to have a game night. Spouses usually come too. It's usually a fun night. Lots of laughing, probably a good bit of swearing if you're up for it.

KINSLEY

Are you asking me out??? 🫢

ME

Uh...well...I mean consider it a fake date with your fake boyfriend? I just thought if we're going to spend the weekend together soon it might be a good idea to get to know you a little more. And you, me. And the team as they're such a big part of my life.

KINSLEY

Do they know?

ME

About us and our arrangement? Yeah, they know. I tell them everything. We're like brothers. There's not much I keep from them. Is that not okay? I'm sorry, I probably should've talked with you about it first.

KINSLEY

Nonsense. Of course, it's okay. It's your life. I'm the one who put you in this sticky situation.

ME

Trust me. You're helping me out just as much as I'm helping you. Don't sweat it. Just come hang out. I promise it'll be fun if you're into games with friends.

KINSLEY

I'm always up for having fun. I'd love to come! 😊

ME

Perfect. I'll touch base tomorrow and work out the details.

KINSLEY

Alright. Sounds good. G'night Quinton.

A part of me was really enjoying chatting with her, so seeing her say g'night brings a quick stab of disappointment to my chest. I swallow back the weird feeling and send her one last text.

ME

G'night KINK.

KINSLEY

LOL I'm sooo going to regret telling you that.

ME

7

KINSLEY

"So where are we on the fake boyfriend thing? Did you take him to meet your parents?"

Meredith sips her coffee from the back porch of her home while I sit at my desk in my studio.

"Oh, my God, yeah I did and he was fantastic!"

She pulls a blanket over her lap and snuggles into her seat. "Tell me everything and don't you dare leave anything out."

"First of all, my parents were annoying as hell trying to woo him, you know how they do."

Meredith rolls her eyes. "Yep. Totally know what you're talking about."

"Yeah, but it didn't bother Quinton at all. He matched their energy and gave it right back to them. Also, he's a silent investor in a Hawaiian resort that his sister owns."

Her eyes grow huge. "Giiiirl tell me you're getting yourself an invitation there?"

"Nah. That wasn't anything we discussed, but..." I lean forward with my pointer finger in the air. "My dad was so impressed that he knew about business investments that he invited Quinton to Breckinridge for the grand reopening of Silver Pines Resort and he said yes!"

Meredith spits her coffee all over herself. "WHAT?" She looks down, irritated with herself and wipes coffee off her pajamas. "Wait, back up. So, your parents invited him to come to their resort in Colorado and he accepted?"

"Yeah. But they didn't just invite him. They invited us, Mere! Us...as a couple."

She laughs. "Oh, this is too good. And he said yes?"

"Yep."

"And how do you feel about that?"

"Well, not nearly as nervous about it as I was that night, especially when he said he's doing it because he needs my help too."

"Ouoh so tit for tat." She winks. "I like it."

"Yeah. He has this charity event he goes to every year and doesn't want to go alone because his ex will be there. She works closely with the charity too so he asked me to be his plus one and I said yes."

Meredith twists her mouth, her eyes narrowing.

"What? I can tell you're thinking something over there."

She leans forward and whispers, "Did he kiss you?"

"What? No."

She falls back into her seat. "Damn."

"What is so upsetting about that?" I laugh. "We're not a real thing."

"I know, but wouldn't it have been nice if you could've gotten a little happy ending out of the night? Some one-night stand action or something?"

"Uh, not when I have to see him again, Mere! What if the sex is bad and then we're forced to spend a weekend together?"

"Sex with Quinton Shay? Hockey player for the Chicago Red Tails?" She shakes her head. "No fucking way is he bad in bed. I'm calling it right now. I bet he could make you come for hours."

My cheeks pinken at her comment. "I bet he could make me come with just the sound of his voice if I'm being honest, but I can NOT go there."

Meredith laughs. "Oooh this is going to be so much fun watching you figure this out."

"Oooh my gosh, Kinsley! You turned me into a sexy minx with these pictures!"

I smile at Ada, my latest boudoir client. "Honey I didn't do anything but point and shoot. The sexy minx staring back at us is all you."

"But who even is that girl? My God, I don't even recognize her."

"Well, I certainly hope after today you start accepting how absolutely fucking stunning you are. You blew this session out of the water," I tell her as we flip through more of her finished photos. "I mean these are centerfold worthy if you ask me."

I catch a glimpse of Ada's face just before she bows her head, a tear slipping down her cheek.

"You know I never thought I would ever do something like this," she states, swiftly wiping her tears away.

"No?"

"Huh uh."

"Tell me what makes you emotional about seeing these now?"

"I just..." She shakes her head. "I had someone who made me feel like I was his everything, you know? I never doubted myself with Luke. But when he passed away I fell into this rabbit hole of grief and depression and I kind of... lost myself."

I met Ada a year ago when I adopted Nutsack at the animal shelter. She was so kind and enthusiastic about the animals she was caring for. She introduced me to every cat there but my heart fell for Nutsack the moment I met him. I knew Ada was newish to Chicago like I was at the time, but I had no idea where she came from or what her story was. Hearing her talk about losing a loved one tugs at my heart-strings. I squeeze her hand in mine as a show of support.

"I am so incredibly sorry for your loss, but even more than that, I'm so glad you're finding your way back to who you are. You are a beautiful human being, Ada. Planning this session with you was so much fun and I love that you can use this experience just for you. For your eyes. For your heart. For your soul. People like you are why I do this."

She sniffles. "Really?"

"Absolutely." I nod. "Sure, there are tons of women out there who want to do something unique for their significant others, and I even get couples who come in to have this experience together." I lean closer to her and whisper,

"Those days it's usually hot as hell in here and I have to remind the couples that I'm still here behind the camera because geesh!"

Ada laughs. "Oh my God!"

"Yeah. The struggle is real. But the main reason I love doing this job is to help women just like you. For the woman who has lost sight of who she is or who she wants to be. For the woman who looks at herself in the mirror and doesn't see the beauty she undoubtedly has. If I can get people to trust me to take pictures of them in their most vulnerable states, I value that opportunity to show them their worth. Their value. Their beauty. And Ada, you are gorgeous."

She brushes her hair back and sits up a little straighter collecting herself. "I feel beautiful in these photos Kinsley. I can't thank you enough."

"You are absolutely welcome," I tell her, clicking off the slide show on the screen. "I will compile all of these into an album for you and order the prints you want and then I'll call you when it's all in and ready for pick-up."

"That sounds perfect. Maybe we can have coffee or something. Being relatively new to the city I wouldn't mind a new friend."

"It's a deal! I would love to have coffee with you. I've only been in the city a couple of years so I know exactly how you feel."

"Great." She smiles. "So, I'll talk to you next week sometime?"

"Yep. I'll call you as soon as these are in and ready."

"Perfect. Thank you again. This was a marvelous experience. I can't wait to see the finished products."

I stand from the sofa as Ada does and reach out to give her a hug. "I am so glad I met you, Ada. Thank you for trusting me with your boudoir session."

She walks to the door where Nutsack is waiting on the nearby counter. She gives him a little scratch on the side of his face and says with a giggle, "I can't believe you renamed this poor boy after you adopted him."

"Of course, I did." I laugh. "He definitely wasn't a Sam kind of cat. He likes Nutsack, and he's so happy you introduced him to me last year."

She laughs. "I bet he loves it, and if he ever needs a playmate there are plenty more kitties at the shelter."

"Hmm." I hold my chin between my thumb and forefinger. "Nut sacks do usually hold...two...nuts."

Ada laughs. "See you later, Nutsack." She waves one more time before stepping outside. "Bye Kinsley!"

"See ya, Ada!"

"I should probably warn you," Quinton says after opening my car door. "These game nights can get pretty umm..."

I raise my brow. "Raunchy?"

"Yeah." He grins. "We're basically a group of middle school boys when we're together. I probably should've told you that before I invited you to come with me."

"Wouldn't have changed my mind, Shay." I wink at him and let him lead me to the front door. "I can do middle school boy. How raunchy are we talking? Like, penis jokes and porn references or is this more like a spin-the-bottle kind of evening?"

The front door swings open and a hot guy with several tattoos stands on the other side, an excited expression on his face. "I mean I'm totally up for spin the bottle if it means I can make out with Charlee." He winks just as another guy comes flying down the steps and tackles the guy at the door.

"You'll do no such thing, fucker."

Guy number one cackles. "Gotcha, Bro. I'm just teasing you. Besides, I saw what you did to the last guy who did Charlee wrong."

I turn to Quinton with an amused yet questioning glance. He smiles and gestures to the two guys playfully arguing at the door. "Kinsley this is Dex Foster and Milo Landric."

Dex rights himself and fixes his shirt after Milo's tackle and bows to me, opening the door further. "Welcome my lady. Please excuse the audacious behavior of my friend, Milo here. He's usually the perfect host."

Milo backhands Dex's upper arm. "Fuck you, Dexter." He laughs, shaking his head, and offers his hand to me. "You must be Kinsley."

"Yes. Kinsley Kendrick. Pleasure to meet you...again."

"Right." He nods. "The wedding. Your pictures were great by the way."

"Thank you so much. I had the best time that day."

"Well come on in."

Milo leads Quinton and I upstairs to where the rest of the group are already hanging out, but first we're greeted by two excited golden retrievers.

I squeal in excitement. "Oh my gosh! Hello babies! You

are so beautiful!" I tell them, scratching them both behind their ears. "Yes, you are. I love you already. You're my new best friends, okay? I promise to love you, pet you, and give you all the snackos whenever I can."

Milo chuckles. "Liza, Darcy, sit." Both dogs follow Milo's command and sit watching me, as if waiting for me to do tricks.

"Oh, you two are the sweetest things in the whole wide world. Liza and Darcy, huh? Those are beautiful names." I rub my hand on their chests. "It's so nice to meet you guys."

Quinton gives the dogs a few rubs and kisses while I take in the room we've walked into. Holy balls, it's gorgeous in here. Vaulted ceilings, spacious, natural colors. I can only imagine what it looks like during the daylight hours with the sun coming in off the lake. I bet it's a peaceful haven. I give hugs to Carissa, Rory, Tatum, and Charlee, having spent time with them snapping pictures during Rory's wedding, and marvel over how very pregnant three of them are.

Wow! Time Flies!

Then Milo reintroduces me to Colby, Hawken, and Zeke. It's remarkable how everyone makes me feel at home as if we've all been friends for years.

"Where's Summer?" Quinton asks Dex when we're all together.

"Oh, Rory and I have a friend from school who babysits for me sometimes so we can have a date night, so she took over tonight for us."

"Excellent."

"Kinsley, can I get you a drink?" Charlee asks me. "Beer? Wine? Margarita?"

"Margarita? Are you serious?"

She wags her brows. "Us preggers are drinking virgin, but you get the special stuff if you want it. Strawberry, raspberry, mango, or lemon-lime?"

"Oh my gosh, I'll gladly take a mango. Thank you so much!"

"Coming right up. Quinton? What can I get you?"

"Beer is fine. Thanks Charlee."

Quinton offers me a chair next to him that I gladly take as everyone seats themselves around an oversized dining room table.

"Kinsley, have you played Scattergories before?" Carissa asks me as Milo opens the box.

"Yep. All the time as a kid."

"Well, this ain't your kid version," Dex proclaims. "When we play, it's the adult version only. The more inappropriate the better."

I look at Quinton who winks and leans in to whisper, "See? Middle school boy."

"Right." I nod with a snicker and then smirk at Dex. "This is a challenge I think I can accept."

"Hope you know what you're getting yourself into Kinsley," Hawken warns. "Dex loves to unleash his inner horny teenager when we play this game."

"Bring it on, Dex. Let's see what you've got."

Dex rubs his hands together. "Oooh I like her already, Quinton."

Milo hands us our lists and rolls the lettered die. "Alright all answers have to start with...C." He taps the button on the timer. "Go!"

I read down the list of questions and try to come up

with my answers.

Something you keep hidden.

Song lyrics or title about sex.

Swear word.

Something found in the bedroom.

Reason for being late.

Sexual position.

Word with double letters.

Something you scream during sex.

Where not to be caught having sex.

Pet name (term of endearment).

The timer goes off and everyone lays down their pencils. Milo acting as the leader for this round calls off each question allowing us to give our answers.

"Alright something you keep hidden."

"Cock rings!" Charlee blurts out, making the entire group fall into a fit of hysterics. Hearing them all laugh makes me laugh as well.

"Oh my God, something tells me there's a story there."

"Nope." Milo shakes his head adamantly though his face is beet red. "No story whatsoever. My wife has a penchant for practical jokes is all."

"She's a dirty, dirty girl," Dex laughs. "And that's why we love her."

"Okay, okay. How about song lyrics or a title about sex?" Milo reads down the list.

"It's totally *Closer* by Nine Inch Nails," Hawken states proudly.

"Well, that's better than what I had," Quinton laughs. I peek over at his list.

"'Can You Feel The Love Tonight'?" I burst out laughing. "How old are you? Fifty?"

"Hey now!" he scolds me with a smirk. "Old enough to smack your ass if you get my drift. And who doesn't love Elton John? He's a classic."

Milo continues down through our list and when he gets to sexual position, Dex shouts, "CHICAGO WIND TUNNEL!"

Everyone at the table goes quiet. Eyebrows furrowed.

"Dude, do I even want to know what that is?" Colby chuckles.

Rory mumbles, "It's Dex. I think we know that answer."

Tatum shoots her hand in the air. "I just want to be the first one to say whatever the fuck the Chicago Wind Tunnel is, we've never done it in the bedroom because I have a feeling whatever it is, it's something pretty nasty."

Dex shoots me a challenging glance and I take him on. "Alright, De—"

"Wait." Quinton's hand is squeezing my thigh and holy hell did my body just ignite. "Are you sure you want to go there with him?"

"Oh, come on," I tell him. "Look at the poor guy. He's dying to tell us all what a Chicago Wind Tunnel is. You can see it all over his face."

Quinton holds his hands up in defense, scoffing out a laugh. "Don't say I didn't warn you."

"Okay Dex. Inquiring minds want to know—"

"I don't want to know." Zeke shakes his head, sitting back in his chair.

"I'm not sure I want to know either," Tatum says, covering her face with her hands.

"Good God he's going to tell us anyway." Rory gripes playfully. "Just get it over with already."

I turn to Dex. "What is the Chicago Wind Tunnel?"

A Cheshire-cat type grin spreads across his face. "It's when you're titty-fucking a girl. But instead of kneeling over her stomach as you do it, you kneel over her face and move back and forth between her tits. That way your ass crack rubs back and forth over her nose like she's in a wind tunnel."

I blink my eyes a few times, letting Dex's explanation sink in, and then slowly shift my gaze around the table. Tatum has her eyes closed and is trying not to laugh while Carissa giggles next to her. Rory palms her forehead shaking her head in disbelief and poor Charlee looks like she could vomit, but at the same moment, every guy at the table bursts out laughing. Quinton included.

"Oh fuck!" Milo cackles. "I can't breathe!"

"Where the hell did you come up with that, Foster?" Colby asks wiping tears of laughter from his face.

"Oh, I learned it from Hawken."

"The fuck you did!" Hawken shouts with a goofy smile on his face. "That's some highly messed up shit right there, bro. You did not learn that from me." He turns to Rory and mumbles, "I swear to God he did not learn that from me."

"NEW GAME!" Colby shouts. "We can't keep going after that one."

"Alright, I've got one." Rory reaches down under her chair and throws a stack of cards on the table. "This one is basically like Would You Rather but these are all, well, you

SUSAN RENEE

know. Not work appropriate whatsoever. Everyone takes a card from the pile and that's the question you ask. I wrote everyone's name down on a piece of paper folded up here, so you'll pick a name and pick a question. I'll go first."

She picks up the first card as well as a tiny slip of paper. Unfolding it, she reads the name. "Okay, Milo this one is for you."

He grins. "Bring it on."

"Would you rather watch a couple kiss for five minutes straight or watch an explicit sex scene with your parents."

Milo cringes but then tilts his head in thought. "Hmm, that depends. Who's doing the kissing? Are we talking Quinton and Zeke or—"

"Fuck yes," Quinton nods with an amused grin. "I'll kiss Miller for five minutes if it means you'll watch, Landric."

Milo waves his pointer finger. "You know I would almost be willing to call your bluff man."

Quinton laughs and suddenly I'm wondering why the idea of Quinton and Zeke kissing is turning me on. Seriously, two big burly hockey players swapping tongues? Phew! I'm getting hot just thinking about it.

"You know, I think I might have to say the sex scene with my parents. Mom reads the same kind of books I do so it's not like we're not familiar. She'd be cool with it. We'd probably just giggle about it anyway."

Colby laughs. "And then poor Charlee here would be getting railed for a week."

Charlee keeps a straight face when she says, "What's so poor Charlee about that?"

The ladies all pass around a fist bump and a couple cheers of agreement because who doesn't love hot sex? Then Rory passes the deck to Milo.

"Alright, Milo, you get to ask the next question."

Milo takes the next card on the pile and grabs one of the pieces of paper with a name written on it. "Smallson, this is for you."

"Smallson?" I lean over and whisper to Quinton.

"Carissa's maiden name. She was Smallson when we met her so she'll always be Smallson to us."

"Ah."

"Would you rather have sex in the shower or on the kitchen table?"

"Definitely not her old apartment shower, that's for damn sure," Colby chuckles, his hand rubbing Carissa's leg. "Remember that?"

"I didn't need sex in the shower with that old bathroom, babe," she grins. "The leaks were sometimes like jet powered tubs. No penis necessary."

"Good thing because Nelson has a teeny weeny anyway," Dex says with a wink.

"Whatever helps you sleep at night, Foster," Colby retorts with a smile. "And Milo, her answer is kitchen table."

"It is?" Carissa asks her husband.

Colby turns to her with a peaked brow. "Do I need to remind you of that night when I—"

"Nooope. I remember." She nods, her cheeks blushing. "He's right Milo. Kitchen table for the win and now it's my turn." She takes a card and a slip of paper and unwraps it.

"Dex, this is for you."

"Perfect! Hit me!"

Carissa snorts. "Oh my God. Okay, here we go. Would you rather have sex with a goat and nobody ever finds out, or not have sex with a goat but everyone thinks you did?"

The entire room falls into hysterics as Dex deliberates his answer. "I mean, is it one of those big ass Billy goats or one of those fainting ones that always falls over?

Tatum whacks Dex's arm. "Listen here dumbass, I don't fuck goat fuckers so there better be only one answer here or we're going to have a problem!"

He wraps his arm around his wife smooching her cheek. "But you're my goat, babe. Literally the greatest of all time."

She melts into him a little bit after that explanation. "Alright, I guess I can give you that."

"Believe me, I'm confident enough in my manhood that I don't give a fuck what everyone thinks I may or may not have done. My dick belongs to Tate, forever and always."

Satisfied with his answer, Dex grabs a card and a folded-up name from the center of the table.

"Kinsley darling, this one is for you."

"Uh oh. I'm on the hot seat."

Please don't let this be too embarrassing.

"Would you rather only ever have really loud sex or absolutely silent sex?"

"Oh, that's easy. Loud all the way," I answer. "Who wants silent sex? Silence is boring. Silence is no fun what-soever. I don't think I could be silent if I tried."

Quinton catches my eye and I wink at him, wondering

what he might be thinking right now. He doesn't say a word but the look on his face says he's both impressed and curious. Also, I'll just pretend I don't notice that he's shifting in his seat.

8

QUINTON

She likes loud sex.

Fuck if her answer isn't affecting me in ways I did not anticipate.

"Wait, wait, wait," Hawken waves his hands in front of him. "What if you're in public?"

Kinsley giggles. "Then we better not be in the library."

Dex leans forward on the table, narrowing his eyes at Kinsley. "Give me three places in public you could be loud enough and not get caught."

"You taking notes, Foster?" Charlee asks.

"I might be, yeah."

Kinsley taps her fingers on the table. "Parking garage during rush hour. Cemetery at night, and a—"

"The fuck?" Dex's face contorts. "A cemetery?"

"Yeah."

"Sweetheart, a cemetery is even quieter than a fuckin' library."

She smirks. "Yeah but nobody's going to interrupt you or tell you to go away in a cemetery. Everyone is dead."

Dex slaps the table amused and then points at me. "Your girl's got a little kink in her, Shay. I like it."

Kinsley and I both snicker because if Dex only knew what her initials spelled she would never hear the end of it.

"Third place," she continues, twisting her mouth as she thinks. "In the bathroom of a bar? Or maybe a storage closet or something. Nobody's going to concern themselves with you when they're that busy."

Hawken clears his throat and Rory's cheeks flush as she averts her eyes. Clearly there's something there I don't know about, but I don't bother bringing it up. What those two love birds do is their own business. Besides, I'm having trouble concentrating on not getting a chubby right here at the table at the thought of Kinsley Kendrick screaming my name at the top of her lungs in public as I have my way with her.

Jesus Christ.

Why am I even having these thoughts?

We're not even a real couple.

But damn...if we were, I'd absolutely want to take her home and see just how loud she can get.

We go through a few more questions for everyone including myself before switching to the game Carissa brought with her.

"Alright, listen, don't judge me...actually..." She twists her mouth. "Judge me all you want fuckers. I don't care. This game was made for this group!" She pulls the game from under her chair and if everyone's brows could shoot straight off their heads, there would be eyebrows all over the damn floor right now.

"What the fuuuuuck?" Dex half laughs half gasps.

Charlee, Rory, Tate, and even Kinsley are cackling and clapping their hands in excitement.

"Oh my God!" Charlee squeals. "There's no way this won't be good!"

"Cum Face?" Hawken cocks his head as he reads the box. "It's really called Cum Face?"

Carissa bursts out laughing. "Yes! It totally is!"

"Is this played the way it looks like it's played?" I ask, curiously noting the picture of dueling plastic penises.

She nods. "It absolutely is."

"Oh fuck. This is amazing!" Dex bellows, rubbing his hands together. "I approve. Who's going first? Please let it be the ladies because this is something I have to see."

Carissa places a plastic stand holding two purple dicks on the table and grabs a bottle of water, pouring a bit of it inside the stand.

"Now, this can be a drinking game but since there are several preggers at the table, I'll just use water. Rules of the game are easy. Two people pump away trying to get the other person's penis to...well, you know."

"So, the loser gets sprayed in the face?" Milo asks while his wife giggles next to him. "Is that what happens?"

Carissa smirks. "Yep."

"Sorry guys." Nelson shakes his head. "I couldn't convince her not to buy it."

"Are you kidding? This is fantastic!" Dex exclaims. "Best game I've ever seen! Kinsley's going first."

"What?" I'm ready to defend her at all costs but when I turn my head, she's biting her lip trying not to smile and pushing up her sleeves.

"Bring it on big guy. But only if Quinton fists the opposing dick."

Oh fuck.

'Cause my own dick hasn't twitched enough tonight.

I shake my head in amusement. "As you wish." I lean closer to her and whisper, "Prepare to get creamed."

"Okay, on three," Carissa says. "One..."

Kinsley whispers back, "I bet that's what you say to all the girls."

"Two..."

With a mischievous smile, I scoff out a quick laugh. "Apparently, only to you, Kink."

I have just enough time to wink at her before Carissa says, "Three!" And then we're both pumping our fists up and down as fast as we can as our friends cheer us on anxiously awaiting which one of us will be victorious. She may be trying to win this one but the way I see it, I win no matter the outcome. She could pump faster and harder than me, my eyes already fixated on the grip of her hand and fluidity of her movement as I picture that hand around my own cock. On the other hand, maybe I'll cream that beautiful face of hers and get a first glimpse of what she would look like if she were to take my load like the sexy, kinky woman I think she might be.

There's no way she's conservative about sex.

She's too fun and carefree to be uptight in bed.

Plus, she said she would rather be loud than silent.

Fuck, I bet she's a monster in the sack.

Why am I thinking about this again?

My arm is getting tired.

Look at her over there...unrelenting...

The grip she has on that thing.

Strong...tight...

God, she can grab my dick like that any time she wants.

Is it hot in here?

It's hot in here.

Fuck, I think I'm sweating.

Not wanting to be outdone, I try to pick up my speed using more of my forearm, but it seems my friends are all turning on me in favor of Kinsley.

Chants of "Blow that load! Blow that load!" are being sung around the table, while Dex does all he can to encourage Kinsley to keep going and unload all over me.

Shit! I'm failing at this!

How does a man fail at this?

A man knows how to get himself off.

He should be able to do it better than anyone.

No fucking way can she win this.

All it takes is for her eyes to shift from her hand in front of her to my face. Her stare. Her mossy green orbs accentuated by long soft lashes call to me in a way they never have until now and all of a sudden I'm a goner. She gives her plastic dick a few more pumps and suddenly my face is a wet mess and everyone is clapping and cheering.

Carissa throws me a towel to dry my face and when I look back at Kinsley, her smile is wide and beautiful and... did she just lick her lips?

"Sorry about that, big man," she says with a laugh and a cute as hell shrug. "Bet you've never been on that end of an orgasm, huh?"

Laughing with her, I shake my head. "I can't say that I have. Not like that anyway."

"Well, you're welcome then. For the experience." She giggles as I take one more swipe at my face and then playfully snap the towel at her arm.

"Don't worry. I'm sure I'll find a way to get my revenge."

She gives me another playful smile but it's the doe eyes that are totally reeling me in with every single glance tonight. I can't tell if this is just her personality or if she's actively flirting with me, but seeing her smile and knowing I had a hand in putting it there gives me this weird possessive feeling I did not anticipate.

I don't hate it.

In fact, I think I kind of like it.

And that's how I know I need to get a grip.

Kinsley Kendrick is not my girlfriend.

She's doing me a favor as I am for her.

Anything more than that is dangerous and I'm smart enough to know it.

She's not my type anyway.

Right?

She's not.

And this is not one of those times where I should fuck around and find out.

"Charlee really enjoyed having Kinsley at game night," Milo tells me as we're suiting up for tonight's game. The sounds of Taylor Swift comes from across the room as Dex goes through his pregame routine.

"Yeah, I think she really enjoyed herself."

"Fits right in and she handles Dex like it's nothin'."

His comment makes me laugh. "That she does."

Colby lifts his shoulder pads over his head. "Yeah Smalls really likes her too." He shrugs and positions his pads on his body. "But she's liked Kinsley for a while. I think she kind of knew she would fit in with our group."

"Sooo." Zeke laces his skate. "Tell us the good stuff."

"What good stuff?"

He cocks his head but Hawken is the one who huffs from his spot on the bench. "He means did you kiss her yet?"

My brows pinch. "What? No. Why would I do that?"

"What do you mean why would you do that?"

"She's not my girlfriend. We're not a thing."

Hawken chuckles. "Yeah. Okay."

I spin around to see him pulling on his jersey. "What?"

"So, you're a fake thing then."

"Yeah."

"Not at all a real thing."

"No."

"So, you weren't thinking dirty thoughts watching her pump that purple dick the other night?"

"I..." *Fuck yeah I was thinking dirty things.*

"OH!" Dex points to me. I didn't even notice him walk over here. "He hesitated."

"Alright, alright, of course I was thinking dirty thoughts. How could I not be? But that doesn't mean I did anything about it? Like I said, we're not together. She's just doing me a favor. Plus, she's five years younger than me."

"Who cares how old she is?" Zeke asks. "I mean...as long as she's legal." He cringes. "She's legal...right?"

Rolling my eyes, I huff out a laugh. "Yes she's legal dumbass. She wouldn't have been in Pringle's otherwise and plus, I'm not a perv."

"Okay so again...who cares how old she is? You think she's pretty, don't you?" Zeke asks. "I saw you looking at her more than a few times."

"Of course. I thought she was pretty the first time I saw her. That's half the reason I talked to her in the first place."

Colby pulls on his sock. "Five years is nothing. It's not like you're old enough to be her dad."

Hawken shrugs. "Maybe more like an older brother."

I throw Hawken the double bird and smirk. "Fuck you, Malone. Like Rory hasn't been like a sister to you for years."

Dex makes eyes at Hawken who throws his hands up in defense. "Hey, I didn't say it bro. Shay did. And no, I've never viewed her like a sister. She's too hot to look at her that way."

"Fuckin' Malone," Dex mumbles with a laugh.

"Anyway," Colby continues. "She makes you laugh. I saw it myself. In fact, I think you may have laughed the other night more than you have all season."

Dex leans over my shoulder. "She could and probably would do you a few extra favors if you played your cards right, dude. Just sayin'."

"Right, 'cause that would make me look like a stellar guy. This isn't *Pretty Woman*, you know. She's not some female escort I bought off the street to do whatever the hell I want with. I don't own her for fuck's sake."

Wouldn't mind introducing myself to parts of her though.

"Don't get your panties in a bunch, Shay." Dex chuckles. "We're just saying..."

"What? What are you saying exactly?" Honest to God this is getting irritating.

Zeke shrugs. "We're saying it's okay if you were to want...you know, more than something fake."

"Well, I don't."

"Why?" Dex asks. "She's hot."

It takes all I have not to round on him and get up in his face. "Because I don't, alright?"

He holds up his hands in defense. "Okay man, whatever you say."

I take a deep breath and release it with as much control as humanly possible. I don't know why I'm letting the subject of Kinsley get under my skin. The guys are only curious, but they're not in my head.

They don't know.

"Look, I'm sorry, alright? You're right. Yes, I find her attractive. Immensely...attractive. But we have an arrangement and I'm not going to screw that up just to get into her pants. I won't treat her like some casual fuck buddy. She deserves better than that and that's all I'm going to say on the matter."

"Well, alright." Zeke stands and cups my shoulder. "If that's how you feel, then it's done. Now let's go kick some Louisville ass."

9

KINSLEY

MEREDITH

Good luck this weekend! Can't wait to hear all about it!

ME

Thanks. Gah! He should be here any minute. I'm wearing leggings and a sweater…good or no good?

MEREDITH

Let me see.

ME

pic of me standing in front of a mirror

MEREDITH

Perfect. Comfy for flying. Not too overdressed but you don't look like a hobo. Shabby Chic looks good on you.

ME

Thanks Mere.

MEREDITH

eow.

"I know buddy." Nutsack jumps onto my bed and watches as I pack my suitcase for the weekend. "I promise, Ada said she would stop by and take care of you while I'm gone, okay? You like Ada, remember?"

Meow.

I fold myself down onto the bed so I can be at Nutsack's level. "And you're not going to do anything stupid for her while I'm gone, right?" I give him a little scratch behind his ears and he lifts his head to boop my nose with his own before curling up right next to my suitcase. "I know. I love you too, buddy. It's just for a couple days. If I could take you with me, I would, but I think this weekend will be weird enough without having a Nutsack running around our cabin."

My stomach flutters inside. Quinton should be here any minute and the more the seconds tick by, the more nervous I feel. I trust Quinton completely and know he has my back, but my mother is the wild card here. Not knowing what kind of mood she'll be in or what she'll do or say at any point throughout the weekend heightens my anxiety and makes me antsy. On any other normal day, I don't mind going wherever the wind takes me but knowing what could be in store over the next few days, I hate not feeling like I'm in control.

No.

Scratch that.

I hate that my mother puts me on edge to the point of feeling out of control.

I hate that I allow my mother to make me feel like I'm always on the proverbial hotseat.

I hate that she can't see how happy I am simply being me.

I hate that I'm always disappointing her no matter what I do.

And I hate that I've dragged Quinton into the middle of my family bullshit.

The last time I was with Quinton we had a fantastically fun night with some of his teammates. I don't think I've laughed that hard in an exceedingly long time. With Quinton's friends it was so easy. They made me feel as if we had all known each other for years. But what I haven't been able to stop thinking about since that night was Quinton's face when we were playing our last game together. My hand wrapped around that purple penis. The water spraying his face when I won. His promise of revenge.

Yeah, I'd be lying if that comment didn't make me feel warm in all kinds of places.

Maybe it was just the nature of the games we were playing but I spent the rest of that night wondering what it would be like to kiss Quinton. And because my mind can't stay in one lane for very long of course I thought about what he must be like in bed.

A take charge kind of lover.

A beast in the sheets kind of guy.

Likes to play rough but doesn't mind the occasional soft and slow sometimes.

He's the kind of lover who takes care of his woman in more ways than she probably knows exist.

That's the kind of lover I think Quinton Shay might be.

But I could be totally wrong.

I sit up on the edge of the bed, a slight wave of nausea hitting me. "And now I'm second guessing this entire weekend plan," I say to myself...or I suppose Nutsack if he's really listening. "How could this possibly go well? Quinton and I are not a couple. We only barely know each other yet we're supposed to make it look like we're madly in love? How?"

I stand and pace the bedroom area while haphazardly tossing the rest of my clothes into my suitcase. "Oh God, we never talked about any of the physical parts of this fake arrangement. Should we hold hands at some point?" I ask Nutsack who blatantly ignores me. "Will he be okay holding my hand? Putting an arm around me? Maybe a sweet kiss to the side of my head once in a while? Shit we never talked about kissing. I always think it's so sweet when guys do that. I would want that from my fake boyfriend. He should kiss me, right Nutsack?"

Of course, he doesn't answer me so I tip my head back and squeeze my eyes closed. "I'm rambling. Fuck. Get a grip Kinsley." I pull the top of my suitcase down, having finally thrown my toiletry bag inside, and then wring my hands together.

"But what if we need to kiss, kiss? Like, on the lips and everything. It would be weird if we went the entire weekend and never kissed. My parents would surely notice that, right?"

Should I ask him?

How would I mention that?

Shouldn't we practice something like that?

We should totally practice a kiss.

Otherwise, it could be awkward.

We can't have awkward.

It has to look real.

Knock, knock, knock.

"Shit. How am I going to bring this up?"

Nutsack raises his head at the knock on the door and stands up on the bed, stretching himself, before jumping down and walking with me to the door. Along the way I step on one of Nutsack's toys and then trip over the leg of my easel knocking it over as it crashes to the ground.

"Shit!"

The crash scares Nutsack who bolts backwards and then darts across the room by way of the coffee table. When he springboards off my box of positive potatoes to get to the couch, he knocks it to the floor spilling them everywhere. He's cautiously walking across the back of the couch when I pull open my studio door and find a fresh faced and totally handsome Quinton Shay smiling at me.

"Hey Kink." He's dressed in a pair of black jeans that effortlessly hug his strong legs, a white button-down collared shirt with a gray sweater over top, and a pair of white sneakers. His camel-colored cashmere overcoat is the perfect addition to his outfit.

"Wow." His hotness catches me off guard. "You look great." I look down at my choice of clothing for our flight this afternoon. Black leggings and an oversized green cable-knit sweater. "Maybe I'm underdressed."

He shakes his head as his eyes rake over me. "Nonsense. You look adorable."

Nutsack meows at my feet like he agrees with Quinton, but I know his game. He's just playing cute because he made a mess and caused me to make one as well.

"Hi Nutsack. Good to see you again."

Meow.

"Uh...come in. I just need umm..." My voice is unsteady and my brows pinch as I struggle to decide if I should bring up my thoughts to Quinton or just let whatever happens happen. I hitch my thumb toward the kitchen. "I need to feed Nutsack and then grab my bag and then I guess I'm ready."

"Alright."

Quinton steps inside, closing the door behind him, and then reaches down to pet Nutsack.

The minute I grab the can of his favorite wet food, Nutsack ignores Quinton and rubs himself between my feet purring like this is the biggest treat I've ever given him. It's not. I empty the can of food into his bowl and then set it on the floor so he can chow down.

Clearing my throat, I rub my sweaty hands on my pant leg and then move to clean up the mess I made before answering the door. "I hope you're ready for the weekend. You know I really do feel badly for putting you through this so if you decide you would rather not go through with it... well, you know, my parents will totally understand. I can easily tell them you got sick or you had an injury or you're busy making some little dying kid's hockey dreams come true and can't make it."

I flit around the studio never standing still because

having Quinton here is making me hella nervous. I scoop the last of my positive potatoes into the box and lift my easel back in place, and then tug on my sweater a few times to air myself out because hell if it isn't getting hot in here.

"Kinsley everything is fine. I'm more than happy to—"

"I mean sometimes my mom can be off her rocker and there's no telling what might come out of her mouth and then Dad," I laugh nervously. "Dad's like a human lie detector. He's probably already figured out that we're totally making this up and I don't know what he might say and—"

"Kinsley..."

My face is heating and I feel all sweaty and I can't stop rambling about utter nonsense because at some point I have to kiss Quinton and oh my God what if he thinks I'm the world's worst kisser or what if we just don't jive and there's no chemistry there and we're like the poster children for couples that should never exist together.

Rambling. I know.

"I'm just grabbing my suitcase and then we—Dammit!" I pull my suitcase off the bed forgetting that I never zipped it closed and now everything is spilled out of it all over my bedroom floor. "Shit." I shove my hands through my hair. "I'm sorry Quinton," I say, crouching down to scoop up my clothes and toiletries, literally shoving them back inside my suitcase with shaky hands.

Quinton is by my side in less than a second calm as a cucumber. "Let me help you."

"No. Really. It's fine. Silly me. I just forgot to z—"

He grabs my wrist gently. "Kinsley."

"Yeah?"

"What's going on?"

"Nothing's going on. Wha-what do you mean?"

He chuckles. "I mean you seem out of sorts. What's going on in that pretty little head of yours?"

He thinks my head is pretty?

Or does he think my head is little?

Is that a compliment or not?

"Do you think we should practice?" Yep. I just blurted that out because fuck my life.

He cocks his head. "Practice? Practice what?"

I try to swallow but my mouth feels like it's filled with cotton. There is literally no saliva in there. How does that even happen? Where the hell does it all go?

"Practice. Yeah. You know. Because what if we have to do it this weekend in front of people? I mean they'll think we've been doing it for months when really we've never..." I shake my head not knowing exactly how to spit out what I'm thinking.

Quinton's brows lift. "Do it in front of..." He shakes his head. "I'm sorry Kinsley. I don't think I'm following."

"Kissing, Quinton. Should we practice kissing...er...I don't know." I wring my hands together again. "I mean what if people think we're this serious couple and we have to kiss in front of them? We've never done that because you know, we're not really real, you know? So, it would be like an awkward first kiss in front of everyone and I don't want to make you look bad or—"

"Whoa, whoa, whoa." Quinton stops me, his hands on my shoulders. "First of all, I'm not certain you've taken a breath since I walked through the door so take a deep breath for me, alright?"

I do as he asks but I still feel hot and my stomach is all quivery.

"So, you're saying you want to practice kissing?"

I squeeze my eyes closed. "God it sounds so stupid when you say it back."

"Not stupid, Kinsley," he says gently, shaking his head. "Is that really what has you tied up in knots right now?"

Can this be any more embarrassing? "Yeah. I'm sorry. My mind just...stupid irrational fears, I know."

"Don't apologize. You're right. We should definitely practice."

"We should?"

When I open my eyes, Quinton is nodding. An empathetic smile on his face. His hands now cradling my cheeks. "Absolutely."

"Umm, okay. H-h-how do you want to—"

"I'm just gonna go for it," he murmurs. His face within mere inches of mine. "That okay?"

I nod. "Yeah. Yep. Yes. That's uh...that's good. That'll be good."

He moves close enough to me that I can smell his minty toothpaste. "You ready?"

"Mhmm."

He tilts my head slightly and I close my eyes again in anticipation and before I can conceive another thought his lips are on mine.

Holy balls!

Quinton Shay is kissing me!

He's ever so soft as his lips tenderly brush with mine. His mouth is warm, gentle, and slow as he coaxes my lips with a sweet affection that sets off all the bells, whistles, and sirens in my head and a swell of heat through my body I did not expect. This kiss is...well, it's everything I didn't expect from a big husky hockey player, but it's also sweet.

And delicate.

And affectionate.

And everything.

And then just as quickly as he started, he pulls away and I'm frozen. My eyes closed, my lips parted. To be honest, I'm not even sure I'm still breathing. Quinton's hands still hold my face. I open my eyes and find him gazing down at me. Like he's searching for something deep down inside me. His eyes are dark and his breath quickened. He glances down at my lips and swallows before he mutters, "Maybe one more time. To make sure we have it right."

"Yeah," I whisper.

One of his hands slides into my hair while the other trails down to my neck and he's kissing me again and holy shit if I don't get weak in the knees. He starts off slow and soft and then his tongue trails against my lips, slipping between them, lazily exploring, tasting.

Quinton picks up his pace and I follow his lead and this practice kiss is starting to feel less fake by the second. My hands rest on his muscular chest and I groan into his mouth as my tongue collides with his. I don't mean to make a sound but hell. Kissing Quinton Shay is kind of like having an out of body experience. He presses his body firmly against mine in response and oh my God. Can we just cancel this weekend and make out right here for the next couple of days?

Because damn! Quinton Shay is an excellent kisser.

I don't ever want this moment to end.

But it does.

It ends.

And then he's watching me.

The same darkened stare he had before.

But he doesn't say anything.

Is he waiting for my reaction?

"That was...uh..." I lightly pat his chest a few times. "Yeah. Good. Okay. I think we've got that down. Let's go."

I bend down and grab the handle of my now closed rolling suitcase and lead us both to the door, not giving him a chance to say anything.

Because I don't want to know what he thought.

I don't want to know if he thinks I'm a good kisser or a bad one.

I don't want him to laugh over my need for a practice kiss.

I don't want my new favorite thing to be tainted by the fact that none of it was real.

I want to fly to Colorado and float over the clouds while I'm living a dream in my head and in my heart.

"See you later, Nutsack. Be a good boy."

Quinton loads my suitcase into the car while I strap in and try to calm the voice in my head that keeps screaming repeatedly, "Oh my God! Quinton Shay's tongue was just in my mouth and it was all the things!"

10

QUINTON

I don't know what the hell happened when I walked into her studio today but I think kissing Kinsley Kendrick might be my new favorite thing. I haven't been able to stop thinking about it since the moment she brought it up.

A practice kiss.

It was a clever idea and one I hadn't thought of.

Now it's *all* I've thought of.

Driving to the airport.

As we lifted off the runway, her hand gripping mine because she hates the take off and the landing.

When she fell asleep on my shoulder for a half hour during our flight.

And now in the backseat of the SUV we're riding in on the way to the cabin.

I wish she wouldn't have been so good at it because fuck me, now I have to spend the weekend with a woman I liked the taste of whose lips were soft and supple and warm against my own, and I have to control myself.

Or...

I have to find a reason to practice again.

"In case I forget to say so several hundred times over this weekend, thank you for doing this."

I glance over at her, taking note of her flushed cheeks and her nervously wringing hands. It's not lost on me that I'm the one who should be nervous here, being the new guy and the fake boyfriend in front of her family, yet I'm eerily calm. To be honest, I'm excited for this weekend. It's been a tough and grueling season so far and I appreciate the break while the All-Star games are going on to relax and not have to think too much about hockey. Kinsley on the other hand, has been a ball of nerves since I showed up at her door today. I cover her fidgeting hands with my own and give her a reassuring smile.

"It's my pleasure. Everything's going to be fine, Kink. I promise." I lean over and whisper so our driver can't hear me say, "I can be a fucking good boyfriend when I want to be."

Kinsley finally relaxes a bit, letting out a small laugh. "Well thank God for that. I'll expect nothing less than your A-game then."

Rubbing my knuckles on my chest, I wink at her. "Let the wooing commence."

Our driver drops us off at the main house of the Silver Pines Resort where we check in and get our keys and directions to our cabin. The main lobby isn't too busy but Kinsley makes a beeline to the exit, not wanting to make eye contact with anyone hanging around.

"Everything okay back there?" I ask when we're outside on the path to our cabin.

"Hmm? Oh yeah. Fine," she answers. "Just noticed a few familiar faces and didn't want to go through the whole back and forth of 'Hey, hi, hello. I'm great. You look fabulous! What am I doing now? Let me tell you what I'm not doing which is living off my rich parents and doing whatever it is they tell me to because I'm a fucking full-grown woman and deserve to live a life of my own.' You know. Those conversations can get awkward."

"That all spilled out of you quite quickly. Almost like you rehearsed it. Did you rehearse it?"

She shakes her head, pulling her suitcase behind her. "No need to rehearse it when it's the same conversation I end up having with all of my parents' friends."

"Right. Got it."

Personal note: This is harder on Kinsley than I thought it would be. Help her relax this weekend.

"Well, if you find yourself needing to be saved from whatever conversation you're having with someone and I'm around, I'm more than happy to help steer things in a new direction. You know, take the focus off you a little, or talk you up as the absolute love of my life."

"Uh huh. And how will you know when I need that to happen?"

"I don't know. How about a code word or something?

She halts halfway up the stairs and looks back at me. "A code word?"

"Yeah. What's wrong with a code word? Just slip it into the conversation and then I'll know."

"So, it should be something easy like, uh, doughnuts? Or maybe rainbows?"

I shake my head. "Nah. Those are too common. You might actually use those words this weekend and I'd hate to interrupt for no reason."

"Alright then." She turns back around and continues up the stairs in front of us. "Penis."

"What?"

"Penis it is. Penis is the code word."

"Penis."

"Yep."

"Why penis?"

She laughs. "Because why not penis? I can't think of the last time I used penis in a sentence with anyone so I think that's a safe word."

Shaking my head in amusement even though she's not currently looking my way, I concede. "Alright. Penis it is."

"Oh my gosh!" Kinsley gasps after climbing the steps to a walkway leading to our cabin. "Treehouses, Quinton! Look! They're beautiful."

Situated among a group of bridges within the edge of the forest is a collection of luxury tree houses. They look like tiny chalets situated among the trees. Each one offering gorgeous tree-top views of the snowy mountains below from an outdoor deck and nighttime stargazing from modern-day turrets on each structure. I must admit, Kinsley's parents hit the nail on the head with the layout of this place. Assuming it's equally as nice inside as it is outside, this is a winter paradise and every skier's dream.

"It is pretty damn nice."

"Should we check out the inside?" Kinsley dangles the key to the door.

"Lead the way."

Following her inside, I'm impressed with the grandeur of the place. To the left just inside the door are the stairs to the turret and a small bench with attached cubbies for storage of ski gear and winter coats. Kinsley walks further into the expansive great room with a cathedral ceiling and floor-to-ceiling windows. She runs her hand over the pine mantle above a large wood-burning fireplace that is lit and crackling. She turns, her jaw hanging open, and then smiles.

"It literally feels like we're living in the trees."

Though the amenities here are modern with some even being high-tech, the all-around feel of our surroundings is nothing but luxurious comfort. This is the perfect place for someone like her. Someone who enjoys seeing the beauty in the world around her.

I like that about her very much.

She's not the kind of girl who needs or wants extravagance.

She enjoys simple. Small. Intimate. Personal.

"Knock, knock!" We both turn to see Mr. and Mrs. Kendrick at the door.

"Mom," Kinsley stammers. "What are you doing here?"

Mrs. Kendrick cocks her head giving her daughter a pitying look. "I own the place, darling. Did you not expect to see us when we personally invited you here?"

Kinsley shakes her head. "Sorry, I didn't mean it like that. I just...we just...anyway we just got here."

"I know, dear. I asked Joffrey at the front desk to keep me informed of your arrival so I could check in on you both myself." She walks further into the great room where

Kinsley and I are standing and offers me a weak hug. "Quinton, it's so nice to see you today. Welcome to Silver Pines." She gives me some of those stupid fake kisses on each cheek and I want to fake-wipe them off just to see her reaction.

"Thank you very much Mrs. Kendrick. You've truly outdone yourselves. This place is immaculate and the views are breathtaking."

"They are, aren't they?" She smiles and then gestures to the walkway between our chalet and the one directly beside us. "We'll be your neighbors for the next few days. You'll notice the enclosed walkway connecting our cabins through this window, so please feel free to come and go as you please. Mi casa es su casa, as they say."

"Thank you." I nod.

"Hopefully, you two will find the time to join us for dinner. Oh!" she winces. "I should've asked but just assumed, there's only one bed so yo—"

"Mom..." Kinsley starts but I wrap a gentle arm around her to stop her.

"It's perfect. Thank you again." I lay a kiss to the side of Kinsley's head for good measure.

"Definitely take advantage of the hot tub on the back deck. We've had a few rare and spectacular views of the northern lights over the last couple of nights. You might just get lucky."

I wouldn't mind gettin' lucky.

I don't know how Kinsley would feel about that though.

"Great, well, we need to unpack now so..." Kinsley's tone says everything her blank face doesn't say. She clearly doesn't like being around her mother.

SUSAN RENEE

"Right. We'll see you at dinner then." Mrs. Kendrick turns to leave but as she reaches the door she turns back. "If you need anything—"

"I know who to call," Kinsley groans.

Not wanting to come across as a dick, I smile at Kinsley's mom and thank her again for the weekend invitation.

"You didn't have to do that, you know." She grabs her suitcase and wheels it back to the bedroom.

"Do what?"

"Be nice to her like that."

"Oh. I'm sorry. I didn't mean anything by it, I just—"

"I know what you meant. I'm just saying. She's never nice to me. What you just witnessed was all show for you so..." Kinsley steps into the bedroom and I follow behind her until she stops abruptly in the doorway, turns, and looks behind me, her brows pinching.

"What is it?"

"One bed."

"Yeah. Your mom said that, remember?"

She tilts her head, looking at me like I don't get it, but I do. It sucks but it is what it is and I know how to be a gentleman. "It's fine. You take the bed. I can sleep on the couch."

"What? No! You're not sleeping on the couch."

"Why not? It looks large enough. I'm sure it's comfortable."

"Quinton Shay you are one of the national hockey league's premier players and I'll be damned if I ask you to come with me on this trip and then make you sleep on the couch. I'll sleep on the couch."

104

"Like hell you will. And you didn't invite me here. Your parents did and I accepted."

"Right but we still have to look like a couple and couples—"

"Sleep together. Yeah. I get it."

"So—"

"We share the bed then." I shrug like it's no big deal because in all reality, it's not. I can control myself for a few nights. It might be hard...literally...but I can man up and pull through.

"Seriously? You're really suggesting we sleep... together?"

"We're both adults, aren't we? I think we can handle it. I mean I know you can't keep your eyes and hands off me but—"

A laugh finally bursts from her mouth and she playfully smacks my arm. "Shut up!"

Phew. Finally broke that ice.

"What do you say, Kink? Will you sleep with me for the weekend?"

She laughs again. "Okay, okay. We can do this." She points a stern finger at me. "But you better not snore."

"Scouts honor. I don't snore."

"Okay good."

"Can't promise I won't Dutch oven you though."

Kinsley falls into a fit of giggles, shaking her head. She's damn cute when she's happy and laughing. "We're leaving the door open at night then. This girl's going to need some fresh air."

"And let the wild animals inside? I don't think so."

"There are no wild animals here."

"Kinsley..." I cock my head and smile at her. "We're in the mountains of Colorado. There are plenty of wild animals out there. Bears. Mountain lions..."

"They're all hibernating. It's winter, remember? Hence all the snow."

"Uh huh. That's what all the campers think until the big ass beast is climbing up to your treehouse and letting himself in so he can enjoy your heat while he feasts on your limbs."

She snorts this time. "Oh my God, you're incorrigible."

I gesture to my hands and legs. "These are million-dollar limbs you know."

"And I wouldn't dream of hurting them."

She places her suitcase along the wall near the closet and waits for me to set mine up on the other side of the room. With her hands on her hips, she releases a big sigh and then asks, "Well, what should we do next?"

"We should explore," I tell her. "There were a bunch of shops when we came in. You want to go look around? Show everybody what a cute couple we are doing coupley things?"

"Yeah." She nods. "That sounds fun. Let me grab my purse."

Frowning, I shake my head and move to take her hand in mine. "You don't need a purse. Come on."

"What? Why?"

"Because as of right now, I'm your doting loving can't-get-enough-of-you boyfriend and I pay for everything."

"What? No, no, no, no, no. That was not the plan. I am fully capable of paying for my own things."

"I know you are." I place a chaste kiss on the back of

her hand. "But if we're going to come off as a serious couple, I want to do this. A rich boyfriend who's crazy about his girl would want to buy her things, so let me do this. It's not a big deal."

I step forward but she doesn't move causing a tug between our hands. "But it is a big deal, Quinton."

"Why?"

"Because I didn't ask you to do this for your money."

"I know you didn't." I step back up to her and smooth my hands down over her soft brown hair. "Stop over-thinking this, Kinsley. We're just two people heading out for some casual shopping. Enjoying each other's company. None of this is about money. It's more about convincing the public that we're a committed couple. Stop worrying and let's go have some fun."

She stares into my eyes for a few seconds and I begin to see the vulnerability she doesn't want anyone else to see. "I'm not like anyone else here, Kinsley, alright? I'm two hundred percent here for you and you only. Okay?"

Finally, she nods. "Yeah. Okay. I'm sorry."

"There's nothing to be sorry for." I lean forward and kiss her forehead. "Let's go buy you something nice."

She laughs a little and rolls her eyes but acquiesces, following me out the door and then stopping on the bridge between the trees.

"Kinsley? You okay?"

"Yeah. Just...look how beautiful it is here. The snow glistens out there under the lights." She gestures to the ski slope to the east of our set of tree houses. "And it looks like tiny diamonds hanging from some of those trees, doesn't it?"

"Yeah, you're right. I guess it does."

"It's stunning." She breathes in. "And you can smell the burning firewood coming from everyone's cabins. I love a good winter where you can snuggle up in the comfort of your home and read a good book or paint or you know, do whatever."

Sex.

Sex in the wintertime is fun.

Sex anytime is fun.

But particularly wild naked sex in front of the fire.

I watch Kinsley take in nature's beauty around her and for a few seconds allow my mind to picture what life might be like if Kinsley Kendrick was really my girlfriend.

First off, we wouldn't be out here and we wouldn't be about to go shopping. I would've had her naked and in bed by now enjoying the backdrop of the snowy mountains while tasting every part of her. In fact, we probably wouldn't go shopping all weekend because we wouldn't be leaving the cabin at all. We'd be enjoying three lustful days of being completely naked and snuggling together under a pile of soft fuzzy blankets. The agenda would include hot steamy sex on all possible surfaces including on the back deck at night under the northern lights.

And then we would probably...

"Seth?"

"Kinsley?"

"What?" I ask as I feel Kinsley's hand squeeze mine. She yanks back on my arm having stopped on the bridge connecting our cabin to the others in our community. Finally seeing what she's looking at, I halt my steps too and nearly gasp as my heart falls through my stomach.

Fuck I wasn't paying attention.

"Quinton?"

"Lexi..."

The shock on Kinsley's face finally registers with me as I peer back at the couple in front of us. Lexi Stock, my ex-girlfriend, is walking arm in arm with Seth Lockhart, a B-list celebrity actor who I assume Kinsley knows.

"Wha-what are you doing here?" she asks him.

"Your parents invited Lexi and I months ago after our wedding. I've always supported their endeavors. You know that."

Kinsley's staring at this guy—speechless—and I'm not quite sure what to do so I offer him my hand. "Hi. I'm Quinton Shay."

"Hey, man," he says with a huge smile. "I know who you are." He shakes his head. "I didn't know I would be in the presence of hockey royalty this weekend. Pleasure to meet you. I'm Seth Lockhart."

Hockey royalty?

Now who's sucking up?

Although I know who the guy is, I pretend I've never heard of him. Yep, it's a petty thing to do but I never said I wasn't the pettiest of them all. This is the douche Lexi left me for, so as far as I'm concerned I owe him nothing. Gesturing between Kinsley and Seth I ask, "And how do you two know each other? Family friends?"

"Uh, no." Seth smiles awkwardly.

Sighing beside me, Kinsley finally answers. "Seth and I dated for a while several years ago."

Oh fuck.

He's the ex.

The ex who is now with my ex.

And Kinsley clearly didn't know any more than I did.

Clearing my throat, I nod. "Oh. Okay. Uh, Lexi this is Kinsley Kendrick, my—"

"Fiancé!" Kinsley blurts out, shaking Lexi's hand. "We're getting married."

Oh shit.

Ooh shit.

Yep. I said fiancé.

I said it out loud.

"Oh! How adorable. Congratulations to you both," Lexi says with a smile.

Adorable? Why the hell would she say that?

Is she serious?

Or is she being a complete bitch who doesn't believe a word I said?

Honestly, I can't tell if she's genuinely excited or if her face contorts like that when she smiles all the time.

"Thank you," Quinton murmurs, giving me a smile and hopefully reminding himself to breathe. I want to take back the words and apologize profusely but no way in hell can I do that in front of my ex. No way will I admit defeat now. We're all in.

"Yes congratulations," Seth tells us. "I'm sorry, your parents didn't say anything when we saw them last night."

"Oh, we didn't want them to say anything because we haven't announced it yet."

Good save.

That's a good save, right?

"Can I see your ring? I bet it's stunning. Quinton always had wonderful taste in gifts."

Fuck. Fuck. Fuck.

I pull my hand behind me unable to think of what I should say because there are exactly zero rings on my finger at the moment.

"The ring was being sized. We're actually on our way to pick it up right now. I had it flown here with a jeweler friend coming this weekend."

Wow.

Quinton's fast on his feet.

"You don't mean Albert do you?" Seth asks. "Albert Nial?"

Of course! Albert is a good friend of my parents. There's no doubt he'll be here this weekend. "Yes. Quinton had the ring custom made by Albert."

Seth pitches his thumb over his shoulder. "He's here. I saw him walking into the Pine Jewels just a little bit ago. I didn't know you knew him."

"Perfect timing then." Quinton smiles, ignoring Seth's other patronizing comment, and squeezes my hand in his.

"So how did he pop the question, Kinsley?" Lexi asks me. "I bet it was very thoughtful. Was it a huge grand gesture? I would've thought the media would have reported on that right away." Her brows pinch. "But I don't remember hearing anything."

Shit! She needs a story?

A quick romantically sweet story?

"Well, it was uh...it was so sweet."

My mind is drawing a complete blank.

"We were umm...together one night and...and then he..."

What do I say?

"Uh..." I shake my head and blink a few times. "Penis."

Everyone looks at me in confusion including Quinton and now I'm freaking out and staring back at him not understanding why he isn't saving me.

I said the word!

I said penis!

Penis! Penis! Penis!

That's still the code word, right?

I didn't change it, did I?

"I'm sorry," Lexi snickers softly. "I must've misheard you."

"She meant nutsack," Quinton says, finally coming to my recovery.

Thank God.

Lexi laughs. "Nutsack?"

"Yes! Nutsack! Yes!" I shout a little excitedly. "My cat," I add, feeling the relief of Quinton's help. "I have a cat named Nutsack. It's a whole thing. Long story."

"Right." Quinton nods. "Anyway, the proposal was a lowkey thing because we wanted to enjoy our engagement for a little while without the media feeding into it. So, after dinner one night while I was feeding her cat, I slipped the ring on his collar, waited for him to be done eating, and then tossed one of Kinsley's yarn balls across the room knowing he would run after it. Kinsley caught him and when she picked him up and noticed the ring I was already on my knee."

"Oh my gosh, it was so incredibly sweet!" I press a hand to Quinton's cheek and kiss his lips gently. "And of course, I said yes."

Lexi clears her throat, looking uncomfortably between us. "Well congratulations to you both. I'm sure you'll be incredibly happy together."

"We are." Quinton returns my kiss with another and then rubs his nose against mine. "And we will. Every minute of every day." He never stops gazing at me and I can feel myself getting flushed in my cheeks wondering what he might be thinking.

Because I'm now thinking all kinds of things I shouldn't be.

Like how I wouldn't mind going right back into our cabin and making out with Quinton Shay for the rest of the night.

Like how his kisses make me weak in the knees.

Like how his hands on me make me feel safe and protected. Like nobody can hurt me.

Like how his eyes always seem to be able to see right through me down to my soul.

I could get lost in Quinton's eyes.

I could get lost with Quinton.

"Well, we'll let you two lovebirds get on your way so we can get back to our cabin." Seth breaks up our moment. In my head I'm mentally flipping him off. "It was good to see you, Kinsley. Congratulations again."

"Your cabin? Are you in one of these?" I gesture towards the other cabins in our area.

Seth points to the one right next ours on the opposite side from where my parents are staying. "Yeah we're right there. Is this one you guys?"

Fucking wonderful.

"Yeah."

"Okay. Well maybe we can hang out one night or something. You know. Have a beer and share stories."

Quinton shakes his head still staring at me. "Oh, I don't think that will be possible Seth," he says. "You see, once I get Kinsley's ring back on her finger I don't plan to let her out of our bedroom until it's time to fly home... unless, of course, she wants sex in the shower or sex by the fire or sex on the kitchen counter. Whatever my girl wants, she gets."

Seth scoffs out a laugh. "Well, a man's got to eat sometime, am I right?"

"Oh, I plan to eat," he answers, licking his lips and wagging his brow. "I plan to eat all weekend. See you Sethy."

Swoooooooon!

I don't even bother to say goodbye because that ass muncher doesn't deserve any of my attention. Even Quinton gives them both a quick grin, much to Lexi's surprise, and leads us across the bridge and down the steps toward the shops we passed on our way up here earlier. Once we're in the clear I let out a huge breath.

"Quinton, I am so sorry!"

"I know."

"I didn't mean to just blurt it out like that. I don't know what I was thinking. I just saw him and everything came back and I couldn't let him think I was—"

"I know, Kins. I know." He squeezes my hand. "Trust me, if you wouldn't have said it, I probably would have."

"Also, I swear to God I didn't know your ex was with my ex. I had no idea who he dated after me. I kind of blocked him from my life after I left."

"I knew," he tells me. "I knew who she was with, but I didn't know he was your ex."

"I'm sorry they were even here. That we ran into them. That they're our fucking neighbors for the weekend."

Quinton chuckles. "I'm not the least bit worried, but I promise you by the end of this weekend they're going to wish they were nowhere near us."

"Uh oh," I snicker. "What's that supposed to mean."

"Just tell me you trust me and you're willing to play along with me."

"To piss off those two? Hell, yeah I'll play with you. Whatever your game is, I'm in."

"Perfect. Come on."

"Where are we going?"

He stops and cocks his head. "You can't leave here without the best ring Pine Jewels has to offer."

My smile falters. "Quinton, you might want to rethink this. The regular clientele here are people who have stupid amounts of money and spend it on just about anything. There won't be anything cheap here."

"Good. I have stupid money and I don't want cheap."

"Quinton!"

"It's just jewelry, Kinsley. Consider it a thank you gift or an I'm sorry gift or whatever you want it to be, but we're in this now. You need a ring on your finger tonight so the question doesn't come up again. And then for the rest of this weekend, I'll be making certain that anyone who sees us together knows you're mine without a doubt."

"What do you mean? How are you going to—"

"Like this." Quinton stops just outside Pine Jewels and spins us around so my back is against the wall of the building. His fingers thread through my hair and I'm damn sure if it weren't winter here, my entire body would break into a sweat. His warm lips press against mine and I can feel his confidence. His power. His protection.

He trails one hand down my back, gripping my waist and pressing into me with the weight of his body. I slide my hands up to rest on his firm, tight chest and tilt my head to give him a better angle. He takes full advantage, swiping his tongue against my lips as if asking for access to more of me. Access I unequivocally grant him because oh my God! This does not feel like an I'm-your-fake-fiancé-so-we-have-to-kiss type of kiss. Quinton is kissing me with full-on tongue and there is nobody here to see it.

His hand smooths down over my ass and he groans against my mouth. His touch heats everything in me, sparking my desire and melting it into a pool of moisture collecting between my legs. I can feel how turned on he is as we become a tangled mess of lips and tongues and hands, gasps, and moans and groans.

Jesus, thank God nobody can see us but also, even if all of Silver Pines was watching, I don't think I could stop. I have no idea how long we stand here, kissing like our lives depend on it, but I allow myself to get lost in him if only for a few fleeting moments because this kiss, it's everything.

If I didn't already know everything between us is a fake

arrangement I would swear he was claiming me as his own with this kiss.

Like I'm really his.

Like he's really mine.

When he finally slows his movements and our lips separate, he leans his forehead against mine and we catch our breath. His eyes close and his brows pinch as if he's confused.

"What was that for?" I ask breathlessly.

Quinton's chest rises and falls in tandem against mine. He doesn't answer right away. He swallows hard and then murmurs, "That's how hockey players kiss their fiancées."

I touch my fingers to my swollen lips. "Oh. Really?"

He nods. "Yeah. You got a problem with that?"

"No." I shake my head slowly, my gaze never leaving his. "Not at all, Quinton. Practice is good."

"You should probably prepare yourself Kinsley."

"For what?"

"I saw the way that asshole looked at you back there and I didn't like it." He shakes his head, his eyes squeezing shut like he's struggling with his thoughts. "Call me possessive if you want, but now that I know he's in the cabin next to us and will be watching for you, I plan to show him what he's missing every fucking chance I get."

Ho.ly. Shit.

"Quinton..."

"I don't even know the guy but I know you deserve so much more than anything he's ever offered you, Kinsley."

"I know I do. I don't care about making him jealous. I walked away from him because he was a douche. He said some hurtful things during our time together and..." I bow my head, a bit embarrassed. "Look, I know I'm not perfect. I don't look like Lexi and other women like her, but a girl can only take so much, you know?"

Quinton lifts my chin with his finger. "Hey."

"It's really okay. I'm good now. I'm in a good place. I didn't want to live like that anymore so I left. End of story."

"That doesn't mean it doesn't sting a little." He tries to give me an empathetic smile. "Trust me. I understand that just as much as you do."

"Did you love her?"

He takes a breath before answering. "I thought I did."

When I don't say anything he elaborates. "She's the reason I haven't wanted a relationship in years. She broke me. Right there on the red carpet for the G.A.M.E. Night Gala. Literally walked out of my arms and into the arms of another man in front of everyone."

My breath hitches. "Oh, my gosh. I'm so sorry Quinton."

"It was probably the most humiliating and heart-breaking night of my life." He inhales a deep breath. "I haven't had a serious relationship since her because I don't trust very well, but I got through it. I worked through my pain. Focused on my game. I moved on. It doesn't make seeing her here any easier though. I'm over her, but it still stings, you know?"

I nod. "Yeah. I get it."

"Yeah. I know you do."

We stand here for several minutes staring at each other, lost in our own thoughts, but sharing a connection neither one of us could have planned.

He gets me.

He understands my heart.

"Can I ask you something?"

"Of course." His brows furrow. "Anything."

"What made you trust me?"

He chuckles lightly. "You weren't looking for something. You didn't even know I was there behind you that night. You never asked me to lie for you. You were apologetic from the get-go. You were just...you. Adorable and fun." He lifts his hand, smoothing my hair back from my chilled face. "I thought you were pretty and something about you made me want to say yes. Made me want to take the leap."

How on earth this man can kiss like a hungry beast one minute and then be this tender the next, I may never know but damn, if I'm not starting to wonder what life would be like if Quinton Shay was more than just my fake fiancé.

"I'm really glad you're here, Quinton."

"I'm glad I'm here too." He leans forward and presses a kiss to my forehead and then grasps my hand. "Now let's go find you a ring."

"Hey that reminds me. How did you know Albert Nial would be here this weekend. Do you really know him?"

He shrugs with a laugh. "Would you believe me if I said I didn't?"

"No!" I burst out.

"Well, it's true. I totally pulled that one straight out of my ass and Seth went with it, so I guess I got lucky."

I wink at him on our way inside the jewelry store. "With an ass like that, of course, you did."

12

QUINTON

"You have got to be kidding me with this one." Kinsley holds up her left hand, cringing at the hefty rock on her finger.

"No, you're right. It's not you." I pick another one from the tray. Slightly smaller but with tiny diamonds surrounding the three-carat princess cut stone in the middle. "What about this one?"

She shakes her head before she even holds it and leans over to whisper, "I'm just not the look-how-many-diamonds-are-on-my-finger kind of girl. I don't need to look like I'm marrying a rich guy. I don't need the show and tell. If this is going to be believable, we need to find something that is unmistakably me."

"Something you..." I stand back and allow my eyes to roam over her for a moment, noting all the things about her that attract me.

She's not a diva.

She's not into the rich and famous lifestyle.

She appreciates the smaller things in life.

She takes time to look at glistening snow.

She loves treehouses.

She takes pictures of flowers and trees and grass and all things natural.

She has a profound sense of humor.

She has a cat named Nutsack and she crochets positive potatoes.

And she can pump a purple plastic penis like nobody I've ever seen.

Okay maybe that last part isn't important when it comes to buying a ring.

But it's a core memory that will always remain unlocked for me.

I hold up my pointer finger and step aside Kinsley. "Give me a minute. I can do this." Considering all the things I like about Kinsley, I peruse the custom ring collections one more time until one particular ring catches my eye.

Yes!

That's it!

I pick the ring up and hold it between my fingers, confident it's the perfect one for Kinsley.

"This one. This is the perfect one for you, Kink." I hold the ring out to her and her breath catches. Her eyes grow wide and the smile that crosses her face...it tells me everything I need to know.

"Oh, Quinton. It's..." She shakes her head. "It's unbelievable."

Wispy vines of eighteen-carat gold entwine towards lustrous marquis shaped emerald buds that surround a three and a half-carat diamond.

"You are one who appreciates nature's simple beauties. And you're an artist so your ring needs a little color. The emeralds look like leaves on these golden vines and plus emerald is my birthstone so..."

Her brows shoot up. "No freaking way. Emerald is my birthstone too! You were born in May?"

I nod. "Yeah. Twenty-second."

Her jaw drops open and she laughs. "Shut up. Have we talked about this? Are you joking with me?"

"Uh, I don't think so. You told me you were twenty-eight, but that was the extent of our conversation."

"That's right, sugar daddy!" She giggles. "Are you sure I didn't tell you my birthday was also the twenty-second of May?"

"Are you being serious? It really is?"

She nods with a beaming smile and something inside me shifts. Like two lost pieces of a puzzle finally clicking together.

We share the same birthday.

Who is this girl?

And how on earth did I find her?

"Sooo, is that a yes then? To the ring? You like it?"

"Like it?" She scoffs as I slide the ring on her finger. "I absolutely love it. It's perfect."

I bring her hand to my lips and kiss the ring on her finger. "It's perfect for you." Turning to Mr. Nial, the owner and custom jeweler of Pine Jewels, I give him a friendly nod. "We'll take it."

Snowballs.

That's the only word floating through my brain right now.

Not because it's snowing outside much to Kinsley's enjoyment. I'm not going to lie, it's picturesque out there. A beautifully serene night and one where I would usually be home in front of the fireplace watching whatever hockey game I can find on cable. But Kinsley's in the shower and now here I am alone with my thoughts and all I can think about is how much this...thing...with Kinsley has snowballed.

We were just two people laughing in Pringle's Bar nearly a month ago, producing a fun plan to deceive her parents. Since then, things have quickly snowballed, so not only are we in a fake committed relationship, but we're also now fake engaged for all the world to know.

Oh, and we've kissed.

More than once.

And I admittedly enjoyed it each time.

I haven't been in a sincere relationship since Lexi, and for good reason. She was the first girl I considered having a life with. The first girl I seriously considered marrying. But then she yanked my heart right out of my chest the night she walked away from me. She betrayed my trust having had an affair with another man. I grieved our relationship for months and I vowed to myself I would never trust the love of a woman again. My sister used to say that love and relationships weren't practical. She preached it to all her podcast listeners and I used to laugh about it because I was in a serious loving relationship at the time.

Until I wasn't anymore.

By all means, I should stick to my guns and avoid Kinsley Kendrick. We made a deal to help each other out and we should stick to that agreement, but that's a lot easier said than done. No matter how many times I tell myself not to make us into something we're not, I can't seem to stop thinking about her.

Her smile.

The way she snorts when she laughs.

Her sense of humor.

Her affinity for the simpler things in life.

Her creativity.

Even the way she flusters when she's nervous.

There's something about her that makes me want to be around her all the time. I like hanging out with her. I like laughing with her and I like making her laugh.

And fuck, I like kissing her.

I wouldn't mind more of that.

She steps out of the en-suite bathroom in a pair of skimpy pink sleep-shorts and a tank top that says, *I'm good in bed. I can sleep all day.* I'm pretty damn sure she's no longer wearing a bra and now I'm regretting the gray lounge pants I'm wearing.

Maybe I should've packed my athletic cup.

The steam billows behind her, illuminated by the light above the bathroom sink. She looks like someone straight out of a hot porno.

Not that I would know.

And I'm definitely not complaining.

"Oh, my God, that shower is amazing," she hums, squeezing the ends of her wet hair in her towel. "The water pressure is..." She pinches her fingers together next to her mouth and kisses them. "Chef's kiss."

"Judging by the amount of steam coming from behind you I'm guessing there's no more hot water anywhere in this resort. Well done, Kink."

"Listen," she chuckles. "That just means none of our neighbors on either side of this cabin will have enjoyable shower experiences and I can't even say I'm sorry for that, so win-win."

"Damn right. Welcome to team petty. Where Schadenfreude is our favorite word."

She giggles some more as she grabs a bottle of lotion from her bag and props her foot up on the chair next to the balcony doors. She pours some into her hand and rubs them together before smoothing them down her leg.

Fucking Christ.

I don't know if I'm supposed to be watching her right now or not but at this point I'm not sure I could be paid to look away. She's literally bent over wearing those skimpy pink shorts, with no bra, and I can see the silhouette of her breasts underneath her tank top. Fuck, if she turned just a little bit more toward me, I would be able to see right down her shirt. This is a show I was not at all prepared for and it's causing my dick to twitch in my pants.

Yep. Should've brought my cup.

"Keep that up, Kink, and I'm going to have to take a dip in the snow before I fall asleep tonight."

"Hmm?" She glances at me as I teasingly lick my lips and then she rolls her eyes and laughs. "Mmkay. Because you've never seen a woman in pajamas before?"

Her question gives me pause. "Actually...besides Lexi or my sister?" I shake my head. "No."

She tosses her lotion back in her bag and moves to hang her towel in the bathroom. "Well, if you've seen Lexi in pjs, then you've seen far better than all of this." She gestures to herself. "Lexi's a bombshell. I'm just me."

She says it so matter-of-factly.

Like she actually believes that.

"Whoa, whoa, whoa." My brows furrow "Let's get one thing straight right now, Kinsley. Lexi doesn't hold a fucking candle to you."

"Okay." She scoffs out a laugh. "Whatever helps you sleep tonight."

Sitting up straight on the bed, heat flushes through my body as I watch her coming back out of the bathroom. Now she's just pissing me off. "No. Not whatever helps me sleep tonight because God already knows I won't be doing much of that anyway with you lying next to me, but if you for even one second think you don't look absolutely breathtakingly sexy as fuck right now then maybe it's you who needs to take a dip in the snow to clear your muddied sense of self-worth."

She's frozen in place next to her side of the bed, her jaw hanging open, her arms folded across her chest, which sucks for me because up until now I was getting a very nice nipple show.

"Uh...I don't...know what to say."

"First of all, you can get in here so you're not freezing," I tell her, folding down the blankets so she can climb into the bed.

"Don't you want me to sleep somewhere else?"

"What? No." I shake my head. "That's not what I want at all."

"But you said you won't get much—"

"I know what I said, Kins. And I meant it." I stare at her. "I don't usually sleep next to gorgeous women without fucking their brains out first and even after that, I still don't sleep with them. They leave or I do, so this is new for me. And yes, it will be uncomfortable for me because I happen to find you fucking attractive. I didn't plan it, but I can control myself, and I want you here, alright? So please... get in."

Jesus, why am I so fucking word-vomity all of a sudden?

Kinsley's not making eye contact with me. Her head is bowed but I see the smile when it happens. I watch as her grin grows across her mouth and her cheeks pinken. I notice when she bites her lower lip between her teeth. It's then she finally looks at me.

"What are you thinking?" I ask her.

"You find me attractive?" Her question is almost a whisper.

"Painfully so," I answer. "Yes."

"Painfully?"

"That's what I said."

"Have I hurt you, Quinton?"

"I haven't given you the opportunity to hurt me Kinsley."

You can't hurt me if you're not mine.

She lets my confession soak in, her head nodding slowly. "Is that why you kissed me earlier? Because you find me attractive?"

Yes.

"No." My eyes fall to her lips. "I kissed you because I had to."

"You had to?"

"I wanted to."

"Because you're attracted to me."

What's not to like?

You're cute as fuck and your kisses are like sunshine.

When I don't answer right away she tucks her fingers underneath her tank top and pulls it up over her head letting it slip from her hand and fall to the floor.

Hooooly fuck.

Trying my best not to smile like a horny teenage boy, I too bow my head. "Kinsley, what are you doing?"

"I'm not ashamed of my body, Quinton."

"Good. You shouldn't be. You're perfect. Put your shirt back on."

Sooo goddamn perfect.

She's standing less than six feet in front of me with her beautifully curved breasts on display. Her pink nipples pebbling in the chill of the air. Fuck me, what I wouldn't give to hold them in my hands and warm each peak with my tongue.

"Do you always sleep in pants?" Her question catches me off guard.

"I never sleep in pants."

"Then why are you wearing them now?"

"Because I'm trying to be a gentleman."

She giggles. "You don't have to be a gentleman with me. Nobody is here. It's just you and me. What do you usually sleep in?"

"When I'm not nude? My underwear."

"Then take off your pants."

"I don't mind wearing them."

"I want you to be comfortable, Quinton. This bed is yours as much as it is mine."

"Are you seriously asking me to take off my pants?"

She looks up at me from underneath her long lashes and gives me a hint of a smile. "Yes."

Standing up from the bed, with Kinsley standing on the opposite side, I untie the strings at my waist and let my pants fall to the ground, my feelings on the beauty in front of me now evident in my erection.

She walks around the bed toward me and just when I think she's going to stop in front of me she takes a few more steps and then holds out her hand.

"You up for a little fun, Quinton?"

My mouth twists up in a smirk. "With a half-naked woman who just instructed me to take off my pants?"

"Hell yeah." She snorts and takes my hand. "Come on."

13

QUINTON

I help Kinsley take the cover off the hot tub outside and watch as she turns up the heat knowing I'm about to get all kinds of wet with this beautiful almost-naked woman. She steps in front of me, her eyes filled with amusement and says, "Tell me again why you kissed me earlier Quinton."

I don't know what makes me do it but I reach for her and pull her body against mine. Her hardened nipples brushing against my chest. Her skin velvety soft under my touch.

Jesus she feels good.

"I kissed you because I couldn't stand the thought of Seth ever tasting you. He's a douche and he doesn't deserve you and I guess I was a bit possessive in the heat of the moment. I'm sorry if I—"

"No." She lays a finger over my lips. "Do not apologize for your feelings and by God, do not apologize for that kiss because it was..." She fans her face with her hand. "Phew! It was hot. Not going to lie."

Feed my ego a little more why don't you.

"Is that why you brought me out here? You want me to kiss you again?"

She bobs her head. "Yes...and no. You had your moment of...shall we say irritation with the exes, and now this is mine."

"Oh? You didn't like Lexi?"

She crinkles her face. "Hell no. I mean, I'm sure she's a nice person and all, but I don't like her on pure principle. She hurt you and that's no bueno for me. So, she's enemy number one. And also, you were right when you said Seth needs to see what he lost out on. But not because I want him back. God couldn't pay me enough to be with him again. This is simply me wanting to be petty as fuck because we can." She pitches her brow and smirks at me. "So...fake sex wet and wild edition. You in?"

Fuck yes.

That's my girl.

Bring on the petty fun.

With a Cheshire cat grin on my face, I nod. "I am one hundred percent in."

"Good." She slips out of her shorts and then takes my hand to steady herself as she climbs into the hot tub wearing nothing but a pair of blue bikini briefs. "Oh, God, yeah," she moans, closing her eyes and welcoming the warmth on her body. I could stand right here in this spot and watch her in there all night. "Turn off the light and get in here, Shay. It's time to get loud and make a mess."

"You want the light off?"

"Yeah. That way pictures of us won't end up in some tabloid."

"Smart thinking."

"I know. Don't worry. I promise they'll hear us but they won't see us."

Following behind her, I climb into the hot tub, enjoying the warmth of the water mixed with the chill in the air. Kinsley leans back against the edge of the hot tub, her arms stretched out to her sides, and looks toward Seth and Lexi's cabin.

"There!" She points. "See them? They're in the kitchen."

"Yep. I see them."

"Okay. How should we do this?" she asks me.

"You'll have to ride me. It's the only way there's no chance they'll see clothing."

She shrugs. "I could take it off if that would help."

Huuuumunah hummunah hummmunah.

I don't think I could be any fucking harder right now if I tried.

"Are you trying to kill me here, Kink?"

She snorts. "Oh. Right. Sorry."

"Don't be sorry. Just get over here and straddle me." I pull her body against mine and she wraps her arms around my neck, her silky wet breasts sliding against my chest. I have to take a deep breath and remind myself to stay in control.

Kinsley moves against me and freezes. "Uhh, Quinton?"

"Yeah I know, but you just wrapped your nearly naked body around mine, your beautiful tits are practically in my face, and you just offered to take off you're your panties. What's a man supposed to do with that?"

"Shit. You're right. I'm sorry." She moves to back off of me. "Is this a bad idea?"

"Fuck no it is absolutely not a bad idea."

It's a goddamn wonderful idea.

"But if you expect my dick to not enjoy this even a teeny tiny little bit, you're off your rocker."

She nods giving me a goofy smile. "Right. Ten-four on the happy dick. I've got you little buddy."

I grab Kinsley's waist holding her in place and shake my head. "Kinsley Kendrick, you will never again refer to my dick as little buddy."

Giggling she palms her forehead. "Fuck. Did I say little buddy? I meant monster cock."

"That's more like it." I playfully smack her ass. "Now saddle up and let's have some fun."

Kinsley slaps the water hard with both hands and throws her head back, an emphatic lustful moan emanating from inside her.

"OH GOD YES QUINTON! MMMMM! GIVE IT TO ME! GIVE IT TO ME! MORE!"

Bucking against me she slaps the water a few more times and then brings her hands to my head, threading her fingers through my hair.

Shit. This might be a terrible idea.

What was I thinking?

"Fuck, you feel so good, Kink."

She pulls my hair and murmurs, "Louder. Be louder."

"OH, FUCK BABY! IT'S SO GOOD. YOU FEEL INCREDIBLE!"

"YES QUINTON! UNH, UNH, UNH, UNH, YEAH...OH MY GOD!"

My hands around her ass, I hold onto Kinsley's body as she thrusts up and down on my way too excited cock so she doesn't rock herself completely off me. I'm not going to lie. As ridiculous as we are being right now, Kinsley's idea of a fake fuck is very convincing.

Deep breath.

You can do this, Monster Cock.

I know it feels nice but no, you cannot come out and play right now.

Be a good boy.

"Anything?"

I peer at Lexi and Seth's cabin behind Kinsley. "Not yet."

Kinsley wraps her arms around my head and squeezes me to her, essentially pulling my face into her chest, and moans again as she rocks against my cock.

Yep...I'm totally motorboating Kinsley's tits right now.

Should I make noises?

I feel like I should make noises.

Also, holy fuck, my face is in Kinsley's tits.

"QUINTON!" she shouts. "OH, FUCK RIGHT THERE! YES!"

Splash, splash, splash.

"YOU WANT TO RIDE ME, BABY? TAKE MY COCK. TAKE IT ALL. FEEL HOW HARD I AM FOR YOU."

I look up for just a moment when I notice a light flick on behind her.

"I think it's working," I whisper. "A light just came on over there."

SUSAN RENEE

Kinsley throws her head back, her chest pushing into my face. "OOOOH SHIT, YES!"

Splash, splash, splash.

"FUCK, FUCK, FUUUCK YES! RIGHT THERE! OOOH RIGHT THERE! YES! YES!"

Splash, splash, splash.

"DON'T STOP, QUINTON! DON'T STOP!"

Mother fucking Jesus Christ, if this is even close to how she actually fucks, I am a dead man. An incredibly happy, completely satisfied, all out of fucks to give dead man. This is too good. Her body...shit. It's like she's made for me and I haven't even claimed her yet. Not that I'll get the chance to physically claim her, but a man can dream and right now I am fucking dreaming because her vibe, her energy, and holy shit, her tits rubbing against my chest is enough to make me lose control.

God how my cock wishes there were no barriers between us right now.

Yeah okay, it's not just my cock. I wish that too.

"SQUEEZE MY TITS, QUINTON!" She moans. "HOLD THEM. SQUEEZE THEM. OH GOD, YOU'RE GOING TO MAKE ME COME."

Splash, splash, splash.

Doing as she asks, I palm Kinsley's tits in my hands, watching her face contort at the pleasure I'm giving her.

That's right, Kink. Not everything about me is fake.

I know how to touch a pair of tits.

"MMM YEAH!"

I spot two bodies in the window of the cabin next to us and know without a shadow of a doubt we're being watched even if they can't see us entirely.

"They're watching," I whisper.

"Great! Big finish. Ready?"

"Ready. Kiss me."

She doesn't hesitate to crash her lips against mine as she ramps up her rocking against me. Together we put on one hell of a show for our neighbors. Even with our lips locked and our tongues swirling against each other, her high-pitched moans are loud and clear. At one point her sounds stop and she looks at me. Yeah, it's dark out here but not dark enough that I can't tell she's looking down deep into my soul as if we were really fucking inside this hot tub.

All the blood in me rushes to my cock and I swear to God I'm about to explode.

"Kinsley..."

"I'M COMING, QUINTON! I'M COMING! OH GOD YEESSSSSSS! UNH, UNH, UNH UNH, UNH! UNGHHHHH." Her movements stop and she squeezes me tightly against her. My arms clasp around her back holding her to me as she gasps for breath.

I smooth a hand down the back of her head, reminding myself not to move a muscle lest she get a real taste of what the monster of steel, which is aching for relief, might do.

As we sit here holding each other I catch the faces of Lexi and Seth from their side window. Neither one of them is smiling. In fact, they look a bit forlorn which only makes me want to laugh. I guess our job here is done.

"I think it worked. They don't look happy, that's for fucking sure."

She giggles against me. "Good. They deserve it." She releases her hold on me and puts a bit of space between us. I miss the feel of her chest against mine already.

"Phew," she sighs, smoothing a few rogue strands of hair from her face.

"Yeah. Are you okay?"

"Yeah, I'm great. That was fun. Go team." She offers me a fist bump and I want to laugh out of pure…embarrassment? Nervousness? Awkwardness? I don't know but Kinsley Kendrick just wet-humped me into oblivion on the balcony of our treehouse for the entire resort to hear and she wants nothing more than a fist bump.

Instead of reciprocating her fist bump, I kiss the back of her hand and then kiss her forehead. I give her a few taps on her ass and then offer to help her out of the hot tub so we can dry off. Is it uncomfortable as fuck to step out of this thing with the biggest erection of my life? Yes. Yes it is. So, I'm grateful for the five to ten seconds of pitch blackness out here as well as the frigid air immediately assaulting our skin as we make our way back inside. Kinsley excuses herself to the bathroom to change and rewash her face and what do I do?

I rub one out in less than twenty seconds giving Monster Cock some much needed relief.

Thank God for the socks I took off earlier.

14

QUINTON

TENLEY

What the hell Brother? We don't talk for a
few weeks and all a sudden you're
engaged?

I tap out of my text app and scroll through a few social media posts and just as Hawken said, there we are in several shots throughout the resort. At dinner with Kinsley's parents, kissing in front of the jewelry store. Fuck. I didn't think anyone saw us there. I had a nagging feeling this could happen. There's no way Kinsley could tell my ex or hers that we're now engaged and it wouldn't end up in every tabloid available.

ME

Oh. Uh about that.

TENLEY

😂 I didn't even get to meet her first?
WTF? Ugh! I know Hawaii is far away but
the internet does exist you know?

ME

It's not real.

TENLEY

What? What's not real.

ME

My engagement.

TENLEY

What do you mean it's not real?

ME

Remember you and Teagan and the arrangement you had the first time you visited Kamana Wanalaya Resort?

TENLEY

Oooh. So, you're helping someone out?"

ME

Yeah. It was supposed to just be a fake dating thing between us so she could show me off to her parents and get them to stop hassling her.

TENLEY

Who is HER?

ME

Her name is Kinsley. She's an artist/photographer here in the city. I met her at Pringle's one night when I overheard her telling her mom on the phone that she's been in a committed relationship with me for some time. I thought it was humorous so I told her she better introduce me to her parents. 😏

TENLEY

LOL only you would do something like that.

ME

I needed a little fun in my life. Things were getting boring. Anyway, she accidentally slipped this weekend at an event for her parents that we're engaged sooo we're turning it up a notch.

TENLEY

Ok...so you think maybe this fake thing will turn into a non-fake thing? Like Teagan and me?

ME

Doubt it. But I suppose never say never. I'd be lying if I said she wasn't filling a void right now. She's fun to hang out with so I don't mind. Just do me a favor and don't tell anyone it's fake alright? If anyone asks, you've met her online and she's a lovely fun girl and I'm ridiculously happy.

TENLEY

Your secret is always safe with me, Quinton.

ME

How's Hawaii?

TENLEY

Gorgeous every single day. I feel like I've added another twenty years to my life since moving here. So much less stressful than NYC.

ME

You can say that again!

TENLEY

Well, it's late here. I should get to bed. I was just looking at hockey scores and your name came up. Had to see what was going on.

ME

Yeah. All good. I'm sorry I forgot to tell you about it just in case. Sleep well, Sis. 🤍

TENLEY

Night big brother. 🤍

HAWKEN

Q! Uh…it looks like congratulations are in order, man.

COLBY

I was wondering about that too.

DEX

Right? That shit escalated quickly!

ZEKE

What the hell happened out there Quinton? You're engaged?

HAWKEN

Quinton! Earth to Quinton!

HAWKEN

Hey Q! Are you still alive? You haven't been taken hostage in some remote cabin out in the middle of nowhere, have you?

DEX

Dude, you watch too much TV.

HAWKEN

Fuck off Dexter. What if Kinsley is really like that chick from Misery? *whispers to Quinton* Lock up all the sledgehammers!

ZEKE

But what if she's like that deranged doctor from Human Centipede? #fecesfordinner

MILO

Zeke man...you're not right.

ZEKE

Of course, I'm not right. I spend my off time watching princess cartoons and shows with British pigs and Australian dogs...at least I think they're dogs.

ME

Morning fuckers.

COLBY

HE LIIIIVES!

HAWKEN

Bro, you can tell us...is it horrible out there? You're engaged? What the hell happened?

ME

Uuuh...no. It's not horrible. A little weird, yes. Horrible? No.

HAWKEN

The entire hockey nation is talking about Quinton Shay finding love. It's all over social media. Picture of you two kissing somewhere in the resort and all.

DEX

Bow chicka wow wow. 😉

MILO

Hey if Quinton is gettin' some, more power to him. This third trimester for Charlee is no joke. She's dead set on keeping Fuck Norris far away from her until the baby comes.

COLBY

I feel you there. Duncan McKokinner is getting no action at the moment either.

HAWKEN

Sucks to be you assholes. Long Dong Silver gets all the action he wants.

DEX

Do NOT talk about fucking my sister. 🤬

QUINTON

I didn't say anything about getting fucked…although…shit. I think I might be in trouble.

COLBY

Tell us everything. How can we help? Do you need us to fly you out of there?

DEX

Yeah man. Operation Quinton's Quest… just say the word.

ME

No. I'm fine. Really. Kinsley's fine. She just had a slip up last night because Lexi is here.

ZEKE

Oh shit. As in your Lexi? She's there?
Really?

ME

She's not my Lexi and yes. Really. And
what's worse...she's with Kinsley's ex!

HAWKEN

drops jaw on the ground WTF?

ME

I know. Neither one of us knew. Also,
they're staying in the cabin next to ours.
Guests of Kinsley's parents.

ZEKE

That's some next level shit right there.

ME

Tell me about it. Anyway, Kinsley got
nervous and blurted out that we were
engaged sooo...

MILO

This fake relationship just turned into a
fake engagement?

ME

Yep buuut there's more. Fucking hell, you
guys, I think I might like her.

MILO

Charlee says, "Duh Quinton." We told you
this would happen.

COLBY

It's ok if you like her, man. Have some fun.
See where it goes.

SUSAN RENEE

ME

But I don't do relationships.

ZEKE

Correction. You did do relationships until
Lexi burned you. Kinsley is not Lexi.

ME

Yeah...I know.

DEX

Zeke's right. You deserve to be happy Q,
so if you like her, go for it. If you don't like
her, still go for it. At least get some action.

HAWKEN

smacks Dex upside the head Don't
listen to Dex. He's a walking horn ball. But
I'll agree with Zeke. Kinsley is not Lexi. So
don't push away too hard. Think about it.
Maybe she would be open to the idea of
something real. Doesn't mean you're
getting married tomorrow.

ME

Yeah. Maybe I'll think about it. I should go.
She's starting to wake up.

HAWKEN

😮 Umm...you slept with her? Dude, there
is so much more to unpack there...but
later, Q!

146

15

KINSLEY

The world outside might be covered in snow but I am the toastiest I think I've ever been. When Quinton suggested sharing a bed as two perfectly normal consenting adults, I may have failed to tell him that I'm a cuddler. It's not like it's something I can control. What I do when I'm asleep is beyond me. I've woken up on several occasions holding onto something, be it Nutsack or just the other pillow on my bed. This morning is no different...except I'm holding onto a human.

As the world of dreams fades away and I wake to reality, I can feel the rise and fall of Quinton's chest under my head, the sinews of his perfectly defined abs under my fingers. He's warm and cozy and comfortable in a way that makes me feel protected and cherished. Especially with his hand feathering up and down my back, like this is a position we get ourselves into all the time.

Earth to Kinsley!

This is NOT a position you get into all the time with the hot hockey player!

Wake up!

My eyes finally pop open and I inhale a deep breath, pushing off Quinton's chest enough to look up at him.

Please don't be pissed.

Please don't be pissed.

Please don't be pissed.

"Morning Kink," he says with a lazy smile. "Sleep well?"

Not completely awake yet, I rub my eyes and peek at him again. "I'm…" I shake my head huffing out a soft laugh. "I'm sorry. I didn't mean to…you know."

He lifts his arm away stashing his hand behind his head when I try to sit up next to him. "It's alright. I didn't mind. You were shivering last night so I pulled you over here. It must've worked because you fell asleep hard and slept all night."

"What?" My eyes grow huge before I hide my face in my hands. "Quinton you should've pushed me off."

"Why? You were comfortable and to be honest…" he says with a shrug. "I didn't mind the cuddle."

I drop my hands, watching Quinton for a minute. He appears to be much more awake than I am. "How long have you been awake?"

"About an hour or so."

"You could've woken me up you know."

"Nah. You were sleeping so peacefully and like I said, I didn't mind. It was…nice."

"Nice?"

"Yeah. I guess I forgot how nice cuddling with someone in bed feels. It's not so lonely, you know?"

"Yeah." I nod, still watching him. He's freakishly attractive just the way he is right now. No shirt. Boxer briefs. Messy sleep hair. The stubble on his face darker than it was yesterday.

"You're pretty," I tell him with a dazed grin.

His brows shoot up. "I'm pretty?"

"Yeah. Like some kind of hot super model or something. You know...like when they do those underwear shoots."

"So, I'm an underwear model now?"

I mean...you could take the underwear off and be a nude model...

Wouldn't hear me complain even a little.

"I'm sure you would make a damn good one if some underwear company offered to pay you enough."

He chuckles and even his morning laugh is sexy.

Raspy...warm...

Okay, I really like morning Quinton. Morning Quinton is hot.

"Well, thanks I guess. Maybe I'll consider it someday."

An idea hits me that has my brows shooting up in excitement. "You know what I think?"

"What?"

"I think you guys should do a boudoir photo session with me. The whole team."

"Why would we do that?"

"Uh...why not?" I hold up my hand, ticking off my reasons on my fingers. "First of all, it's just plain fun. Secondly, you're all a bunch of hot guys and I'm one hundred percent certain they would sell like hotcakes.

Third, you could make a shit ton of money for some kind of charity. You know, like those firemen do with their shirtless uniform photos where they're holding puppies?"

Quinton's brows pinch. "That's a thing? Firemen and puppies?"

"Yeah, it's a thing!"

"Why puppies? Why not kittens? Isn't the firefighter always saving kittens stuck in trees?"

I smile. "I suppose you have a point. I have no idea why it's puppies and not kittens. It just is. You guys should think about it. I'm telling you, a calendar with all of you in it would make millions."

"Maybe I'll mention it to the guys and see what they think."

"Yay!" I clap my hands excitedly and jump off the bed.

"Where are you going?"

"Relax Mr. Clingy, I have to pee."

"Oooh no." I gasp, scrolling through my phone. My cheeks burn as I shake my head.

"What?" Quinton is stretched out on his side of the bed. His hands are behind his head as we continue to enjoy a well-deserved lazy morning.

Biting my lip, I frown and lower my phone to my lap. "Quinton it's all over social media."

"What is?"

"Us. You and me. News of our engagement."

"Oh, yeah. I saw it."

I toss my phone beside me and turn my whole body so I can see all of him, a pit of nerves growing in my stomach. "Quinton I'm so incredibly sorry." I palm my forehead. "I'm so stupid. I never considered what would happen. It just...came out of my mouth and—"

"Don't worry, Kink. Everything is fine."

"But it's not fine. The entire world now thinks we're engaged."

"Okay." He shrugs. "Let them think whatever they want."

"But this was just supposed to be something funny to get back at my parents, Quinton! And last night—"

"Was fucking fun so don't say anything that might spoil it for me because I have zero regrets." He finally turns toward me, his arm now open for me to slide in against him. I stretch myself out next to him, my head in the crook of his shoulder. He kisses the top of my head and smooths his hand up and down my arm. He does everything a perfect boyfriend would do. "It's no big deal okay? We just might need to make a few changes."

"Changes? Like what?"

"Well, for starters we'll need to make sure we spend as much time together as possible. We'll need to up the game a little so there's no doubt we're a serious couple. So, plan to come to my next game. And anything you want or need me around for, as long as I'm in town, I'm there. In fact, maybe you should plan to come with the ladies to an away game or two. No wait..." He stops to think. "They're all super pregnant. I'm sure they won't travel anymore so maybe having you here with them just in case is better."

I huff a laugh. "You say that like I'm going to deliver all their babies when they come."

"Stranger things have probably happened. Did you know Dex delivered his first child?"

"Uh no! He did?"

"Yep. Right on Tatum's bathroom floor. You should ask him about it sometime. It's a remarkable story."

"Don't worry. If I happen to be in the same room with all three women when they all go into labor at the same time, I promise I'll go all *Grey's Anatomy* on them. They won't know what hit 'em."

"Seriously?" He chuckles.

"Seriously."

We lay quietly for a moment, neither of us talking before out of the blue Quinton asks, "Do you think you should move in with me?"

I shoot up in total shock and when I do, my hand pushes off what I think is his thigh...but instead I slip and basically punch him in his nuts. He gasps and rolls inward toward me, his hand protecting his jewels and his eyes squeezed shut.

"Fuuuuuuuuuck."

"Oh my God! I am sooo sorry, Quinton. Shit!" I cover my mouth with my hand. "Fuck! I'm sorry! I'm so sorry." He lays his head in my lap and I smooth my hand over his hair.

"Are you okay? I'm so sorry! I didn't mean to do that. My hand slipped when you asked me to move in and—"

"I'm dying," he groans. "Look at me, Kink. Shriveled up and dying."

Is he kidding?

"Are you kidding? I don't think I punched you that hard but if I broke you...fuck, did I break your penis? Did I break Monster Cock and turn him into a little buddy for all the rest of his days?"

"I don't know. I think you did. I think he needs CPR. Definitely some mouth to mouth. That's probably the only thing that will keep him from eternal flaccidness."

Okay now I know he's kidding.

"Oh, but did I not tell you?"

"Tell me what?" he croaks out.

"My mouth is like a horse's mouth."

He tries not to laugh but I can feel his chuckle. "What?"

"Yeah, if I put something in my mouth that doesn't belong there, I can't unhinge my jaw. I have no choice but to bite down on it."

He sits up from my lap immediately and hops off the bed. "Aaaaand I think I'm healed! Huzzah!"

I burst into a fit of laughter and then give him a sympathetic look. "I really am sorry though. Don't hold it against me too long."

"Don't worry, Kink. At some point I'll get a good nipple twist in and we'll be even."

Oooh! A nipple twist! I like the sound of that.

"Is that a threat? Or a promise?"

"You're going to find out if you're not careful." He lifts me from the bed and throws me over his shoulder, slapping my ass as I laugh and squeal against him. "Come on, Kink. Let's find sustenance."

He doesn't bring up moving in with him again for the rest of the day, thank God. I can't even fathom what that might look like. Me, living with a hot as balls professional hockey player. Him coming home to my hot mess of a life. Nutsack running rampant in his home.

Yeah, no. I can't do that to Quinton.

I wouldn't do that to him.

I think I like him too much.

ME

MEREDITH!!! Omg Quinton Shay is a fucking dream boat and we pretended to fuck in the hot tub last night because FUCKING SETH IS HERE and HE'S MARRIED TO QUINTON'S EX! YES I KNOW I'M USING SHOUTY CAPS!

MEREDITH

GIF of shocked Chris Pratt Oh my God you're like a living breathing episode of Paradise Island. Oh, hey congrats on your engagement by the way 😂 Where did that come from?

ME

🤦 my big mouth when I blurted it out to Seth and Lexi last night.

MEREDITH

LOL well played. Did that piss off Quinton?

ME

Not at all. He took it all in stride. He said we'll just up our game until after his charity event.

MEREDITH

Have you kissed him yet?

ME

GIF of Jimmy Fallon saying Maaaaaybe

MEREDITH

I KNEW IT! You're gonna fall for him. I'm calling it right now.

ME

Am not.

MEREDITH

Mmkay. 😶

ME

I'm serious.

MEREDITH

Who are you trying to convince babe? Me or you?

ME

Har har...gotta run. Ribbon cutting in ten.

MEREDITH

Good luck!

Although Silver Pines Resort has been open during renovations, the grand reopening ceremony was, of course, a lavishly decorated ribbon cutting for my parents with a reception that includes every resort guest, more celebrities than I care to count, and of course my perfect sister. Mom has been doting on her and showing her off to her friends for the last hour while Quinton and I work the room speaking with out-of-town guests, but the minute Kennedy has the chance to pull me away, she does, excusing us both to the lady's room.

"Are you out of your mind?"

"What?" I whisper shout, yanking my arm from Kennedy's grip as she walks us to the restroom. "What are you talking about?"

Waiting until the door closes behind us and checking the stalls for extra people my sister rounds on me. "You're engaged?"

"What does it matter to you?"

"Uh, it matters a lot! First of all, do you even know this man?"

I scoff. "What the fuck? Do you think I would be marrying him if I didn't know him?"

What she doesn't know won't kill her.

"How long have you two been together?"

"Long enough," I spit back at her. "And I can tell you this. Quinton is far better of a man than Seth ever was. That asshole can rot in hell for all I care."

"That asshole has made no bones about telling everyone that you and Quinton are engaged and planning a secret wedding...oh, and that you were uh...umm..."

"Well?" I toss my arms out to my sides. "Use your words, Kennedy. God knows you know a lot of them."

She huffs. "He said you two were fucking loud enough for the entire resort to hear you last night."

I stare at her face blankly for a hot second and then start to laugh. "He's just jealous."

Kennedy's eyes go wide. "So, it's true then? The entire resort was able to hear you?"

I shrug. "Maybe. Maybe not." I pat her on her shoulder.

"I mean if you didn't hear me, then obviously not the whole resort."

She rolls her eyes. "Ugh!"

"Trust me, Sis, when you're being fucked as good as I was last night, you'd be screaming too. To be honest, I'm lucky I can walk today."

Or unlucky because oh my God, if last night had been real I swear I wouldn't be able to stand up straight for days.

"One day you'll see."

"Very funny, Kinsley. You know Mom isn't going to be happy with this wedding."

"Oh, I disagree. She'll be extremely happy simply because Quinton makes millions."

"But—"

"No." I stop her with my pointer finger. "You're just jealous because my fiancé makes millions doing something he loves instead of working day in and day out for a family business he has no passion for. Now if you'll excuse me, I need to get back to Quinton."

I don't wait for a response. I check my hair quickly in the mirror and then hurry out to find Quinton. I quickly scan the room and when I find him my eyes bulge and a pit forms in my stomach. My mother is standing with him and has given him a dessert that looks a whole hell of a lot like...

"Coconut," I whisper.

It's all happening in slow motion in front of me and I can't seem to make it across the room in these heels fast enough to stop him. I shuffle through the crowd, my eyes on the fork in his hand as he brings it to his mouth.

"Quinton!" I breathlessly pant in front of him and shake my head. "You shouldn't—"

"Mmm...Mrs. Kendrick, this is delicious." I watch in horror as Quinton takes a huge bite of the coconut cheesecake my mother clearly gave him, because Lord knows he wouldn't choose it himself.

"Well after Kinsley told me it was your favorite and you accepted our invitation for the weekend I asked our chef to add it to the dessert menu for the reception."

"I'm honored," Quinton tells her, taking another big bite before he acknowledges me. "What were you saying, babe?"

"Uuh...You shouldn't...uh, spoil your dinner," I tell him. "I hear the prime rib is to die for and you won't want to miss it."

"Oh, don't be so childish, Kinsley. If that man wants to eat his dessert first, he can do whatever he wants. Nothing is off limits for our new son-in-law."

Son-in-law.

Oh God.

Was I gone that long with Kennedy?

Did Mom already get to him?

What on earth did she say?

"I can't believe you didn't mention anything yesterday when you got here, or perhaps a simple phone call to let us know. We certainly didn't expect to find out our youngest child was engaged on the internet this morning." She pats Quinton's arm. "Not that I'm blaming you, dear. Kinsley has a habit of doing whatever pleases her regardless of how it affects the rest of her family. Honestly now that she'll have a wonderful husband like you to help her, maybe she'll finally grow up and realize her place in this world."

Quinton gives her a questioning glance.

"I'm sorry. I'm not following. Her...place?"

"Well, I'm sure by now she's told you about her grand plan for selling her art." Mom rolls her eyes. "As if she can really make a solid living selling paintings like that. Picasso she is not, am I right?"

"You know what, Mother? I'm standing right here," I announce a little louder than I probably should considering we're in a resort hotel reception room. "And you don't need to—"

"Let me." Quinton tenderly squeezes my arm before turning on my mother.

"Mrs. Kendrick," he starts, his tone deep but even. "Except for the few hours I've spent in your presence I can't say I really know you; however, I can already say with one hundred percent certainty that I've never met anyone more catty, self-righteous, narcissistic, and just plain hateful as you."

Mom's jaw drops. "Excuse—"

"No, I'm not done here," Quinton snaps, shaking his head.

"Your daughter, on the other hand, is one of the most selfless, helpful, kind, beautiful souls I've ever had the pleasure of meeting. Kinsley is fun and funny and cares about even the tiniest details."

Aww, that's sweet of him to say.

"She takes pleasure in simple things and sees beauty in things any of the rest of us take for granted every single day," he fumes. "She's a friend to anyone she meets, and she lights up a room the moment she fucking walks in it, which is more than I can say for you."

Wait. Is he—

"She makes me happy just being around her and I don't give two shits what she does with her adult life. If she wants to sell pictures of her feet for money, I say go for it! If she wants to open a store to sell her art, I'll be her biggest investor. And if she would rather spend the rest of her life crocheting a shit ton of positive potatoes to hand out to everyone she meets, I'll be right by her side helping her pass them out. So, you, Mrs. Kendrick, can kindly fuck all the way off with the way you constantly disrespect your own flesh and blood. I put up with your passive aggressive attitude the first night we met but I refuse to allow it one second longer. If you don't want anything to do with your daughter anymore, that's fine. She's better off without you. I'll take it from here. Oh, and no, you're not invited to the wedding."

Whoa. He's pissed.

Quinton grabs my hand, his eyes tight and his nostrils flaring. "Come on. You don't need to put up with this shit for one more minute."

Oh my God. He's really angry.

His hand clasped firmly with mine, I follow him out of the main house and up the path to our cabin.

"Quinton..."

He doesn't answer me.

"Quinton, wait."

"I can't wait, Kink," he says as he shakes his head and quickens his pace. "My wips are swewwing and I can't feew my tongue."

"Your...what...oooh. Oh God! The coconut!" I palm my forehead with my other hand. "I almost forgot. Wait, do I need to call a doctor? Why did you even eat it, Quinton?

I'm sure they have medicine back in the gift shop. I could run back!"

"Don't need it, Kinswey," he says. "Have some in my bag."

Kinswey. Shit. Allergic reaction Quinton is so cute.

And I'm totally going to hell for thinking so.

"Okay. Okay. I'm right behind you."

16

QUINTON

Fuck!

Kinsley's mother pissed me off for the last time. I refuse to let her disrespect Kinsley anymore. God, the look on her face...I'll never be able to drag it out of my mind. The accepted defeat that she should never feel from the person who raised her. Who should have loved her every minute of every fucking day. Who should want every bit of happiness her daughter could ever have in this life.

Fuck!

I knew that cheesecake was coconut the minute the bitch handed it to me. But no way was I about to let Kinsley look like a liar, allergies be damned. I would've stuck around the party to make sure everyone knew Kinsley and I were madly in love, but I also knew my lips and throat would never make it. I have to get medicine in me before the swelling gets any worse.

Or before I have to hug the toilet for the night.

I make a beeline for my toiletry bag, grabbing a bottle of

water from the kitchen counter on the way. Combing through my shit, I find my Epipen and quickly give myself the injection that will calm this swelling down and allow me to breathe easier. Loosening my tie, I tear off my suit coat and step into the bathroom splashing a bit of water on my face, my words on repeat through my head as a wave of uncertain feelings washes over me.

...She makes me happy just being around her.

...One of the most selfless, helpful, kind, beautiful souls I've ever had the pleasure of meeting.

...I'll be right by her side.

I don't even think I was listening to myself as my feelings for Kinsley slipped out of my mouth but dammit, I meant every fucking word.

Wait...Kinsley.

I turn around assuming she'll be in the bedroom waiting for me but she's not there. Taking a deep breath and reminding myself I'm okay, I step into the hallway and spot Kinsley near the fireplace with her hand on her chest at the base of her neck as she watches the dancing flames.

Christ, she looks beautiful.

Her brown curls pulled back to show off her slender neck.

Her dark green sequin dress leaving nothing to the imagination when it comes to the elegant shape of her body.

The rosiness to her cheeks.

She finally turns and sees me in the entryway of the room.

"Are you alright?" I ask her, slightly worried that I may have upset her.

Clearing her throat, she stands a little taller and nods. "Yeah. I'm fine. Are you okay? How are you feeling? What can I do?"

"I'm fine."

More than fine with you here.

A soft chuckle emerges from her lips and she takes a few steps toward me. "You don't look fine," she murmurs. "Your lips are swollen. And your face...it's a little splotchy."

"Yeah. It'll go away." She holds my stare and I wonder if there's any chance in hell she's thinking what I'm thinking. Because I'm kind of wondering what her pussy feels like under my fingers...tastes like under my tongue. I know I shouldn't be thinking about all the dirty things I want to do to her, but I can't stop myself. I wish we were on the same page right now. I wish she would come over here and give me a sign. Anything that tells me it would be okay to kiss her again because I really want to kiss her again. I'm guessing we're not thinking the same thing, though, so I shake away my thoughts, squeezing my eyes closed, and remember how angry I am with Mrs. Kendrick.

"Kinsley, your mother..." I run my hand through my hair. "I couldn't let her talk about you like that. I'm sorry if I—"

"Don't." She brings her finger to my lips and places a warm hand on my reddening cheek. "You were wonderful, Quinton. Nobody has ever done something like that for me before."

Nobody?

Why the hell not?

"You shouldn't have to explain yourself to anyone. You

owe them nothing, Kinsley. You know that, right? You are perfect just as you are."

"You're right. I don't owe them a damn thing and I need to remind myself of that often. But you...I owe you everything."

My brows furrow slightly and I shake my head. "No, you don't. That's not at all why I—"

"Tell me you can breathe, Quinton."

"What?"

One hand now on my chest, she leans in so that our lips are almost touching. I can smell her perfume, the scent of her making my dick twitch.

Hell. Maybe this is her sign!

She's not afraid to get close to me!

Why is she doing this?

She shouldn't get this close.

I shouldn't let her.

But fucking Christ I would give anything to lay her out on this floor and spend the rest of this night making her scream.

"Please. Tell me you can breathe before I lose my mind."

You mean before I lose mine.

Inhaling a deep breath through my nose I release it out my mouth, drawing her gaze to my lips. "See? I can breathe just fine, Kink. I'm okay. I promise."

"Good," she whispers to me. "Then you'll be okay if I do this."

"Do wh—"

She presses her lips to mine, her tongue dragging across my lower lip in a soft stroke, testing our connection until I open my mouth and welcome her in. And I sure as fuck welcome her in with enthusiasm.

I tilt my head to get better access, sweeping my tongue against hers, tasting her, needing her, wanting her.

"Kinsley..." Her name is a quick release of my breath between kisses, my hands threading through her hair holding her in place so I can deepen our connection.

"I don't even care if it wasn't all real." She groans against me when I drag my lips across her chin, her cheek, down her neck and across her shoulder. "Or maybe it was. I don't know, but what I do know is that whether or not you meant what you said, Quinton, you didn't let my mother disrespect me. You stood up for me. You advocated for my happiness and that means something to me. It means more to me than you could ever know."

Whoa, wait.

I halt my kisses and look her dead in the eye. "Kinsley..." I brush her hair away from her face, her plump pink lips open as she breathes heavily. "Make no mistake. I'll never say something I don't mean."

She stares back at me, her eyes flitting between mine, and then she slowly reaches behind her and pulls down the zipper to her dress until it falls to the floor.

Hoooly shit.

My eyes fall to the stunning black corset and thong she was hiding beneath her dress.

"Touch me, Quinton."

Swallowing the knot in my throat, I trail my finger from the base of her throat through the center of her chest. She arches her back, her eyes fluttering closed as her breasts are pushed into my hand.

"Did you wear this for me, Kink?"

"Of course, I did. Do you like it?"

I wipe my hand down my face. "I fucking love it." I tell her, raising her hand and gesturing for her to turn all the way around so I can get the whole picture. "I think the question is, do you like it? Because I'm about to tear it to shreds so if it's a favorite of yours, you better speak now or forever hold your peace."

A slow smirk spreads across her face. "Take your best shot, Shay."

Taking a moment to appreciate the beauty in front of me, I hold her at arm's length and allow my gaze to wander over her entire body.

"Jesus Christ, Kinsley. You are stunning."

"Please Quinton..."

Her plea is my undoing. God, I want this girl.

Tugging at the seam of her black lace corset, I pull it apart ripping it right down the middle. Clasps and buttons sprinkle the floor, her breasts now exposed as I toss the garment to the ground. I palm her right breast, dragging her nipple into my mouth, stroking it with my tongue.

Quick.

Slow.

Quick.

Slow.

And then I move to the other side and repeat.

"You're overdressed Quinton," I hear her moan as I lap at her pretty pink buds, but I don't have to tell her what to do. She's already unbuttoning my dress shirt and tugging at the belt around my waist. She pulls at my shirt and I don't have the patience to get out of it nicely so I rip it apart too, the buttons scattering everywhere. I pull my arms through and then watch as she lets it drop to the floor.

And then I can't wait anymore.

"Fuck, I'm an impatient man, Kinsley. And I want you so fucking bad."

"Then take me, Quinton," she breathes. "I'm yours. All yours."

My hands under her legs, I scoop her into my arms and carry her in front of the fireplace, laying her out on the plush fur rug, the light of the fire flickering over her smooth warm skin. She peers up at me, her doe-like mossy green eyes watching me with a sense of longing and lust all rolled into one.

"You're so beautiful. You're body..." I say, feathering my fingers over her skin watching as her nipples pebble beneath my touch. "It's fucking perfection."

She runs her hands down my chest and over my abs until her fingers reach the waistband of my pants. Having already unbuckled my belt, she unzips my pants and slips her hands down around my hardened cock. I gasp in a breath at the feel of her touch.

Her hands on me might be the best thing I've ever felt.

"I want you inside me, Quinton. I'm dripping for you. Please don't make me wait."

Smiling down at her I wink and then lean down to kiss her lips. "Greedy girl, eh, Kink?"

"I know what I want." She spreads her legs wide open, her black thong glistening between her thighs.

"I like a girl who isn't afraid to go after what she wants. I really wanted to take my time with you, Kink. Touching and licking and sucking every inch of you." I position myself between her legs, kissing down her stomach as I rip her thong apart at her hips. "But I did tell Seth I would be spending my night eating...and since you said please..."

She smells like absolute heaven as I dip down and press my tongue against her pussy, lapping up all she'll give me and selfishly taking even more.

"Oooh...God!" Her head falls back and she arches off the rug as I part her with my fingers and stroke her soft smooth clit. "Quinton..."

"You're gorgeous, Kink," I whisper, pushing my finger inside her, rolling it against her inner wall. "And I cannot wait to sink myself deep inside you."

"Yesss..."

I push two fingers inside her this time. "Feeling you squeeze my cock so fucking tight."

"Quinton, yes, please..."

"Milking me until I can't hold back anymore. Until I explode and you're screaming for more."

"Shit, I'll scream right now if it means you'll take out that sexy cock of yours and—" I yank down my pants, freeing my cock, and her jaw drops.

Yep. That's exactly the reaction that feeds a man's ego.

"Holy...come to mama." She wiggles herself down between my knees until she can reach my cock, wraps her hand around the base, and then practically swallows me whole.

"Mother fuuuuuck. Kins..." I gasp as her mouth slides off my cock and her tongue swirls around me. She squeezes her hand, applying the perfect amount of pressure, and then sucks me back in and Jeeeeesus her mouth...her tongue. She doesn't stop. She takes my cock as far back as it will go, gagging when it reaches the back of her throat, but never stopping. Threading my hand into her hair I hold it back from her face because this view...fuck, it's everything.

"You take my cock like a fucking goddess, Kinsley. A mother fucking beautiful goddess." I can't tear my eyes away for the life of me. Watching her sweet lips take me in over and over again, the sound of her little gags, and the hunger in her moans is a fucking dream come true. She looks up at me from under her lashes and as fshe knows I'm watching her, slips her hand between her legs. Her fingers stroke through her drenched pussy and drag circles around her clit. She moans even louder than before, the vibrations causing my dick to become a rod of steel.

"Fuck, Kinsley. You're such a good girl. Mmm the best fucking girl. You're going to make me come."

She pops off my cock and moves to take me back in but I don't let her. Pushing her back I crash my mouth to hers in a hungry, hard kiss. "I need to grab a condom."

"No." Her hands grab my ass, keeping me in place. "I'm on the pill. I've been on the pill for years. I didn't want to have Seth's babies."

Looking down at the skin-on-skin connection between us, I catch my breath. "You're sure?"

"Fuck me, Quinton. Put your monster cock inside me and fuck my brains out. Please!"

A girl does not have to ask twice.

Lifting her thighs I line myself up with her entrance and plunge deep inside her, listening to her gasp and sigh all in one movement.

"Yessss. Oh my God, Quinton."

I lean my forehead against hers as I pull out and thrust back in. "Fuck, Kinsley your body takes me perfectly."

"It was made for you, Quinton. I was made for you. Take me. All the way. Take me to the end."

Wrapping my hands around hers, I squeeze them tightly as I thrust my hips forward and back.

In and out.

In and out.

In and out.

Over, and over, and over again until our rhythm is so fast, so tight, neither one of us can stop until we've reached the end.

"QUINTON! OH GOD, YES! YES! OH FUCK!" she screams. "I'm going to come so fucking hard!"

Fucking hell, the way she isn't afraid to scream out and be loud is a huge turn on.

"Squeeze my cock, Kink. Come for me. Grab me inside of you and squeeze me. Milk me." I lean my head down and lick across her breast teasing her nipple, thrusting inside her with sweat beginning to slide down my back until a loud and long moan escapes her. Her body quivers and her eyes squeeze closed and Jesus Christ she is beautiful when she comes apart for me.

Her body squeezes me from the inside out and I only last another few seconds before my balls tighten, my spine tingles, and I'm coming inside her harder than I think I've ever come in my life.

"Shit! Oh...fuck! Kinsley. Fuck!" I buck against her, shattering inside her while trying not to simply drop my body weight on top of her out of exhaustion.

Holy shit.

We're panting against each other, trying to catch our breaths and soak in the moment that just happened between us.

I just fucked Kinsley Kendrick.

And it was...everything.

She is without a doubt the best sex of my life.

And I think I might be in love.

17

KINSLEY

"**S**o why boudoir photography?" he asks me. Our legs entwined and our bodies facing each other in bed after our fourth round of some of the hottest sex I think I've ever had. After our first round we decided to sit in the hot tub which resulted in Quinton sitting me up on the edge and eating me until I came, and then we moved to the shower where he took me against the wall under the cascade of hot water. And time number four? Reverse cowgirl in the middle of this bed and holy hell was it amazing. Best ride I've ever taken. I knew hockey players were fast on their feet, but holy hell, he's fast with his fingers and his tongue and pelvic thrusts too.

After our afternoon and evening workouts, Quinton suggested we order room service and spend the night relaxing before tomorrow's flight home. Since the moment we walked back into this cabin earlier this afternoon, he hasn't left my side. And I'd be lying to myself if I said I wasn't feeling anything for him.

Because I am.

I'm definitely developing feelings for my fake fiancé.

And unless I'm completely wrong, I think there could be some feelings on his end as well. I just don't know if I'm brave enough to ask him yet.

"Honest answer?" I finally ask him.

"Always."

"It was Seth who got me into it. Inadvertently anyway. He didn't know it and still has no idea, but it was the way he treated me when we were together."

Quinton frowns. "Why do you say that?"

I roll onto my back, staring up at the ceiling, Quinton's hand feathering across my stomach. "Seth made no bones about my body not being the perfect model-type body. He was quick to make comments about my height. My weight. The curl of my hair. You name it and I'm sure at some point or another, he's said it."

"But you stayed with him?"

"For a while, yes."

Quinton swallows, his gaze dropping to my stomach and his brows pinching. I can tell he's wrestling with his thoughts.

"It's okay. You can ask me."

"Why? Why did you stay? Why didn't you just leave him?"

I give him the most honest answer I can. "Money. I was still living with my parents then. I made a plan for myself. Saved every penny I could working as many different jobs as I could. I was hardly around for Seth to be able to say anything but then he would say new things because I wasn't around to give him...well, you know."

"Mother fucker."

"So, I promised myself in two years or sooner, I would move out. Get away from my parents even if it meant not having their money to live off of. Because I knew money didn't equal happiness. I was living proof of that. I left Seth a year and a half later."

"And he didn't try to hurt you when you told him you were leaving?"

"Physically? No. Seth isn't that kind of guy. He uses his mouth, not his fists. Quite frankly, I think he was relieved. At least I don't see why he wouldn't be. He was free to find his walking talking perfection."

"I'm proud of you for putting yourself first."

"I'm proud of me too."

Quinton leans over and tenderly kisses my lips and then leans back onto his elbow.

"So, once I moved to Chicago I had the idea to give boudoir photography a try. I had a feeling there were lots of women like me who either didn't think highly of themselves and their bodies and needed a positive reminder to look at, or they were confident in their own skin and wanted to show it off for themselves or as a gift for their partners. The first year I advertised the experience, I had over one hundred clients."

"That's incredible."

"Yeah. It is."

"Do you supply their outfits?"

"Sometimes, yeah. If they have something they want to wear that's great, but there are many who don't usually wear lingerie because they don't think they look good in it and they need a little confidence boost. I'm more than happy to help get them into something special that will make them feel like a million bucks so I keep props and clothing of all sizes on hand just in case."

"And you do that all in your studio?"

"Mhmm. It's not the biggest or best space, but it's what I have and I make effective use of it. Every once in a while a client will ask if I'll do a session in their home and I almost always say yes. They want something more intimate. More personal. In a space that's meaningful to them."

Quinton shakes his head, his eyes marveling, but he's not saying a word. The warmness in his expression causes my heart to swell in my chest.

"Did you always know you wanted to play hockey?"

He nods. "Yeah. Since I was like six or seven."

"Wow that young?"

"Yeah. My dad took me to a game and I watched the guys on the team moving around the ice like they were superheroes and that day I told my dad I wanted to learn to skate. Picked it up quickly and then joined a team when I was eight. I've been skating ever since. It wasn't always easy but it's the world I know. The world I love."

"I love that for you. You've clearly done an outstanding job. You must've had a good support system."

"In the beginning I did, yeah." He leans back against the pillows, his hands behind his head. "Then my parents divorced and things got ugly. My sister and I were all each other had. We got very close and supported each other through it all. My parents don't speak anymore and it's better that way."

"What do you think happened?"

"Honestly?" he asks before inhaling a deep breath. "I think hockey became too much for him."

"Oh no." I roll toward him, my hands on his chest.

"I think my involvement ate up so much of his time, their time, and he just couldn't handle it anymore. We were always at the arena. Practice, games, travel. They spent so much time investing in me they didn't focus on themselves. I'm fairly sure Dad had a side piece. There was this other mom he was always talking to. Sitting next to. I would look up during practice and neither one of them would be there and then a few hours later there they were, sitting near each other, laughing."

"I'm so sorry Quinton."

"I used to blame myself but I don't anymore. He didn't have to choose the other woman. He could've been an honorable man. He was supposed to be my role model, you know? The man I fashioned myself after, but instead my sister and I both grew up with a negative view on adult relationships."

"Is your sister married?"

"She is." His eyes sparkle with amusement. "She entered into a fake relationship with The Love Guru and ended up marrying the guy."

"Shut up!" I sit up, wide eyed. "That's your sister?"

"Yep. You've heard of her?"

"Heck yeah I've heard of her! I've heard of them both! The Love Guru and the Love Grinch?" I laugh. "Their story was all over the place at the time. I had no idea you had a connection there."

"Joke was on her, huh?" He laughs with me. "She married the guy."

"Oh my gosh that's amazing!" I shake my head in wonderment. "And oddly...romantic."

"Yeah, he's good for her. I'm happy for them both."

"I bet Hawaii is beautiful."

"Have you ever been?"

I shake my head. "Nope. It's on my bucket list."

I rest my chin on Quinton's chest while he runs his hand through my hair. "What else is on your bucket list."

"Besides seeing the world?"

"Yeah. Besides that."

"Umm..." My brows pinch as I consider my long-term goals. "Obviously, I want to grow my name. My business. Maybe create a larger studio space eventually. I don't know. I just want to have some sort of impact on others, you know? I want to make people happy. Make a difference in their lives by showing them how beautiful they are and that they matter. I want to remind people how beautiful our world is. We spend too much time focusing on the negative. How much money we have or what our status is. How successful we are. Squirrels don't think about how successful they are. They're simply happy to find an acorn or a comfortable spot in a tree."

"Squirrels?"

"Yeah. Squirrels."

Quinton doesn't say anything. He continues to stroke my hair and when I finally make eye contact with him, he's smiling at me like he's never seen something so peculiar.

I get that a lot.

"What are you thinking about?"

He huffs out a soft laugh. "I'm wondering what my life would be like right now had I not heard you talking to your mom on the phone that night in Pringle's."

I laugh. "Probably a lot less of a hot mess, a lot less complicated..."

"And a lot more boring," he finishes, his hand smoothing my curls away from my face. I watch as he moistens his lips with his tongue and then his lips separate, his smile growing. "Move in with me."

"What?"

"You heard me."

"I know I heard you...but..."

"I know it's fast. I know this arrangement between us never included moving in but think about it. The whole world thinks we're engaged and planning a wedding. So why wouldn't we live together? It would help our story."

"Engaged couples don't have to live together, Quinton."

"But..."

"But what?"

"You don't want to move in? Live with me? I have all the space you could ever want. Then your studio could become a true studio. For all your work. Hell, we could fix it up for you. Make it whatever you want to grow your business."

The thought of using my studio for just a studio instead of also as a living space would be amazing but...

"Quinton what about when this engagement comes to an end? If I spend my money changing the studio space, at some point I have to move out of your place."

"Why?"

"Because this isn't real, Quinton. Remember? At some point we have to...I don't know, stage a breakup of some sort. Which means I would have to move back to my studio."

A look of disappointment and sadness crosses his face and I almost tell him I'm kidding about the breakup part just to see him happy again.

"Quinton?"

"Alright." He inhales a deep breath and then tries to give me a reassuring smile. "Then come stay with me... temporarily."

"Quinton, you know no matter what, I'll make sure I'm available for you, right? Any time you need me?"

"Yeah I get it. But..." He sighs. "My life is boring. And when you're around...I...I forget how boring it is. It's like time doesn't exist when we're having fun together. I laugh more with you. I see things with you I've never seen before."

"Like what?"

"Like...glistening snow. Or the way the sunset hits the mountains and makes the sky glow. I've never paid attention to those kinds of things until I met you. And I remember to have fun when you're around. You beguile me, Kinsley."

"I do?"

"Mhmm."

"It that...a good beguile? Or a bad beguile?"

Quinton's throaty laugh makes me smile. He pulls me on top of him and rolls over onto his back, pushing my hair from my face and kissing me. "It's good, Kink," he affirms. "Very good."

He kisses me again, taking his slow sweet time, rolling his tongue lazily through my mouth and pushing both hands through my hair. This doesn't feel like a kiss from someone only pretending to be my fiancé.

"Quinton?"

"Hmm?"

"I think Little Buddy has become a monster...again."

When he chuckles against my mouth, I feel just how hard he really is. "Put me inside you, Kink. This monster wants to take you for a spin before you give me your answer."

Oh God. Yes please!

I lift on my knees and line his cock up with my entrance and then sink down over him, my head falling back as I gasp at the fullness.

"Quinton?"

"Yes?"

"Promise me that Monster Cock and I can be best friends while I stay with you and the answer is a resounding yes."

Friends with benefits?

We could make this work.

Because I need this cock in my life.

"It's a deal, Kink. Monster Cock and you are now soulmates."

"Monster Cock and Kinsley sittin' in a tree." I glance down at Quinton with a smirk. "F-u-c-k-i-n-g."

18

KINSLEY

When Quinton gave me the address to his home, I had no idea he lived in River North. Known for being one of the poshest neighborhoods in the city, there are high end retail stores, luxury eateries, and art lofts as far as the eye can see. As much as I could see myself owning a space around here one day for my art, I would've expected Quinton to live somewhere a little quieter, and maybe a little less of a popular celebrity hangout. But once I step inside, all my prejudgments disappear.

Quinton's home is breathtakingly serene.

The structure throughout his place reminds me of old Chicago with the brick and wood beams and high-end finishes that bring back a nineteen-twenties kind of charm. Huge skylights are built into his living room ceiling and the rooftop deck is to die for. The perfect evening snuggle spot.

"Is this deck really as private as it feels or am I just being naïve?"

Quinton smiles, his hands in his pockets as he follows

me through his space. "I suppose if paparazzi really wanted to see something out here, they could find a way but it would be tricky," he answers. "Between the overhead trellis and the plants surrounding the deck, we're closed in and cozy without having to share ourselves with the entire world." He gestures to the city below. "Sometimes I like to come out here and read or think or...you know, listen to the sounds of Chicago to drown out my thoughts."

I cock my head and give him a questioning glance. "You have a need to drown out your thoughts?"

"Contrary to your beliefs, Kink, I'm not exactly perfect."

"Oh, I know." I nod, pretending to be empathetic. "Your penis hangs a little too far to the right sometimes."

Quinton's jaw drops and his eyes widen but he quickly figures out I'm kidding and lifts his shoulder. "Right? What can I say? I'm lucky it doesn't get caught in the zipper most days."

His comment makes me snort.

"This really is beautiful, Quinton. Are you sure you're okay with my being here? If this is too much or you—"

"Kins, don't even go there." He brings a finger to my lips and it takes all my control not to cover it with my mouth and suck on it because holy hell, Quinton's presence in this space...in his home...in those gray sweatpants...bare feet...Jesus, he is sexy as sin.

"If I didn't want you here, you wouldn't be. And besides, it's not like I'm here a lot. You'll have the whole place to yourself when the team is on the road and I'll feel better that my fiancée is safe in my home while I'm away."

"Oh, now you're concerned for my safety?"

"Now that there's a ring on your finger? Yes. People are crazy and you never know what they might say. Paparazzi can be even worse when they want to be. The last thing I want is you getting hurt."

"Ugh," I sigh. "I'm so sorry, Quinton. This is all my fault."

"Stop apologizing," he chuckles and kisses my forehead. "We're fine. Everything is fine. I really am glad you're here."

"Alright, well..." I shrug and step back inside his living room. "Why don't you show me to my room and I can at least unpack a few things."

His brow crinkles. "Your room?"

"Yeah." My brows mirror his. "Am I sleeping on the floor ooor..."

"Oh, uh...well, I kind of hoped you would sleep in my room. With me."

My jaw drops and for just a moment I'm speechless but then I remember the deal I made with him in Colorado when I agreed to come here.

"Promise me that Monster Cock and I can be best friends while I stay with you and the answer is a resounding yes."

My lips curl up in a teasing smile and I cross my arms over my chest. "Well, that all depends."

"On?"

"Do you have Make-out Mondays here?"

"Absolutely," he replies deadpanned. He steps closer to me and I watch as his eyes fall to my chest. "And Titty Tuesdays."

"Oh, is that so?"

"Mhmm."

"What about Wednesday?"

"Oh, that's easy. It's Wet-lips Wednesday."

"So, we'll be kissing all day long? I like the sounds of that."

He shakes his head with a heated gaze as he trails a hand through my hair. "No Kink. Those are not the lips I'm referring to."

Fuuuuck me.

"Oh."

"Ask me about Thursday."

Oh God, I'm not sure my girl parts can handle hearing about Thursday. They're hot and bothered already. Swallowing my sudden desire to strip my clothes off and ask Quinton to have his way with me right here right now, I ask, "What's Thursday?"

He pulls me against him and thrusts his pelvis into mine.

Holy shit, I'm not certain he's wearing anything under these gray sweatpants.

"It's Thruster Thursday, Kinsley."

Yes please!

"Aaaand Friday?"

"My favorite day, Kink. Facial Friday followed by another favorite...Suck-it Saturday."

I lick my lips. "Mmm. Can't wait for that day. And what about Sunday?"

"You mean today?" he asks with a wicked grin.

I feign ignorance. "Is today Sunday?"

"All day, Kink. You know what that means?" He bends down and lifts me over his shoulder and carries me down a short hallway, I'm guessing to his bedroom.

"What?" I snort before spanking his tight ass with every step he takes. "Oooh maybe that's it. Please tell me it's Spank Me Sunday."

"Is that what you want, Kink? You want me to spank you?"

"God yes!" I squeal. "Spank me all you want."

Chuckling, he tosses me onto his plush king-sized bed and then crawls over top of me. "It would be my greatest pleasure." He makes quick work of my pants, smiling in approval of the black thong I'm currently wearing. "Now be a good girl and get on your knees."

"Okay let's do one last pose to finish. Are you ready to blow your fiancé's mind?" My newest client, Julia, has been so much fun to work with during this session. I love it when clients come in with no preconceived notions or expectations and are always willing to take my direction. Julia found me online and asked about creating a portfolio for her fiancé as a wedding present and I was all too excited to work with her.

"Oh, yeah. I'm ready."

"Alright, I want you to lay on this rug right here and prop yourself up on your elbows for a minute so you're looking down your sternum."

She follows my instructions perfectly, her white lace bra and thong popping against her tanned skin.

"Great. Now I want you to bend your knees so your feet are flat on the floor and then once you're comfortable in that position I want you to lift your right foot up enough to point your toes against the ground."

She lifts her foot and arches it forward, her big toe feathering on the floor, her left foot slightly arched.

"Yes! Beautiful!" I tell her, crouching down just behind her head. "Now let's bring your head all the way back and use your hands and that beautiful ass of yours to help shift the weight as far back as you can. All the way to the top of your head. It'll look like you're trying to do a back bend."

Julia shimmies herself back and I help position her head on the floor, sprawling her long black hair out around her.

"Like this?"

"Oh, my God, giiiirl you look stunning! Are you okay like this?"

"Yep. I'm good. Where should I put my hands."

"Oh yeah, let's bring your left hand in between your thighs like this," I position her hand for her just inside her left thigh. "And bring your right hand up to your hair...yes. Just like that. Perfect! Alright here we go."

"Close your eyes for me and give me that sultry look we practiced earlier."

I click several shots of Julia from as many different angles as I can and then have her relax. "That's going to be the piece de resistance. I promise you. Look how fucking hot you look."

SUSAN RENEE

I turn the camera around to show her a few shots and her jaw drops.

"Oh, shit! That's me?"

Giggling, I nod. "That is absolutely you, babe. You killed it."

"I cannot believe you just made me look that good."

"No girl, this wasn't me. This is all you. One hundred percent. I'm telling you Tyson isn't going to know what hit him on your wedding night when he opens this photo album."

Julia rubs her hands together and laughs maniacally. "That's the plan."

I help her up from the floor and send her off to change back into her regular clothes while I put all my props and equipment away and then we make an appointment to meet in a few days to go over her final edits and choose the poses she wants for her portfolio.

"Kinsley, I cannot thank you enough. This experience has been mind-blowing and more fun than I think I could have ever imagined for myself. I can actually look at myself in the mirror and tell myself I'm a sexy woman worthy of being desired and that is all because of you."

I wrap my arms around her again already feeling like I've gained another lifelong friend. "Julia you are beautiful in all aspects of the word and if I can take a few pictures of you looking hot as fuck for your fiancé to help you remember that, I'll do it every day for as long as I live."

Waving goodbye as she leaves my studio, I'm all smiles and warm fuzzy feelings because I'm in love with what I do. There's something about fixing another woman's crown and reminding her how beautiful she is that brings me so much joy. Like it's my purpose in this life.

Money or not.

I spend another half hour or so cleaning up the studio and then grab my laptop and camera bag to take back to Quinton's with me so I can work on some editing. I send him a quick text letting him know I'm on my way and within the next fifteen minutes I'm walking through the front door to what appears to be an empty penthouse. Quinton's not in the living room or kitchen from what I can see from the front door, nor has Nutsack welcomed me home as he usually does.

I'm just about to yell for Quinton when I hear the faint sounds of a television from down the hall.

Of course.

He must be going over plays for tonight's game.

I slide off my shoes and meander through the house in search of my guys. When I reach the bedroom my heart nearly melts right out of my chest. A shirtless Quinton is asleep leaning against the headboard and Nutsack is curled up asleep on his stomach.

Be still my heart.

My two guys.

I wasn't sure when I moved in here that Quinton would be okay with Nutsack running around. Having to add litter boxes throughout the space, I'm continually cleaning them so they don't become a burden and I'm always nervous Nutsack is going to get himself into badly timed mischief but this...seeing my two favorite guys curled up and napping together?

Is there really anything sweeter than this?

SUSAN RENEE

I keep telling myself that whatever this is between Quinton and me isn't real. It's just an arrangement we have as two adults, crazy though it may be. Because if it were real, if I really were moved in with Quinton Shay for the near future, if the small touches and kisses and sex we share had any meaning whatsoever, if the way he looks at me really was conveying his sincere feelings, I would easily fall in love with him.

19

QUINTON

"What are you grinning at over there?" Zeke asks, pulling his jersey over his head.

I feel alive today.

Refreshed.

Like I can take on the world.

"Just appreciating the smell of the ice."

Hawken laughs. "Uh, I think that might be Dex's week-old practice socks you smell."

"Nah, that's not it." I shake my head with a knowing smile. "You remember stepping into the locker room for your very first time? That scent of the ice coupled with the leather of our skates? The sound of your blades gliding across the rink or the slap of your stick to puck for the first time?"

The guys nod, nostalgic looks on their faces. "Yeah man," Milo answers. "I think I was scared to death that day."

"I remember watching my brother on the ice," Colby

SUSAN RENEE

reminisces with an amused huff. "He made it look so fucking easy."

Thinking about that very first hockey game my father took me to when I was kid, I give Colby a half smile. "Yeah. Same. I couldn't wait to be a superhero flying across the ice."

Having just joined us from his shower, Dex's eyes slide from Milo to Colby and then me. "Dude, what's with the reminiscing?"

I shrug as I begin to put on my uniform. "Nothing really. I was just telling Kinsley the other day about how I got started and it made me take a minute and appreciate how far I've come. That's all."

"Wow." He laughs and steps over to his spot in the dressing room. "You've got it bad, bro."

"What?"

Dex and Hawken laugh together and Hawken turns to explain. "You slept with her, didn't you?"

I frown. "How the hell did you get I fucked her from me talking about the first time I played hockey?

"Easy. You like the girl and she's making you have all these heartfelt thoughts. You're all up in your feelings."

"So that means we slept together?"

Hawken cocks his head and raises his brow. "Tell me you didn't then."

No can do.

"See?" Hawken points with an ornery smirk. "You fucked and now she has you all up in your feelings."

"What? That's insane."

But so fucking true.

I do like Kinsley.

I think I like her a lot.

"She moved in, right?"

"Yeah." I roll my eyes as I say, "Temporarily."

"Ahhhhh..." Zeke points at me and laughs. "You just rolled your eyes when you said that!"

"Said what?"

"Temporarily."

"So?"

"You like having her there," he challenges.

"Okay. So, I do. It's less...lonely when she's there. So what?"

"Sooo the Quinton I've known for the past couple of years loved being on his own. To do whatever or whoever he wanted."

Correction.

You think I enjoyed being on my own.

Because I'm not about to admit to a team of my brothers that I don't love living alone.

Milo cuts in. "So, I take it things are going well with you guys?"

"Yeah." I nod. "As well as two people pretending to be engaged can be. We're making it work."

"For how long?"

I don't want to talk about how long.

I don't want to think about not having Kinsley with me.

Not wanting to make eye contact, I grab my skate and loosen the laces. "She's attending the G.A.M.E. Night Gala with me."

"Isn't that next month?" Colby asks.

"Yeah."

"And then what?"

"And then..."

My world will be a little less happy.

My life becomes a little more boring.

I go back to being a single Shay.

"I don't know. We'll see what happens from there, I guess. She's already talked about staging a breakup."

Zeke sits down next to me. "And how do you feel about that?"

"I think I don't want to talk about it."

He laughs. "Uh huh. That's what I thought."

"Oooh this is gettin' good." Milo says with a glint in his eye. "It's happening."

My brow furrows. "What's happening?"

"You're falling for your fake fiancé."

"Oh, for fuck's sake. I am not."

I so am.

"It's alright, man," Hawken adds. "You already told us you like her. And it's okay if you slept with her. You do you, boo."

"Boo?" Dex cringes. "Dear God, you better not call my sister Boo."

Hawken's brow raises and a smirk spreads across his face. "You want to know what I call your sister when she's hot and bothered and ridin' my—"

"NOOOOOOPE!" Dex covers his ears with both hands. "I do NOT want to know a damn thing. You keep my sister to yourself."

Hawken chuckles. "Don't mind if I do."

"Giiiiirls alert!" We all turn to the sound of Carissa's voice. None of us are concerned if Carissa sees us in our birthday suits. She's paid to be around, though we do try to remain respectful for Colby's sake. "Is everyone decent?"

"Define decent?" Dex snickers.

"Babe," Carissa shouts. "Is Dex waving his little wand around again?"

"LITTLE WAND?" Dex scoffs. "Listen Smallson! Nothing about my wand is LITTLE, alright?"

"Yeah it's all good, Smalls." Colby laughs and Carissa holds the door open for a small group of women. Tatum and Rory stride in first followed by Charlee and...

Fuuuuck me...she's adorable.

"Kinsley." She's an unexpected surprise. I mean I knew she was coming to tonight's game and that she'd be sitting with the other WAGS but seeing her, here in the locker room, in all her captivating Red Tails glory...Fuck. I'm nothing but a puddle of dopey smiles.

She spots me across the room and waves with a grin as I study her from head to toe. She's the ultimate Red Tails super fan. She's sporting her red Chuck Taylor's and black tights with red leg warmers hugging her toned calves. A red and black tutu sparkles around her waist with a Red Tails t-shirt and a white long sleeve shirt underneath to keep her warm. Her dark curls are pulled up on top of her head in two mini buns each tied with red ribbons. She's not wearing a ton of makeup but she's outlined her eyes with a smokey gray look that entices me more than I should admit. I have this unwavering urge to grab her and kiss those sweet lips right here in front of everyone, but I just told the guys what was going on between us was no big deal.

God, I'm such a liar.

"Hi Quinton."

"You look..." I shake my head slowly, still taking her in when she cringes.

"Too much?" She touches her head. "Oh God, do I look stupid? Is it the buns? I knew I should have—"

"No." My smile widens and I take her free hand, her other holding a bag. "No. You look perfect. Adorably perfect."

"I beg to differ." Hawken folds his arms over his chest studying Kinsley as she stands in front of us.

"What the fuck, man?"

He shrugs. "She's not perfect until she's wearing your name, Shay. Why isn't she wearing your name?"

Shit!

He's right.

Rory swoops in to stand next to Kinsley, their arms entwined. "That's precisely why we're here. When she showed up without your name on her back we told her she should've gone through your things to find something in your closet."

Kinsley frowns, her hand on her chest. "I would never," she tells me, wide-eyed. "That's like a huge invasion of privacy and I would never do that to you and besides..." She pulls at the t-shirt she has on. "This is totally fine. I could just write your name on the back with a sharpie and then everything will—"

"A sharpie." Dex chuckles, putting his arm around my girl. If he weren't head over heels for Tatum, I would kick his tiny balls so fast he wouldn't be able to stand for a week. "That's cute, Kinsley. Tell you what. If Quinton here doesn't have a jersey for you, I would be more than happy to give you one of—"

"Back off, Dexter. She's mine." I'm already pulling off my jersey and maneuvering it around Kinsley's buns. A wave of jitters crash through my chest at the thought of her being mine for real. "I'm sorry, Kink. I should've given this to you earlier."

She peers down at herself now swimming in my jersey. "Hmm…I don't know about this now."

My brows pinch. "You don't like it? You don't have to wear it."

"Are you kidding? I love it!" She smiles.

"Hmm, you're right though." Charlee rubs her hands lovingly over her pregnant belly as she looks over Kinsley's outfit and gestures towards her waist. "The hidden tutu now adds a lot of extra…fluff."

Kinsley shrugs. "I could just take it off. Think the jersey is long enough?"

"For sure, it is." Tatum nods. "Take it off, babe, and wear the fuck out of Quinton's name."

We all watch in awe, highly inappropriate, I know, as Kinsley slides off the tutu she's wearing from underneath my jersey, effectively making it a mini dress.

Holy hell.

She's perfect.

Her legs look fucking great.

What I wouldn't give to be able to bend her over right here and…

"Close your mouth, Shay," Zeke whispers on the other side of me. "You two can celebrate after we win."

"Better?" Kinsley asks the group of us. We all give her an affirmative nod much to her delight. "Perfect. Thank you, Quinton." She reaches up on her tip toes and kisses my cheek.

"Of course."

"Oh! I almost forgot," she says, holding up the bag in her hand. "I brought you all something." She shoves her hand into the bag and pulls out several round brown ball-like objects and tosses one to each of us. "A little reminder of how awesome you guys are."

"I may be a tiny potato," Dex reads. "But I believe in you. Go do your thing."

"You got us tiny, crocheted potatoes?" Hawken asks, perplexed.

Kinsley nods with a smile. "Yeah. Well, actually, I made them. They're positive potatoes. You know, for those times when you just need a little pick-me-up."

Inwardly I hold my breath and pray none of the guys tease Kinsley about her little side hobby. I get that it's unusual but her uniqueness and proclivity for spreading joy are what make her so attractive. She's fun to be around and I don't ever want someone to dull her sparkle.

"These things are fucking cute!" Zeke tells her with a huge smile. "Elsie would love this!"

Kinsley tosses him a second one. "Well give her this one, then. That way you both have one."

Zeke reaches over and gives Kinsley a hug, burying her in his uniform padding. "Thank you Kinsley."

"My pleasure."

"We should probably go." Carissa gestures toward the door. "Time for you all to get your game faces on and bring home a win."

Charlee waves her finger between Milo and the rest of

us. "Hey, you be nice to my brother out there," she says, referring to Oliver Magallan of the Anaheim Stars and our opponents for tonight's game. "He doesn't need any more missing teeth."

Milo laughs. "No promises, Goldilocks, but we'll try to behave if they do." Milo kisses her one last time, his hand palming her pregnant stomach, and then he places a kiss there as well. "Take care of my girl."

"You know I will."

"I'll catch you after the game, yeah?" I ask after chastely kissing Kinsley's lips.

"Of course! Go score a goal for me."

"How about I score three?"

Her brows shoot up. "Whoa. A hat trick, huh? Alright. Let's see what you can do, Shay. Good luck out there." She reaches up on her tiptoes one more time and presses her lips against mine and fuck, if I could just forget about the game and make out with Kinsley right here in the locker room, I would in a heartbeat.

"Thanks, Kink. I'll see you later."

We all watch the ladies leave and finish dressing before preparing for our warmup. When we're standing in the tunnel I catch Zeke staring at me with a puzzled look on his face.

"What?"

"Do I even want to know why you call her Kink?"

Chuckling quietly, I shake my head. "It's not at all what you think."

20

QUINTON

"HUSTLE, HIT, and NEVER QUIT!" We chant our team motto before taking to the ice one at a time as we're called up by the announcer. When my skates touch the ice I can feel the energy in the arena, the electricity in the air.

This is going to be a damn good game.

"Hey Shay!" Zeke calls out to me as he skates backwards toward his position at the net. I turn around to look at him and he gestures to where the ladies are seated near the penalty box. "Take a look at your girl, man."

I turn back and spot Kinsley right away. The two buns in her hair adorned with red ribbons giving her away immediately. She's adorably sexy wearing my jersey as a dress, jumping up and down in excitement but what makes me shake my head in amusement is the black face paint under her eyes like she's about to play professional football and the larger-than-life red foam finger she's got over her hand, waving it around without a care in the world.

How the hell is she so cute?

And how on Earth could anybody not love her?

"Your girl's bringing her A-game tonight, Shay," Landric says with a chuckle.

"Sure is. Someone's got to cover for all those preggers sittin' up there with her."

"Good point!" He laughs. "I don't need any babies coming during this game."

"Babies?" Dex's eyes grow huge and he whips around toward our girls. "What babies? Shit! Is there a baby coming?"

"Relax Dexter. There are no babies. I promise."

I suppose I shouldn't promise. Never say never.

"Phew." Dex brings a hand to his chest. "Scared me there for a second. Thought I was going to have to put my delivery skills to the test again."

"I'll thank you to keep your filthy hands out of my wife's vagina, Foster." Colby laughs.

Dex holds up his gloved hands. "Hey, these hands can do more than shoot a puck across the ice asshole. They can bring life into this world."

"Yeah, yeah, we've heard it a million times. Let's not forget how you freaked the fuck out and had to be put in your place by the screaming mother of your child in the process." Those of us within ear shot of Colby and Dex enjoy a quick laugh at Dex's expense and then Colby's game face is back. "Let's play some hockey, gentlemen!"

Landric and Ledger Dayne, Anaheim's center, face off in the puck drop and Dayne grabs control. Shot over to Griffin Ollenberg, Colby tries to take possession and succeeds snapping the puck to Hawken who gets tripped up but sends it down the ice. Dex and I sprint for the puck alongside Oliver Magallan, Charlee's brother, and Harrison Meers. Dex gets the puck over the line and then circles back around Magallan passing to me and I immediately spot my opening. I shoot the puck toward the net but it's blocked by Barrett Cunningham and returned to Ollenberg. Colby's already on him fighting to regain control. The puck slides across the ice into the far corner and I swoop in to intercept. Flying behind the net, Ollenberg and August Blackstone now on my tail, I swing my stick to the front where I sneak the puck into the bottom corner of the net and score!

"LET'S GOOOOOOO!" I shout, shaking my fists in the air. A sense of euphoria sweeps over me as the crowd rises to their feet celebrating with me as my teammates surround me for a group hug.

"Way to fucking start, Shay!" Milo shouts tapping my helmet.

"Way to slip it in, Shay." Dex beams at me as he wraps his arm around me in a congratulatory hug. "You treat all the girls like that?"

I laugh with him. "S'all in the thrust, Dexter. All in the thrust."

Nearing the end of the second period, Anaheim is up two to one until I score a second time in the last thirty seconds and tie the score, the crowd roaring to life and bringing a renewed energy to the last period of the game. I've been lucky enough to catch small glimpses of Kinsley during the game, her enthusiasm for each of my goals inspiring me to play my best possible game.

For her.

To make her happy.

During a television timeout the crowd noise amplifies, but nothing major is happening on the ice. A quick glance at the jumbotron gives me all the explanation I need and now I'm captivated from my seat on the bench. Remi, our team's mascot, is working his way down the steps toward the group of ladies I now consider family. Charlee, Carissa, and Tatum are all smiles when Remi gives them high-fives and rubs their pregnant bellies. Rory gives Remi a fist bump and a huge hug but it's his playfulness with Kinsley that has me grinning from ear to ear.

Walk the Moon's "Shut Up and Dance With Me" plays overhead and Kinsley doesn't miss a beat. She grabs Remi's arm and he pulls her out to the steps twirling her around as if they're on the world's biggest stage. The crowd starts clapping to the beat of the song and when they get to the chorus, everyone sings the words aloud. Kinsley takes it all in stride, her energy contagious to everyone around her. She's fucking remarkable. When the song is cut short so we can resume game play, Remi dips Kinsley and pretends to kiss her. She comes up laughing and gives him a peck on his feathered cheek and I'm pretty damn sure I've never been more jealous of a human-sized feathered red bird in all my life.

"What is going on with your face, Shay?" Zeke asks when we're seated in the dressing room in between periods.

"Nothing's going on...what? What are you talking about?"

He smirks. "You look like you took a piss in everyone else's Cheerios and you're fucking giddy about it."

"Well from the looks of Barrett Cunningham's face tonight you would think I did piss in his Cheerios."

"Yeah. He's having a bad night. I love the goals, don't get me wrong, but he's played better than he's playing tonight."

Unable to stop smiling I take a deep breath and let Zeke in on my thoughts. "I've never played this game for anyone but myself," I explain. "But once I scored that first goal tonight and I saw the excitement on Kinsley's face..."

Zeke nods. "I hear you, my man. Suddenly you want to work your ass off to keep that smile on her face, yeah?"

"Yeah. It's like I can't get enough. Lexi wasn't at every game, but even the ones she came to, I never felt the positivity that radiates off Kinsley, you know? It's like she makes me feel like I'm a better person than I really am. Or she makes me believe I am, anyway."

"Dude, you're a great guy." Zeke frowns. "And the fact you would ever consider otherwise is bologna." He leans closer to me and murmurs, "So am I to infer that what you said earlier about nothing going on between the two of you is a lie?"

I bob my head cringing slightly. "We haven't exactly talked about it. We've definitely done some...stuff," I tell him, choosing not to go into detail about our wildly fun night in Colorado. "But I think she views whatever we do as two consenting adults having fun together."

"Nothing more?"

"That's what I don't know. We haven't really talked about it."

He nudges me with his shoulder. "Sounds like you two have some chatting to do then because I haven't seen this side of Quinton Shay in quite some time."

"What side is that?"

He winks at me and stands up, ready to return to the ice for our final period. "The in-love side."

In love...

Wow.

I don't know.

Am I in love with Kinsley?

Love feels like a strong word.

Maybe like?

I'm in like with Kinsley.

Like feels easier.

Yeah. I'm in like with her.

That's better.

The first puck drop of the third period is in our favor as Colby maneuvers down the ice and passes to an open and waiting Hawken. He tries for a shot but the puck bounces off Cunningham. Colby chips the rebound back into the goal crease but it stays out and Cunningham covers it up for the save.

"Son of a bitch, nerd!" Colby's outburst makes me crack up laughing.

"Nerd?" Dayne laughs next to me as we fight for the puck. "Who says nerd anymore?"

"Apparently Nelson does...when he's with your mom, dude." I give my opponent a quick wink, not knowing or caring if he notices, and swipe the puck shooting it in Milo's direction. Milo spins and weaves the puck back to me as my teammates do their best to distract Cunningham from the net. I try three times to sink it in to no avail before it glides toward the far corner. Magallan swoops in to intercept and it's played away until I cross the ice and take it back, bringing the puck back toward Cunningham.

"Hat trick, Shay!" Milo shouts. "Get it done!"

The guys rally around me, Nelson checking Magallan and Malone on top of Ollenberg. Foster takes Blackstone and Landric weaves between me and Meers trying to give me room to take my shot. Cunningham is fierce and he's big enough to take up his entire net but he's been playing hard this entire game. He's tired. I can tell his knee is bothering him because he's been slower on the uptake the longer this game has gone on. Cunningham's a great guy but right now his loss is my gain. I bring the puck down the middle passing it to Milo and flying back behind the net where I wait for Milo's move. He spins in front of Meers and the puck flies back to me just in time to shoot for Cunningham's five hole and in it goes!

"FUUUUUUUCK YES!"

The crowd goes crazy as do the guys as they practically pummel me into the glass with their hugs and helmet slaps.

"YOU FUCKING DID IT, QUINTON!"

"HAT TRICK BABY!"

"BAD ASS QUINTON!"

Even Zeke is jumping up and down from his spot on the ice.

The crowd explodes with raucous excitement, a sea of red towels spinning through the air above everyone's heads.

Holy shit.

I did it.

I just scored three fucking goals in one game. Not many

on our team have done that. I should be soaking this in. Every single fucking minute of celebration, but I only have eyes for one person and she's on the other side of the ice waving her foam finger and beaming at me like I'm literally the only other person in the room. She blows me a kiss and throws her foam finger down so she can make a heart shape with her hands as I take my seat on the bench after my shift.

And then she starts yelling something I can't hear above the noise of the crowd. She claps her hands twice and then thrusts her pelvis forward three times in a row. And then she does it all again.

What in the world?

Is she chanting something?

Hawken leans across Dex who is seated next to me and asks, "Dude, what is she saying?"

With an amused chuckle I shake my head. "Fuck if I know, but she's cute as hell and I can't stop watching her."

Kinsley shouts again, this time joined by Rory. Two claps...three pelvic thrusts.

"What the fuck?" Dex asks with a choked laugh.

Carissa and Charlee join in and soon their movements and chants begin to spread throughout the arena.

"Shay, look at that!" Colby gestures toward the jumbotron where Kinsley is front and center doing her cheer and within seconds the crowd around the arena has joined her!

"WHO'S YOUR DADDY" – Clap, clap, thrust-thrust-thrust.

"SHAY'S YOUR DADDY" – Clap, clap, thrust-thrust-thrust.

"Holy shit!" I lower my head in complete disbelief, unable to suppress my smile. "Is she really doing this?"

"She sure as hell is doing this." Milo claps me on the shoulder. "Quinton your girl just brought the entire arena to their feet in a cheer for you."

Fuck me.

This girl...she's an amazing human being.

Selfless.

Caring.

Loving.

Kind.

Funny.

Adventurous.

God, I wish I could kiss her right now.

Lexi never cared about my hockey success.

She only cared about my money and tabloid status.

Forget being in like with Kinsley Kendrick.

I think I might just be in love with her.

21

KINSLEY

"To Kinsley!" Dex raises his glass from his seat at the table. Thanks to the growing baby bellies in this group, Pringle's made sure we had access to the private back room tonight where there is more table space. "And her unbridled enthusiasm for the Chicago Red Tails and the game of hockey." Dex shakes his head in an amused laugh. "I don't think I've ever enjoyed hearing someone say who's your daddy more than I did tonight. Kudos to you, woman. Cheers!"

"Cheers!" the group chants together clinking glasses and taking their sips of beer, or water for the pregnant ones among us.

My smile widens. "Thank you, Dex. You all played a remarkable game tonight. It was fun getting to be your cheerleader."

"Hey if she's going to cheer like that," Hawken says, "Maybe we should take her on the road with us."

"What you should do," Charlee tells him, "is get that girl a shot. She deserves it!"

SUSAN RENEE

"That's a good idea." He nods with a grin and raises both arms. "Shots for everyone."

"Thanks for the compliment, Hawken, but I'm pretty sure I would need to be good and drunk to act like that in another team's arena."

"What?" he scoffs. "What are you talking about? You were a natural."

"Yeah well, it's easy when you're surrounded by fans who cheer for the same team you do, but once you become an outsider in enemy territory, all bets are off."

Hawken chuckles from across the table. "Well, for what it's worth, I think our man Quinton here thought you were hot as fuck up there dancing around in his jersey."

"Truth." Colby states with a nod. "He couldn't keep his eyes off you."

"You guys are just jealous because she had the whole place calling me daddy." Quinton gives me a knowing glance and quick wink. His hand sliding to my thigh underneath the table.

"So, he liked what he saw, huh?" I murmur beside Quinton.

He grunts, his hand palming over my thigh, and then leans over to whisper in my ear. "You can dance like that for me anytime you want, Kink. But I hope the next time is in my room just for me. And I hope you won't be wearing anything at all."

Our server arrives with a tray of shots, placing one in front of each of us. Quinton's eyes fall to my drink as his pinky finger rubs the inner part of my thigh. "Drink up, Kink."

"Tequila, huh?" I raise a brow when I lift my shot, smelling the alcohol before it ever reaches my lips. "You trying to get me drunk, Shay?"

"Hmm," he chuckles. "What happens when Kinsley Kendrick gets drunk?"

"I'll tell you exactly what happens." I lick my lips and match his smile. "I end up on the phone with my mother telling her about my sexy as hell rich hockey boyfriend so she'll leave me the fuck alone and then end up fake-dating the guy just to show her how goddamn serious I really am."

Quinton barks out a laugh. "So that was drunk Kinsley?"

I bob my head. "Meh, it was probably more like tipsy Kinsley if I'm being honest. Drunk Kinsley probably does all sorts of stupid shit and ends up with her head in a toilet the next morning."

"Well then..." Quinton hands me my shot and lifts his from the table. "To stupid shit and all the fun we'll have doing it."

I'm not sure if that's an invitation or some sort of promise for the night we're about to have, but I'm a go with the flow kind of gal so I'm here for it.

What have I got to lose?

"Bottom's up, Shay."

Two beers and several tequila shots later, for me, not Quinton since he drove, we're finally walking through his front door and I am feeling larger than life. I twirl myself into the living room unsteadily, bending over to give Nutsack a few scratches behind his ears.

"This has been one of the best days of my life!"

Quinton tosses his keys onto the table just inside the door. "Oh yeah? What makes you say that?"

"Because I got to watch my super sexy fake boyfriend..." I frown shaking my head. "No...wait. Did I say boyfriend? I meant fiancé! Yeah. I got to watch my super-hot as fuck fake fiancé do what he does best and he was fucking incredible at it, by the way."

He chuckles watching me. "Was he really?"

"Mhmm. And...AND...he even gave me this jersey and I've been smelling it all fucking night long and..." I lift the collar of Quinton's jersey to my nose and inhale a long deep breath. "It smells like what I'm pretty sure Heaven smells like."

"And just what does Heaven smell like, Kink?"

"Like...sex and candy and hockey and everything manly."

"Is that so?"

"It is so. Yes."

"Can I tell you a secret?"

My eyes light up at his request. "YES! I promise not to tell a soul."

Quinton steps toward me, wrapping his arms around my waist and pulling me against his warm strong body. "It just so happens your hot fake fiancé very much enjoyed watching his super sexy fiancée cheering him on in the crowd with his name across her back."

"Mmm..." I grin mischievously. "Did he?"

He shakes his head. "You have no fucking idea how hot you look in this jersey."

Still smiling, I lift on my tiptoes so I can whisper in his ear. "Would it help if I told you I'm not wearing any pants under this thing?"

"Jesus," he murmurs, his forehead leaning against mine. "Body shots."

"What?"

"Body shots. I think I need to catch up to you. How many shots did you take tonight?"

I giggle stepping back from him. "Uh...I wasn't keeping track. Three? Four? Six?"

"You definitely didn't have six, Kink. If you had had six, I'm quite sure I would've carried you in here asleep."

"Ouoh, but would you though? I mean, have I never told you how many nights I used to go out drinking with friends when I lived in California?"

Smiling as he heads to the kitchen he answers, "No. I guess you haven't. Were you a party girl, Kinsley?"

My face reddens as I bite my bottom lip. "I did my fair share. That's all I'll say."

"Good to know."

I watch him grab a bottle of tequila, a container of salt, and a few limes. He pulls a knife out of the knife block and cuts the limes into small wedges and then brings all the ingredients he needs to his larger-than-life dining table. Once he has everything situated, he comes back for me, lifting me into his arms and carrying me to the table where he sits me down on top.

"What are you doing?"

His pupils darkened, he licks his lips and answers, "Catching up."

Quinton lifts my arms slowly above my head. "Keep those there for a minute. I need to get this off." He tugs at the hem of my jersey and lifts it over my head and arms, tossing it to the floor and revealing my deep red satin bra and thong underneath. A heated smile on his face, he shakes his head in disbelief. "You're telling me this is all that's been under my name all night long.

"Mhmm." I nod methodically. "Do you like it?"

He rakes a hand down his face, holding it over his mouth. "Kinsley you are so goddamn gorgeous I can't even think straight half the time. You literally take my breath away so yes. Yes, I like this very much. Now lay down so I can pleasure your body until you're coming so hard you forget your damn name."

I swear in this moment all the air leaves my body.

And I can't form words.

No words.

Nope. There's nothing there.

I can't even think of something witty to say.

So, I do as he asks and lay back on his dining room table. He rotates my body so I'm parallel to the edge, granting him easier access to all of me. He trails his hand down my neck and over my sternum between my breasts and then down my stomach, feathering between my legs just enough to tease me.

"Quinton," I breathe.

He leans over me and kisses each of my breasts covered in soft satin material and then he pulls the cups down effectively plumping them. He squeezes a lime, letting it drip over each of my nipples as I gasp in response to the cool wet feel against my skin.

"A little salt I think." Quinton focuses on adding just enough salt to each nipple, the lime juice helping the salt stick, and then he places a small wedge in my mouth. "Hold this for me Kink. I'll be back for it."

I start to squirm as heat spreads down my body, pooling between my legs, but his hand steadies me.

"Don't move, Kink. We can't spill the best part."

He lifts the bottle of tequila and pours a shot sized amount into the divot of my belly button.

"Fucking gorgeous." Quinton licks his lips and then smirks at me from above. "You ready for me?"

Trying to keep my body still for him, I nod my head. "So ready."

He leans over my chest and licks across my nipple, my back arching in response to his touch.

"Ah, ah, ah," he says. "You'll spill my drink." He moves down to my navel, lapping up the tequila pooled there, and then kisses me hard, transferring the lime from my mouth to his.

Jesus, Mary, and Joseph that was hot!

"Mmm," he groans. "Delicious."

Finally able to wiggle a little, I bite my bottom lip and beg him, "Please tell me you're going to do that again."

"Oh, I'm definitely going to do that again," he chuckles, pouring more tequila onto my stomach. He licks across my other salted nipple this time, swirling his tongue around and around until I moan before he sucks the tequila off me once again. As soon as he's done, he

SUSAN RENEE

pours more tequila and sprinkles salt right at my thong line.

"And again..."

He trails his tongue lazily across my lower pelvis, licking up the salt before moving up slightly to suck the liquid from my belly button, only this time as his tongue swirls there, his finger dips between my legs and slides through my slick arousal.

"Oh God, Quinton..."

"And again..." he says, sprinkling my chest with salt and pouring more tequila all while keeping his finger between my thighs.

He nips at my hardened peaks before he licks off the salt and then palms them one at a time, rubbing, kneading, squeezing them as he drinks more tequila from my body. As his tongue swirls around my stomach, his finger mirrors his movements around my softened wet clit and hell, if it isn't immediate ecstasy.

"Fuuuuck, Quinton, yes!"

My back arches off the table and my feet bend to a pointed position. My head falls back and my eyes squeeze closed as he pushes a finger inside me.

"Christ, Kinsley. You're so fucking wet."

"Damn right I am." I spread my legs wider for him. "Now be a good boy and clean up the mess you made."

A soft grunt of appreciation emanates from his throat. "Oh, but there is so much more of a mess to be made, Kink."

"And I'll enjoy every minute of it with you, but for the love of God, I need to come and I really need your tongue to get me there. So, please, Quinton. Please I'm begging you."

"You never have to beg for me, Kink," he promises as he turns my body so he's standing between my legs. "I'll give you anything you want anytime you want it." He lifts my legs onto his shoulders and cradles my ass in his hands as he brings his face to my throbbing clit. He inhales a deep breath and growls, "Mother fucking intoxicating."

22

QUINTON

I take my time torturing her with delicate kisses against her swollen pussy, my tongue softly licking, swirling, my mouth sucking. Kinsley's hands slap the table as she writhes beneath me. She releases a moan that not only causes my dick to become a steel rod in my suit pants, but it may also very well have my neighbors on the bottom floor wondering what's going on.

"Jesus...Christ, Quinton!"

Her perfect ass in my hands, I press a thumb against her tightly puckered hole and pulse against it as I flick her clit with my tongue and then suck the same aroused spot intensifying my pressure on her body.

Her back arching off the table, she moans even louder and I chuckle.

She did mention something about being loud a while back.

"Hoooly shit, y-yes...oh, my God, please don't stop."

I dip my tongue inside her, drunk on her arousal as I lap up every drop of her. My cock brushes against the edge of the table and fuck, I'm going to need a release soon. Anything to ease the strain.

"Fuck, Kinsley," I groan against her. "If you only knew what you do to me. You're making me so damn hard." With one hand, I yank on the clasp of my pants and pull the zipper down, freeing myself while continuing to enjoy the meal in front of me.

She whimpers, her eyes squeezing closed as she tries to catch her breath. "Quintoooon!"

"I'm going to make you come, Kink. You're going to come all over my face like it's your goddamn job and then I'm going to sink inside you so damn hard I might lose my balls and black out."

"Yessss, Quinton. Please. I want it. I want you. I want it all. Please."

Palming her ass in one hand, I push two fingers into her pussy and curl them against her inner wall as I relentlessly flick her clit with my tongue.

Faster.

Slower.

Faster.

Harder.

Her body tenses.

Her legs tighten around my head.

Faster.

Harder.

Flick.

Flick.

Flick.

"Ahhhh! Ahhhh! Oh my GOD!" The pitch in her voice

rises until she's nearly squealing and then her body convulses against me and she comes.

All over my face.

Even in her state of bliss, I stroke my tongue against her, eating every drop of her orgasm her body will give me and then as promised, I line myself up to her entrance and thrust inside her so hard I take my own breath away.

"Who's your daddy now, Kink?"

I don't pull out entirely before I thrust back inside her, her arousal coating my stiff shaft. She's warm inside, her body melding to mine like it was made specifically for me. She invites me in like she's known me my whole life. Something flickers in my chest when her mossy green eyes find mine.

She's not looking away.

She's watching me.

Connecting with me.

For the first time as our bodies move together it feels like she can see straight into my soul.

She sees me.

She knows me.

Like two long lost lovers.

Or maybe it's simply that I love her.

Shit.

This won't take long.

Unable to hold back any longer, I bury myself deep inside her as she moans with pleasure. Accelerating my speed, I lean forward, my back tightening, and pull her breast into my mouth.

She lifts her legs into the air tilting her pelvis back so

I'm pumping into her at a deeper angle. "Yes, Quinton. I'm so full. It's too good."

Sooo fucking good.

"You take me perfectly, Kinsley. You're perfect. So fucking perfect."

Her mouth opens and her eyes slide back and suddenly her pussy is clenching me like a vise and I'm no longer in control.

"Fuck, Kinsley." I push her thighs back folding her body nearly in half, and pound against her, the pressure in my cock building until there is nowhere left to go and I'm exploding inside her. Emptying everything I feel for her into her body and praying she'll accept those feelings. Hold them. Nurture them. And maybe one day soon, tell me she feels the same.

"Quinton," she pants, her body coming down from its high, her arms holding me against her chest, her hands smoothing up and down my back. "That was..."

"I know, Kink. I know."

It was scintillating.

Extraordinary.

Bewildering.

I take a moment to catch my breath and then lift myself from her so she can breathe easier. I smooth her hair from her face and soak in her gorgeous gaze, swallowing back the words I'm too afraid to release from my mouth. I don't know how she's having this effect on me but everything about my life has been different since she walked into it.

Good different.

And I don't know what to do with that.

Her eyes flit between mine, the lines of worry

spreading across her forehead. "What is it, Quinton? What are you thinking about?"

I try to give her a reassuring smile but inside my mind is racing and I don't know how to stop it.

"What are you doing to me, Kinsley?"

Her frown deepens. "What?"

She tries to sit up so I offer her my hand to steady her as I stand between her legs. Shaking my head, confounded, I give her a small taste of my inner thoughts.

"For the last several years before you came around I only had sex in hotel rooms. One person, an hour or so of adrenaline release and I'm out the door. It's just been easier that way. No feelings. No connections. Just women looking for a quick fuck with a rich athlete."

"Okay..." Her brows furrow and she cocks her head. "I guess I don't underst—"

"But then you walked into my life," I tell her, my hands cradling her flushed heart-shaped face. "And now I don't know what's happening. I try to think back on what my life was like before you and I can't see it anymore. It's like none of it mattered so I don't remember it."

Hell, am I even saying any of this right?

Am I making any sense to her?

"Kinsley, you're the first woman I've allowed into my home since Lexi. The first woman I've asked to move in with me. The first woman I've slept with more than once and..." My brow furrows. "I like it. I like you, Kinsley. Everything about you, I..." I scoff out a nervous laugh. "Shit, I'm sorry. I must sound like a fucked-up teenager right now."

"No." She shakes her head, her hands on my chest.

"Not at all. I appreciate everything you're telling me, Quinton. I like you too." She gives me a shy smile and brings a hand to her forehead. "God, I don't even know if I'm supposed to be saying this. We never discussed what would happen if feelings got involved. And I'm such a hot mess most of the time. I'm weird and quirky and I see the world so differently from others but somehow..." She looks up at me. "Somehow you accepted that part of me when you could have called this whole thing off and ran. You accepted me, quirks and all."

"I enjoy every one of your quirks. I've never met a woman who makes me laugh the way you do. Your creativity, and imagination, the way you see the world...it's remarkable and inspiring."

"My own family can't accept me for who I am...but you do. You make me feel safe, Quinton. Safe to be whoever I want to be."

"I'll never ask you to be someone you're not, Kinsley."

Swiftly stepping out of my pants that are now down around my ankles, I angle her chin with my thumb and lower my mouth to hers, tenderly swiping my tongue across her soft lips. I slide my hands underneath her, lift her from the table, and carry her toward the hallway to our bedroom.

"Shower with me. I want to wash you."

"Only if I get to wash you too."

"Okay but you know if you touch me I'm going to want to be inside you again."

"Oh darn," she sighs with an ornery grin. "Whatever will I do?"

Being away from Kinsley this long is pure hell. Away games are usually no big deal. Sometimes we're on the road for a day or two. Maybe three days tops but a week? Yeah, it's hell.

Sleeping alone is hell now.

Her scent doesn't linger in my bed or in my room or on my stuff.

Not seeing her everyday sucks.

Time zone differences are a pain in the ass.

Fisting my own dick isn't half as nice as the feel of Kinsley's hand...or tongue...or mouth for that matter.

Yep. It's official.

I'm totally going through Kinsley withdraw.

We've texted every single day and I try to face time her each evening when I can. She seems to be keeping busy which is good, but no matter how busy I am, whether getting in a workout or playing my ass off in a heated game on the ice, I can't get her out of my mind.

I wonder what she's doing at any given moment.

I wonder if she's missing me as much as I'm missing her.

I picture her sleeping in my bed.

I picture her in my shower.

Laying on my couch.

Naked.

Waiting for me.

Okay maybe I shouldn't go that far but dammit I'm addicted to Kinsley Kendrick and I can't fucking help myself. It's been six days and we still have two more to go. Tonight's loss was hard to swallow. We've been doing so well for this entire stretch but we left plays on the ice last night. We didn't give it our all. Colby, Dex, and Milo are worried about their ladies after not being with them for a week. We all know it, and they have a right to feel that way. Carissa, Tatum, and Charlee are nearing the end of their pregnancies so they're no longer traveling with the team. It messed with Dex's head the first time Tatum was pregnant so we all know the guys are a bit on edge. Every time one of them receives a text they all scramble to see if one of the girls is in labor. It's humorous to watch every time but only because I know how much they love their partners. They'll be excellent dads.

"Where's Zeke?" Colby asks after a quick phone meeting with his agent.

"He went up to his room early so he could call Elsie before she goes to bed since it's only eight there."

"Oh right. Poor guy. I'm sure being away from her is hard."

Hawken nods. "He's told me more than once he doesn't love that he has to lean so much on his parents. And they're not getting any younger."

I take a quick sip of my drink listening to Colby and Hawk and then add, "Maybe he should hire a nanny or something."

"Yeah. Maybe."

"Hey, did Kinsley say anything about talking to Tate today?" Dex asks me as he sips his scotch on the rocks at the hotel bar.

"Nope. I haven't talked to her since this morning. She

said she had a full photography day today. I'll check in with her tonight."

"Carissa said they were all having dinner this evening," Colby reports. "So, I'm sure everything is good or we would hear otherwise."

Milo chuckles. "No wonder none of them are talking to us. They're all spending time together."

"Speak for yourself man," Hawken says. "Rory texted me a picture earlier and it was fucking hot. She must've been hanging out with Kinsley because she was wearing nothing but my—"

Dex throws his hand over Hawk's mouth. "Finish that sentence and I'll break this glass and literally slice your balls right off your body."

"Mhmfrmrhmhm mmmmh mhmmrffmrhmhmff."

Rolling his eyes, Dex removes his hand from Hawk's mouth. "What?"

"I said, you do that and your sister will hate you forever for taking away her chance at a dashing brood of tiny humans."

"I'll take my chances," Dex says deadpanned.

Just as Dex takes the last sip of his drink each one of our cell phones dings with a text notification. We eyeball each other wondering what on earth is going on and then all glance down at our phones.

KINSLEY

Thought you might want to see what I was up to today...

Attached to her text is a picture of her wearing my jersey, but this isn't just any picture. She's sitting backwards on my couch, her back to the camera. Her knees are spread apart, treating me to a stunning view of her lacey thong, and my jersey is pulled up and folded under itself like a crop top so the only part of the jersey I can see clearly is my last name. She's looking off to the side, a hand in her hair, and her mouth open slightly. It's the perfect seductive pose and fuck if I'm not getting hard staring at her.

I glance away from my phone just quick enough to notice all the other guys staring at their phones with the same holy shit expression I just had.

Chuckling, I clear my throat and murmur, "I guess now I know what Kinsley meant when she said she had a full photography day."

Hawken laughs as Dex and Colby and Milo wipe the drool from their chins and adjust their junk.

"Uuh, not to bring this night to a close so abruptly," Milo says as he tips back his drink to finish it off, placing his empty glass on the bar. "But I think the text I just received is going to take some further study."

Hawken bursts out laughing and claps Milo on the back. "Be careful upstairs, Landric. Carpal tunnel is a bitch."

> **KINSLEY**
>
> If you like that one, there are plenty more to share... 😊

> **ME**
>
> I'm literally sitting in the bar with a chubby. Does that tell you anything?

KINSLEY

Oh. Sorry. I guess I'll keep the other ones
to myself.

ME

The fuck you will. I'm heading upstairs.
Send away Kink.

One by one each of the guys heads upstairs and I follow right along with them. It might not be the same as feeling her physically touch me, but no fucking way am I giving up the opportunity to spend the rest of this night with my eyes glued to my phone and my fist wrapped around my dick.

23

KINSLEY

"Okay what about this one, Mer? What do you think?" I pose in front of my iPad so she can see the detail of the black and gold dress I tried on for her. She crinkles her nose and shakes her head.

"Nah, that one's not you. It screams rich fifty-year-old cougar wannabe." She laughs. "I think you look way hotter in the purple one."

"Really?"

"Really."

"You don't think it shows too much cleavage?"

"Kink, how many times have I told you too much cleavage is not a thing." Quinton stands in the doorway of his huge walk-in closet, his arms folded over his chest with a grin on his face. "Cleavage is sexy."

"See?" Meredith says through the speaker of my iPad. "Quinton says cleavage sooo cleavage it is. Hi Quinton!"

"Hi Meredith! Good to see you this morning."

"Same. Are you treating my girl like the queen that she is?"

"I'll never tell her no Mere. I promise you that."

"That'a boy Quinton Shay. That'a boy."

"Thanks for letting her try these dresses on for you. She's been a nervous wreck about it for a week."

"So, she tells me. She just needs me to remind her how fucking hot she looks. It's a girl thing."

"Got it. I'll leave you to it."

"See you Quinton."

"Later Mere."

Once he leaves the room Meredith gives me the look that says she's thinking something and I should know what it is.

"Alright, spit it out. I can tell you want to say something."

"I'm just thinking the guy is head over heels for you, Kins. You see it, right?"

"What? No. It's not like that."

"Bullshit. He likes you."

"Well yeah. I know he likes me. I like him too."

"No Kins. He likes you in that way more than like kind of way. And if I'm being honest, which I always am with you, you very much feel the same way."

Not wanting to have this conversation with her while Quinton is so close by, I turn once more in the mirror and ask, "So you think the purple dress is best?"

She scoffs out a resigned laugh. "Yep. It looks great on you and will probably look every bit as good when it's laying at your feet once he's ripped it off you."

"Oh my gosh, Meredith."

"Just sayin' girl. Just sayin'."

The ballroom where the G.A.M.E. Night Gala is taking place is beautifully decorated in an array of color stemming from each of the many different team sports banners hanging along the walls. There must be hundreds if not thousands of different school districts and communities represented here given the decorations alone.

Round tables and chairs are set up and adorned with white table linens and full place settings, and each table holds an impressive centerpiece depicting a different sport. Large clear cylinders on each table are filled with mini sized versions of whichever sport the table is representing. Some are filled with golf balls. Others with mini footballs, baseballs, basketballs, tennis balls, bowling balls, hockey pucks, and even badminton birdies. I even spot a few filled with swimming goggles. On top of each filled cylinder are colored balloons so that everyone can match their seating assignment to the appropriate table.

"Wow they really go all out for this."

"Yeah they do." Quinton nods as he leads me around the room arm in arm. "G.A.M.E. is a nationwide charity so they're able to get tons of people involved. You'll see a lot of celebrity athletes here tonight."

"Oh yeah?" I squeeze his arm with my hand. "You mean some more popular than you? I can't even imagine."

He chuckles and pulls me tighter to him. "I knew I liked you for a reason, Kink."

"Quinton!" a voice calls out that has us turning around. The moment I see her I want to shrink inside myself. She's drop dead gorgeous in her long red gown. The ultra flirty low-cut v-neckline leaves absolutely nothing to the imagination and the dramatic sweeping train means everyone will have to pay attention to her lest they step on her dress.

Quinton loved her once.

And I am so not her.

No. Fuck that mentality.

I'm every bit as good as she is if not better.

"Lexi." Quinton nods stiffly beside me.

She approaches him and kisses both of his cheeks, her hand resting on his chest. Not once does he let go of my hand, his gentle squeeze telling me all the things I know he can't say out loud. "You look amazing, Quinton. Quite the dashing tuxedo. You always did look nice in a tuxedo."

What the fuck, lady?

You have a husband.

You had your chance and you walked away.

There are no second chances for you.

Stop flirting with my fiancé.

Quinton doesn't respond to any of her antics. He merely pulls me to him and says to her, "Lexi, you remember Kinsley."

She smiles but I see the fakeness in her eyes. My mother smiles the same way. "Oh yes. Kinsley. The fiancée."

"Nice to see you again, Lexi."

It's not nice to see her but whatever. I promised Quinton I would be here for him. That's my one and only job tonight and I swear to God if she looks up and down his body like that one more time I'm going to have to punch her out.

That's right.

Sometimes you just have to choose violence.

"How's the wedding planning going?"

"Oh, I don't give two shits about the wedding," I tell her with a sweet smile. "We can get married in a trash-filled dumpster for all I care. I'm more excited for our honeymoon where I can spend all the time I want fucking my husband."

Lexi chokes on a nervous laugh, her eyes flitting between Quinton and me.

"Yeah, I mean it'll be like 'Happy wedding, babe, here's a transatlantic blow job' and then we can fuck again and again all over Europe. We can come in ten different languages!"

Quinton clamps his lips together suppressing a laugh but squeezes my hand in solitude. I'm not sure what's funnier. What I just said out loud, Quinton's control in not laughing, or poor Lexi's horrified expression.

"Uh..." Lexi clears her throat. "Wow. Okay then. That sounds..." She fans herself, her face reddening. "That sounds fun and I'm sure you two will have a great time."

Pretending as if I didn't hear a word she said, I look off into the distance holding my chin between my thumb and forefinger. "I wonder what the world record is for longest blow job. I bet I can beat it..."

This time Quinton can't hold back but confines his laugh to a choked snort.

"By the way, is Seth still taking those penis enhancement pills? He used to eat those suckers like candy. Poor guy." I shake my head in empathy. "Flaccidity is no joke."

Lexi scoffs but I'm not about to let her get a word in

edge wise. I lean forward like I'm giving her my best super-secret advice. "When it gets bad, here's a tip. Just tickle his asshole a little bit and the little guy will come out to play. You should have a solid three or four minutes but that's all it takes, am I right?" I wink at Quinton's shocked and speechless ex and then squeeze his hand. "We should find our seats, babe. Lovely talking to you, Lexi. Maybe we can hang out sometime."

Fat chance.

Quinton takes the lead, his hand on the small of my back as we walk toward the front of the room to find our table. When I glance over at him, he's pressing a fist to his mouth to keep from laughing.

"Hope I didn't say something wrong back there. She wouldn't stop looking at you like she wanted to eat you."

Quinton stops and grabs his side, wheezing in laughter. "Oh my God, I can't breathe." He laughs. "I don't even know what happened back there. That was..." He shakes his head, grabbing a nearby chair back for support. "Oh fuck, that was...ten languages?"

Smirking, I quietly murmur my best European impressions. "Oh, mon Dieu, oui! Oui! Oooh Dios! Si!" Fanning myself I whimper, "Sto arrivando!"

"Okay I got the first two. What was that last one?"

"'I'm coming' in Italian." I wink. "You want Canadian? Fuck me, eh?"

He bursts out in laughter again. "Where the hell did you learn all those languages?"

"I was a rich kid in a rich family who did business all over the place." I give him a meaningless shrug. "My parents made us learn."

"Well for what it's worth, Kink, I think you are a remarkable human being and watching you shock the shit out of Lexi was a much bigger turn on than I anticipated. I don't think I've ever been prouder." He gestures to the table in front of us. "This is us."

Before sitting down, I turn and press my lips to his. "Nobody comes between me and my man, Quinton Shay."

"Possessive, huh?" He pulls out my chair and helps me take my seat and then sits down next to me. "I like it."

Quinton introduces me to the other professional hockey players seated around our table. Some of the names I've heard before and some I'm less familiar with, but each one of them friendly and equally as passionate about the G.A.M.E. organization as Quinton is. The evening officially starts with a speech from the CEO of G.A.M.E. and introductions of the board of trustees. It's a night filled with laughter, pride, encouragement, and celebration but also a successful night of fundraising for the team sports of our communities nationwide. I have the pleasure of watching and listening to Quinton and his colleagues share their experiences as children participating in team sports and how that benefitted their mental health growing up. Their mutual experiences give me a whole new amount of respect for what they do and who they are now as adults.

"Dance with me." Quinton takes my hand and leads me to the dance floor in the middle of the room. He wraps his arm around me holding me tightly against him and I take the quiet moment to breathe him in. These past few months have been happier than I ever could have imagined and I'm saddened to think that tonight marks the end of our official agreement. Quinton asked me to be his plus-one for this event in return for accompanying me to Breckinridge. We never talked about what might happen after all this is said and done, but I know he has a season to finish. I've been a huge distraction for him, I'm sure, at a time where he's otherwise used to being intently focused. It would be wrong of me to expect or even want something more from him. I feel guilty enough as it is having taken up so much of his time and space already.

For all intents and purposes this should be an easy breakup.

We can put out a statement about it being an amicable split.

No one will ever have to know that what we had was fake to begin with.

Though ending this fake relationship is going to feel so very real when it happens.

"You're awfully quiet, Kink." Quinton murmurs against my ear. "What are you thinking about?"

I'm thinking I let my feelings get involved and I shouldn't have.

I'm thinking I'm really going to miss you when this is all over.

I'm thinking seeing you with someone else is going to hurt.

I'm thinking I don't how I'm supposed to just walk away from you.

I've had so much fun with you.

There's nothing about you I don't like.

Except for the fact I'm going to lose you in the next few days and it's going to rip me apart.

Because I think I might be in love with you.

"Uh, nothing. Just enjoying the moment." I force a smile because all I want to do right now is cry. "You're a good dancer."

"Thanks. I guess all those hours practicing with my pillow in my bedroom paid off."

I snort, appreciating that he knows when to lighten my spirits. "Oh yeah? What else did you practice with your pillow?"

He wags his brows. "Wouldn't you like to know?"

"Yes," I giggle. "Because now it sounds like there's something to know."

He pulls me in, bear hugging me while continuing to sway to the music. "Nah, there's nothing good to know. I never practiced a damn thing when I was younger. Back then I thought my shit didn't stink. Even when it came to the ladies."

"Ah. Right." I nod. "Because they threw themselves at you?"

His cheeks redden. "I mean...I'm not trying to be a prick but yeah. I was the captain of the high school hockey team and then I was the captain of the college team. That came with certain...perks."

"I'm sure it did and still does."

He chuckles. "You might be right about that. It brought me you, didn't it?"

"Yeah but if you recall, I didn't throw myself at you. You kind of came on to me."

He tilts his head pondering. "You're right. You were hot and you made me laugh. I liked that you weren't taking life too seriously. The world we live in is too filled with shit to not have fun and laugh when we can."

"Yeah. Sometimes I wish we could just stay in the bubble, you know?"

"We can." He squeezes me in a bear hug. "Tonight, we can go home and you can let me peel you out of this amazing dress that shows dangerous amounts of cleavage in all the best ways."

"Hmm. I might like where this is going."

I'll do anything for one more night with you.

He kisses my temple and then whispers in my ear, "And then I can spend the night with my mouth all over this delectable body of yours until I've got you so wet you're dripping for me."

"Mhmm. And then?"

"And then you can saddle up on the monster cock and ride him all the way to Pound Town, screaming so loud the entire fucking neighborhood hears you."

I gasp in a breath at his suggestion, hot and bothered and already wet thinking about it.

Shiiiit.

Yes please!

"I'm ready when you are."

"I was ready the moment we got here, Kink, but we're going to stand here and dance this out because the thought of spending the night pleasuring you got me a little too excited to be able to detach myself from you without embarrassing myself. So, until my cock calms down enough to walk out of here..."

"Ah. So, this might not be the right time to tell you that feeling how hard you are between our bodies right now is a turn on?"

"Kink," he huffs out a laugh. "No. Not helping at all."

"Okay, well what if I tell you that I would give just about anything right now to pull you into a dark corner, unzip your pants, and put that monster cock of yours in my mouth so I can suck it dry before we even leave this shindig?"

"Fuuuuck, Kinsley."

"I'm going to turn around now, Quinton. And you're going to keep an arm around me and follow me wherever I go, yes?"

"I'd follow you anywhere. You know that, but—"

"Ah-ah-ah. No buts." I lay a finger to his mouth. "Just follow me and trust me."

He loosens his hold on me so I can turn and head off the dance floor, his arm around my waist as he follows close behind. I spot the perfect area to head to; a small curtained off portion of the ballroom not being used, right behind the main stage. Checking around to make sure nobody is nearby that can see us slip through the curtain, I find the opening and step into a cramped but completely darkened space.

24

QUINTON

Without a word, Kinsley spins around and pushes me against the wall, making quick work of my pants and wrapping her hand around my straining cock. I hiss in a breath as she works her hand up and down my shaft and silently release a whispered moan when she opens her mouth and strokes her tongue from root to tip.

"Fuuuuck, Kinsley." I try to get my eyes to focus on her, to watch her as she takes me into her sweet mouth, but I can't see a fucking thing back here. All I can do is feel and right now I feel like I'm having an out of body experience.

"Shhhh," she says, licking the tip of my cock like a lollipop. "They'll hear you. No talking."

Fuck.

No sounds.

Okay.

I can do this.

I lean my head forward and pretend I can see every single move she makes as she makes it. When her mouth opens wide I feel her take me in deep and I feel when I hit the back of her throat.

I feel it when she gags but doesn't dare stop.

She grabs my ass and uses my body as leverage as she opens her throat and takes me in over and over again, in a slow and steady motion.

In and out.

In and out.

In and out.

Mother fucking Christ...

Kinsley...

With lazy circular motions, she explores the entire length of my shaft with her tongue and then tightens her lips around my now throbbing cock. She reaches for my hand and brings it to the back of her head and fucking hell I'm painfully hard. Gripping her hair, I tug on it enough to let her know I can take it from here.

"You want to take this monster cock, Kink?" I whisper to her.

"Mmmhmm..."

"Good. Because I need to fuck this sweet mouth of yours right now."

"Gag me, Quinton," she begs softly. "Gag me until you're raining down my throat."

"Seth, have you seen Quinton and...what's her name again?" We both hear Lexi ask on the other side of the curtain.

"Kinsley. And no. I have no idea where they are. Maybe they left."

For a quick moment, I freeze, but Kinsley wraps her hand around the base of my cock and takes me into her mouth as far back as I can go and fuck if the idea of getting off right on the other side of this curtain while our two exes are looking for us doesn't spur me on. I slide my hand through Kinsley's hair and gently swipe my thumb over her cheek and then I buck against her mouth, hitting the back of her throat. She gags at the fullness of me, but she never stops. I'm mesmerized by the feel of her. The strength of her hand around my shaft mixed with the softness of her mouth.

It's too fucking much.

My head rolls back against the wall and my mouth falls open, but I suppress the moan inside me dying to be set free.

Kinsley doesn't let up.

Not for a second.

My spine tingles and I start to sweat. "Jesus, Fuck, Kink. I'm gonna come." My knees go week and my chest grows tight as my cock swells and explodes in Kinsley's mouth.

"Ahh fuuuck, Kinsley."

She drinks down every fucking drop and rubs the life back into my legs so I have half a chance at walking out of here. As she's tucking my cock back into my pants, the curtain in front of us moves and there are Lexi and Seth.

Lexi's jaw drops and she scoffs. "What the hell are—oh my God." I zip my pants and help Kinsley up off her knees as she wipes her mouth with the back of her hand. She takes one look at Lexi and then smiles at me, her hand on my cheek.

"Thanks for the drink, babe."

"Really?" Lexi chides. Her hand on her hip. "For the

love of God, you two can't control yourselves for one night?"

Kinsley shrugs. "Dehydration is a real thing, Lexi. Surely an athlete of your stature would know that. Plus..." she leans in and whispers loud enough for the four of us to hear. "Have you seen the size of his cock?" She brings her fingertips together to form a large circle with her hands. "I had to use two hands. Pretty sure I just took the gallon challenge and lived to tell the tale." She gently touches Lexi's arm. "Don't worry though. I think I got enough to control myself for the next fifteen minutes or so." She holds her hand out for me and I take it without question. "You ready honey?"

Fuck, I love this girl.

Holding back another laugh at the expense of Lexi and Seth, I squeeze her hand and smile back at my girl. "Ready, Kink."

With a disgusted yet jealous expression on her face, Lexi huffs at the both of us and storms away. Seth trails close behind her. Kinsley could've been horrified at being caught in the act, but holy shit, she took it like a boss, not at all phased. We have a good laugh and then I kiss the shit out of her for what she just did for me.

"You're incredible. Have I told you that lately?"

"Not in the last few minutes, but your monster cock made it quite clear."

"Good. Now let's go home so I can repay your kindness until the sun rises and I have to be on a plane."

Two minutes left in the third period and I'm so fucking ready for this game to be over. This is without a doubt my worst performance of the season. Minnesota just scored on a power play while I was sitting in the fucking sin bin because I wasn't paying attention. They're kicking our asses tonight and I'm partially to blame.

"What the hell, Shay?" Hawken shouts as we near the bench after our shift. "I thought you had that run in the bag."

"No shit, Malone. I thought I did to or I wouldn't have taken the shot. Ramos came out of nowhere. I didn't do it on purpose."

I plop myself down on the bench and reach for my water bottle not giving a care in the world that I just drained part of the bottle over my face.

I get it. The season is tightening up. If we don't keep up a winning record, we won't even have a chance at the play-offs this year and after taking the whole fucking cup last season, that's a hard blow to bend over and take.

Coach Denovah sends me back to the ice for the last thirty seconds of the game and I take off in a sprint, trying like hell to redeem myself in any way possible but to no avail. The buzzer sounds and Minnesota celebrates their three-one victory.

"Fuck!" I'm the first one off the ice ready to take a long hot shower and get the fuck out of here.

I've been in a weird mood all damn day.

It's been three days since I've seen Kinsley in person and it's making me antsy. My mind has wandered back to the gala more times than I can count over the last few days, replaying the whole night in my head.

"Yeah, I mean it'll be like 'Happy wedding, babe, here's a transatlantic blow job' and then we can fuck again and again all over Europe. We can come in ten different languages!"

Yep. That moment is my second favorite of the night next to Kinsley being on her knees behind a curtain with my dick in her mouth. Maybe she's used to dealing with high profile events given her upbringing but I couldn't believe how comfortable she was with me the entire evening. I think I fell in love with her even more that night and having to leave her the next day was killer.

"Hey! Earth to Quinton." Zeke takes a seat next to me in the dressing room. "You okay man?"

"Huh? What? Yeah I'm good."

His eyes narrow. "You sure? Because everyone is dressed to leave and you're still sitting here in your underwear."

"Oh. Yeah. I'm just...I was drying off."

"You want to talk about it?"

Coming back to reality, I shake my head with a huff. "Nah. It was a shit pre-workout leading up to a shit game. I didn't sleep very well last night and I'm pissed at myself for a weak performance tonight. I know better. I should've done better."

Zeke nods. "Yeah you played like shit tonight, but we've all been there. I'm talking about Kinsley."

I whip my head up, making eye contact with my friend. "What about her?"

"You guys have a fight or something?"

"No." I contemplate arguing with him over my performance being anything about Kinsley but I would be lying if

I said it wasn't. "I don't know, man. I think I'm just up in my head about things lately and I hate being away from her."

"Yeah. You miss her."

"Yeah. She makes me feel better when she's around, you know?"

He gives me a sympathetic smile. "I get it."

"It's frustrating because we get into these amazing grooves where we're really enjoying each other and I think to myself yeah, I could have this. We could make a run at it. A real relationship, you know?"

"Yeah..."

"And then I have to leave her and get on a fucking plane for three days and it sucks ass."

He huffs out a laugh. "I hear you. I used to be that way with Lori and now it's even worse with Elsie. She's my flesh and blood and I have to leave her with my parents more times than I can count when we're away. I'm toying with the idea of getting a nanny, can you believe that?"

"Oh yeah? Your parents okay?"

"They're perfect, yeah, but I'm not blind. They're older now. The last thing they should have to do after raising me is raise my offspring too. And I miss having Elsie around. At least with a nanny I could potentially have them travel with us." He shrugs. "I don't know. I haven't decided anything yet, but back to Kinsley. It's clear you've developed strong feelings for her."

"Yeah. I think I have."

"Then a word of advice?"

"Okay..."

"Communicate. Tell her how you feel. Even when you

miss her. Maybe Lori didn't hear it enough from me. Or maybe she's an immature whiney bitch who just wasn't strong enough to handle the lifestyle of a hockey wife." He scoffs, rolling his eyes. "Or that of a mother for that matter. Just tell her. Always tell her. Communication is key."

Shaking my head, I try to take his advice and store it somewhere safe.

"Thanks Zeke."

"Anytime. Now put some pants on and let's go home."

"Oof." Charlee stills in the kitchen, her hand on her stomach, her eyes pinched closed as she takes a deep breath.

"You okay there, Mama?" My Spidey senses have been up ever since I got to Carissa's house where the ladies decided to hang out for the night to watch the game. The very disappointing game. There's no way Quinton is coming home in a good mood after that one.

Charlee nods, breathing through the obvious cramp she's experiencing. "Braxton Hicks. I've been having them more often these past few days. It's got to be my body's way of saying get the fuck out spawn. There's no more room at the inn."

Placing a few chicken tenders on my plate, I give Charlee a sympathetic smile. "It's got to be any time now, right? You're all due around the same time?"

"Mhmm." She nods. "I'm due next week. Carissa is literally due tomorrow and Tate is due after me."

"Wow. Things are about to get exciting around here, huh?"

"Right?" Her laugh is uneasy but Charlee smiles through it. She's such a trooper. "Maybe just not tonight." She pats her swollen belly. "I keep telling this baby to stay in there until Daddy gets home. I'm not having this child without him."

My heart sinks at the realization that unless they come tonight, I won't be around when the Red Tails babies make their debut. The night of the gala was technically the last event Quinton and I needed to get through as a fake couple. I imagine at some point after he gets back from tonight's game we'll have to talk about what happens next. He deserves to have his life back to normal as heartbreaking as that will be for me.

I know Carissa and I will remain friends and through her my friendships with Charlee and Rory and Tate might continue but I'm not sure how much I'll want to spend time with them when Quinton eventually starts seeing someone else. After everything we've done together, I know walking away is going to be one of the hardest things I've ever done. Harder than leaving my own family to come to Chicago.

"Definitely not tonight, okay? Rory and I are not delivering any babies tonight."

An empty plate in her hands, Carissa laughs as she enters the kitchen for a refill. "What's this about babies tonight?"

"No, no." I shake my head adamantly. "I said NO babies tonight. At least not until the guys get home, alright? You just keep those legs together and put up a no-exit sign."

"Deal. I'm not quite ready anyway. We still haven't packed a hospital bag."

Charlee's brows shoot up. "Are you serious?"

"What?" Carissa shrugs. "We've been a little busy with the season and all."

"Girl, you put that plate down right now and let's get you packed. At least put a few things in a bag so on the off chance you go into labor, oh, I don't know, tomorrow morning or something, you'll have what you need with you."

"Ugh. I hate packing," she whines. "I would much rather talk about Kinsley and Quinton." She turns to me with a knowing smirk. "Sooo? Tell us all the juicy details? How are things going with you two?"

I freeze like a deer in the headlights. "Uuh, you know, good, I guess."

"You guess?" she asks. "Why does that not sound so convincing?"

My shoulders fall as does my smile. "Ugh, because I don't know what's going on with us right now if I'm being honest. I mean, things seem...great, but our agreement ended after the G.A.M.E. Night Gala. I can only assume once he's back in town, Quinton will be ready to have his life back."

Charlee scoffs. "That's not what I heard."

"Me either," Carissa says, shoving another cookie in her mouth.

Wait.

What?

This is news to me.

"Uhh...whaaat have you heard?"

Charlee cocks her head. "Milo and I called it the very first night you two spoke. You two are a classic fake relationship trope romance happening in real life."

"What do you mean by that?"

"You don't read romance books?"

I frown. "Umm, not usually, no. I haven't given myself time to read in a while."

"Okay so I edit romance books for a living and Milo reads a lot of them."

"Aww, that's so cute!"

"Yeah, it is. So, anyway, a fake relationship trope is when two people enter into an agreement to pretend to be each other's boyfriend and girlfriend or fiancé or whatever but somewhere down the line they start falling for each other for real."

Interesting.

"Why have I never heard of this before?"

"There's no way you haven't heard of it. Ever seen *Pretty Woman*?"

Carissa points to me. "Oooh or *The Proposal*? I love that movie. Ryan Reynolds? Yummy!"

"Yeah, I've seen them both. And you really think...?"

Both girls raise their brows as I consider the story lines of the movies.

"There's no way he's not falling for you," Carissa tells me. "First of all, it's all over his face whenever you're around and secondly, because of my job, I have the inside scoop and he has been talking about you on several occasions when he doesn't know I'm around and listening." She shrugs. "Not to mention Colby tells me everything sooo..."

"So, the question is," Charlee adds, "do you feel the same way?"

My face heats and something in my chest tingles. Carissa leans over to Charlee and whispers, "I think that's a yes."

"I do like him, yes," I admit. "It's just, you know, scary. We haven't really had a serious lengthy discussion about our real feelings and though sometimes it does seem like we both have feelings involved, I don't want to assume anything."

"We get it. We've both been there."

"For sure." Charlee nods. "And if I had to guess, I would say you have nothing to worry about, but maybe this insecurity just means you both need to sit down and talk about where you go from here."

"Yeah, I think you're right."

"Great!" Charlee claps her hands together. "Now that that is settled, this crazy lady here," she says, gesturing to Carissa, "needs to pack a hospital bag."

"Ugh. You're right. And you're here so you can help me, so let's do it. If I ask Colby to do it, I'll end up with a pair of his sweatpants, which I suppose I don't technically mind, an ungodly piece of lingerie that no longer fits this baby-toting body, a bag of Cheese Nips, and toothpaste with no toothbrush."

While Carissa and Charlee waddle down the hall to Carissa's bedroom, I join Tate and Rory in the living room where they're both lounging on the couch flipping through channels now that the game is over. Tatum snickers over something on her phone.

"Dex is out of the shower and dressed," she reports.

"Oh, and now he's walking to the bus that will take them to their plane."

Rory shakes her head quietly smiling to herself.

"What's that look for?" I ask her.

"Because my brother is a paranoid idiot who has been giving Tatum a play-by-play of literally everything he's been doing since the game ended so she'll know exactly where he is and when he's getting home."

Tatum reads her next text. "The bus driver has started the engine."

"Oh my gosh." I laugh with them. "It's like he's never done this before."

"Right?" Rory says.

Tatum rolls her eyes playfully. "I think he's just nervous something will happen and he won't be here to save the day like he did last time."

"So, he really did deliver your baby in your bathroom?"

"Oh yeah," Tatum giggles. "Absolute scariest and best day of my life. And although he wasn't laughing at all that night, when I think back on how much he was freaking out...Dex...the big strong hockey player." She starts to laugh a little harder. "God, it's funny as hell."

My phone dings with a text that I can only imagine would be from Quinton.

> QUINTON
>
> Can't wait to see you. Should be home around midnight.

His text makes me smile.

ME

Great.

QUINTON

You okay?

ME

Yeah. Sorry about the game. That was a hard loss.

QUINTON

Can't win them all I guess.

ME

Ramos is a douche. You didn't deserve the penalty.

QUINTON

And this is why I love you. You're good for my ego. 😊

Love.

He loves me?

Did he mean that or did he just accidentally use the word love?

An uncomfortable feeling washes over me and I curl into myself on the couch nearly choking back tears as I stare at my phone. This is why the thought of walking away and ending something that was never real to begin with is gutting me. He just said he loves me, something he's never said before in person or text and now I'm freaking out inside.

Do I say it back?

Was he kidding?

Will it be weird if I say it back?

I feel like I'll make it weird, but fuck I wish I knew one

way or another if he meant those words or if he's just being nice. He's told me he likes me before, but like could mean anything from 'Yeah she's nice. I'd ask her to take care of my cat when I'm away' to 'I like her so much I can't stop thinking about her and might be falling in love with her.'

So, which is it?

The back and forth...the not knowing for sure. It's eating at me. I know I should just come out and ask him but the fear of rejection after I let myself fall for him is a hard pill to swallow.

> **QUINTON**
>
> You're quiet. Everything ok? Still hanging with the girls?

> **ME**
>
> Yeah.

> **QUINTON**
>
> Alright. We just pulled up to the tarmac so we're heading to the plane.

"Aaand now they're walking onto the plane," Tatum reports from her Dex messages.

> **ME**
>
> Ok.

> **QUINTON**
>
> You don't have to wait up if you don't want to. If you're tired I understand. I'll try not to wake you when I get in.

> **ME**
>
> Not tired. My brain is in overdrive. Lots on my mind.

QUINTON

> Like what? Need to talk it out? I'm all
> ears. And it'll take my mind off tonight's
> game.

I guess it's now or never. Maybe it will be easier for him if we have this conversation via text instead of crying about it in person. I don't want him to see my tears. If he doesn't share my feelings I don't want him to see how much it'll break me. He doesn't deserve that. I did this. I started this. I put him in this predicament. I can't just walk into some guy's life, turn it upside down to live out a lie with him, and then expect to be able to make a forever home out of the arrangement.

I'm smarter than that.

But I'm beginning to feel like this entire idea was really fucking stupid.

ME

> Sooo I'm just going to send this text
> because...well, it's just easier to type out
> words than have this potentially awkward
> conversation face to face.

QUINTON

> Uh oh...what's going on, Kink? You okay?
> Did I leave towels in the washer again?
> Did Nutsack pull the toilet paper roll off
> the holder and tear through the house
> again?

ME

Nutsack is good. We're great. No worries. Umm, I'm just wondering, now that your charity gala is over, you're probably ready to have your life back and I don't want to be a burden or cause you any more distraction than I already have. So maybe it would be better for you if I just moved my things back to my place while you're gone? I'm sure we could come up with some sort of public statement about an amicable split. Whatever makes you most comfortable.

QUINTON

KINSLEY KENDRICK, DON'T YOU FUCKING MOVE AN INCH UNTIL I GET BACK.

"You GUYS!" Charlee calls from down the hall. Rory, Tatum, and I all share a confused look and then Charlee appears from the hallway, Carissa hanging on her arm. "Carissa's water just broke!"

26

QUINTON

KINSLEY

Sooo I'm just going to send this text because...well, it's just easier to type out words than have this potentially awkward conversation face to face.

ME

Uh oh...what's going on, Kink? You okay? Did I leave towels in the washer again? Did Nutsack pull the toilet paper roll off the holder and tear through the house again?

KINSLEY

> Nutsack is good. We're great. No worries. Umm, I'm just wondering, now that your charity gala is over, you're probably ready to have your life back and I don't want to be a burden or cause you any more distraction than I already have. So maybe it would be better for you if I just moved my things back to my place while you're gone? I'm sure we could come up with some sort of public statement about an amicable split. Whatever makes you most comfortable.

"What the fuck?" I shout from my seat on the plane. My body heats and I break out in a sweat. "What is she thinking?"

"What's going on?" Zeke asks from across the aisle. "Everything okay?"

"No, it's not fucking okay! Kinsley just asked if she should move her shit out while I'm gone?"

Milo leans over his seat and joins in. "What? Why would she do that?"

"I don't know! Wait...fuck! Yes I do. It was our arrangement from the get-go. She said since the charity gala is over she doesn't want to be more of a burden than she's already been, but why the hell would she think she's been a goddamn burden?"

"Have you talked about this at all? I mean, about what would happen when your arrangement came to an end?"

"No, because I don't want it to end so I purposely haven't talked about it." I swipe the sweat from my forehead trying my hardest to keep my cool but just the thought of Kinsley leaving me in the dark of night while I'm not home shreds any amount of self-control I thought I had. "I love her! I don't want her to go anywhere."

Dex and Hawken share a smile. "Aww, he wuvs her."

"Fuck you, Dex."

"For the record," Milo points out, "Charlee and I were right."

I give Milo a deadpanned fuck-you expression as well but he beams back at me unphased. "Okay, continue."

Colby caps my shoulder from the seat behind me. "Have you told her that? Have you told her you love her and don't want her to go? Does she feel the same?"

"No, I haven't told—"

"Why the fuck not, dumbass?" Hawken scolds.

I throw my head back and try to take a deep breath. "Because I'm an idiot, Malone. That's why. I'm a fucking pansy ass pussy who has been too afraid to tell the best thing that's ever happened to me that I'm in love with her because the last time I told someone I loved her, she walked away from me and right into the arms of another man in front of the whole fucking world and it crushed me."

"Well okay then." His voice is calmer now. "At least you're honest, but look, first of all, Kinsley isn't Lexi. Not in a million years. You know that."

"I do."

"Okay so it's not too late. You can still tell Kinsley how you feel and work this out."

"But what if she doesn't feel the same way? What if she doesn't want to stay? What if I'm not enough for her?"

Colby squeezes his hand still resting on my shoulder. "It's the risk you have to take for love, bro. I had a hell of a time telling Carissa how I really felt, but once I opened up to her and told her everything it was like a weight I had been wearing for twenty years was finally lifted."

"Son of a bitch! Why do we have to be on a fucking plane right now? I hate that she's having these thoughts and I'm not there with her. I could be fixing all of this and I'm not fucking there."

"You could just call her."

I shake my head. "No way. I have to see her face to face. I have to tell her and she needs to see it in my eyes. And the only way I'll know if she sincerely feels the same way is if I see hers."

Zeke nods. "Then tell her not to move a fucking inch until you get there. We'll be home soon."

ME

KINSLEY KENDRICK, DON'T YOU FUCKING MOVE AN INCH UNTIL I GET BACK.

"And," Hawken adds with a shrug, "if she's not there when we get back, just do what I did and show up knocking on her door at midnight. Worked for me."

Dex narrows his eyes. "When did you...you know what? Never mind. Probably better if I don't know."

Hawken winks. "Definitely better if you don't know, bro."

I stare at my phone, willing Kinsley to write back to me, but those three little dots that tell me she's typing never appear.

What the fuck?

Did I just scare her off?

I see she read it.

Why isn't she responding?

Shit, was she already in the process of leaving?

Is her stuff already out?

Is that what she did with the girls today?

Surely she wouldn't do that to three pregnant women.

The cabin lights are dimmed as the plane heads down the runway. I lean my head back on my seat and inhale a huge breath telling myself to calm the fuck down but also playing through every worst case scenario in my head.

Fuck it, I'm just going to tell her.

At this point I think I'm desperate.

ME

> Kinsley Kendric, I love you. I know, I'm a giant dick for not saying it to you sooner and an even bigger dick for saying it via text first and not in person but I needed you to know ASAP because I don't want you to go. Please don't go. Just talk to me.

"Holy shit!" Colby jumps up from his seat. "Carissa's water broke!"

KINSLEY

> Not going anywhere. Well...actually I am. Carissa's water broke. We're taking her to the hospital. Meet you there I assume.

KINSLEY

> And I love you too, Quinton. 💜 Talk more later. Will keep you updated!

For the first time in three days my shoulders relax, stiff and painful though they might be.

Thank fuck.

She loves me.

A huge giddy smile spreads across my face.

Kinsley Kendrick loves Quinton Shay.

She's not going anywhere.

Okay. We can do this.

We can have a real shot at this.

Thank God for miracles.

ME

Kinsley

"Oh my gosh, Carissa!" Rory bounds from the couch. "Are you sure?"

Charlee snickers. "Oh, she's sure. Started out as a trickle and then a gush. I just gave her some dry clothes to pull on."

Rory claps her hands excitedly. "Holy shit! You're sooo having a baby tonight! Okay. We should take you to the hospital. Wait." She spins around again. "Do the guys know? Someone should text Colby."

"Already done," Charlee states. "Texted him while she was changing. He'll meet us at the hospital."

"Okay. I've got an SUV. I'll drive. Unless you would rather wait for an ambulance?"

Carissa holds her baby belly like she's holding up a bowling ball in front of her. "Nah. I don't think I need an ambulance. Let's just go."

I help Tatum up from her seat on the couch and we

grab our purses excitedly ready to help our friend welcome her first baby into the world. We climb into Rory's car and off we go back into the city. Halfway there my phone dings in my pocket and I see that it's Quinton.

> Kinsley Kendric, I love you. I know, I'm a giant dick for not saying it to you sooner and an even bigger dick for saying it via text first and not in person but I needed you to know ASAP because I don't want you to go. Please don't go. Just talk to me.

Whoa.
He said it again.
He said it for real this time.
"He loves me."
"What?" Charlee and Tatum both ask as I'm seated between them in the back seat.
"Huh?"
"Who loves you?" Tatum asks.
Carissa turns from the front seat. "Quinton? Quinton loves you?"
I turn my phone around for her to see, my eyes starting to water. "Yeah. Quinton just said he loves me. He doesn't want me to move out."
Her brows crinkle. "Move out? What the hell Kins? Why would you move out?"
"Because it was our arrangement. He accompanies me to Breckinridge and I'm his plus one for the G.A.M.E. Night Gala. We were supposed to break up after that and

I've been a fucking mess thinking about it but he just told me he loves me."

> **KINSLEY**
>
> Not going anywhere. Well…actually I am. Carissa's water broke. We're taking her to the hospital. Meet you there I assume.

"Girl!" Rory shouts from the driver's seat. "Tell me you told him you love him too."

Laughing I nod and wipe the runny nose I now have from crying. "Fuck! No, I didn't yet but I'm crazy about him. I've wanted to tell him for days now."

"Fucking tell him right now!!" She laughs as I type out my text with shaky hands.

> **KINSLEY**
>
> And I love you too, Quinton. 🩶 Talk more later. Will keep you updated!

Charlee raises her arm in a fist pump and sings, "Told ya. Told ya. Told ya! It's a classic fake relationship trope. You two couldn't be writing a better love story if youuuuu ooooh! Shit." She grabs her stomach and squeezes her eyes closed, breathing through the pain.

"Charlee are you sure these are Braxton Hicks contractions? You've had them all night."

"I mean…" She groans. "I assume that's what they are."

"Babe, I'm not convinced," I tell her. "We need to start timing them." I set the stopwatch on my phone. "Let me know when the next one comes."

Charlee laughs. "There's no way we're having these

babies on the same night." She shakes her head. "Not possible."

"Oh, anything is possible Charlee Mags!" Rory laughs. "If you can all get knocked up around the same time, you can all have babies on the same day. Plus, it's a full moon. Weird things happen during a full moon. We're almost there. Hang on ladies and babies. Tate? You okay back there?"

"Yep. Me and my swollen ankles are doing just fine."

"Aright ladies, hold on."

"Umm, Kinsley?"

I glance at Charlee. "Yeah?"

"I'm having another one."

Picking up my phone I read the stopwatch.

Five minutes.

"Oh fuck."

Quinton

KINSLEY

I think Charlee's false contractions might be real contractions. Holy shit there might be two babies born tonight! Don't panic Milo just yet. I'm timing them for her now so we can be sure.

ME

WTF? Two babies? Is Tate still okay because Dex will be off his rocker if...

"Fuck! Charlee might be in labor too?" Dex announces to the cabin. Milo jumps up and grabs Dex's phone, reading an apparent text from Tatum. "What the hell? She's having contractions? Why didn't anyone fucking write me?"

"Take a breath, Milo," I add. "Kinsley said she thinks Charlee's false contractions could possibly be real ones because she's had them all night. She's timing them for her now."

Milo sighs into his seat, his hand pushing through his hair. "Oh fuck. She must be scared out of her mind."

"She's in good hands," I reassure him. "Tate's been through this before and they have Rory and Kinsley with them to help keep everyone calm."

> ME
>
> Aaaaand Dex just got a text from Tate. There is now slight panic on the plane.

> KINSLEY
>
> LOL I expect nothing less. Contractions are 5 minutes apart. I think she's in labor too. Everything is good for now. We're just pulling into the hospital. More soon. 🩶

> ME
>
> We land in 20.

I clear my throat and swallow back the excited nerves in my chest. "Uh hey Landric?"

"Yeah?"

"I don't want you to panic buddy, but Charlee's contractions are five minutes apart. Kinsley thinks she's in labor."

267

"Aww hell." Yeah when I said don't panic, he totally didn't listen. "We've got to get off this plane."

"It's okay guys," Zeke tries to reassure them. "It was like this for Elsie's birth and it took hours after Lori got to the hospital for her to actually arrive."

"Not my kid," Colby argues. "My kid is gonna come in like a fuckin' wrecking ball."

"Okay, they're at the hospital now. I'm sure everything will be fine. They'll all be getting the best care possible."

"Do you think the pilot can land this thing any faster?" Colby asks, obsessively checking his watch.

"Better yet," Milo adds, blowing out a series of breaths and tugging at the collar of his shirt to try to get his growing nerves under control. "Is there a landing strip right by the hospital?"

27

KINSLEY

"A lright Carissa, it looks like your cervix is about seven centimeters dilated. You're doing well," the doctor on call tells her. "I've paged Dr. Kent who's on her way, so now you get to sit back and relax as much as possible. All we can do now is wait this out, see how you progress, and go from there."

Carissa nods, clearly a bit nervous and missing her husband. "Okay. Thank you."

Once the doctor leaves the room Carissa breaks down and starts to cry.

"No, no, no, no, no," I croon, stepping over to her bed to be by her side. "Everything is okay, Carissa. You're going to be perfectly fine."

"I know but," she cries, "I need Colby."

"He's on his way, I promise. They should be landing..." I peek at my phone. "Any minute now, and then I'm positive they'll all be hightailing it to the hospital so he can be with you and Milo can be with Charlee."

She hiccups but nods hearing my words. "Okay. Okay, I can do this."

I grab her hand. "You can do this. And I'm right here, okay? I'm not going anywhere so if you need me, I'm here. You need a back rub? I'm your girl. You need ice chips? I'll bring you buckets full."

Suddenly Carissa's eyes bulge and her mouth falls open as she gasps in pain. "Ooooh fuck!" She grabs her stomach.

"Okay I'm guessing that's a nice big contraction." I start to rub her back. "Just breathe. Take as deep a breath as you can and let it out in short bursts."

"Oh God, it hurts!" she cries. "I can't do this. I don't want to do this."

"Yes you do, Carissa. You want this baby and you're going to make it happen. We're going to help you through it."

Her head falls back to her pillow, her hands still gripping her stomach. "I need Colby and I need fucking drugs!" She tugs at my shirt pleading with me desperately. "Drugs, Kinsley. I need the drugs. Please, for the love of God tell me it's not too late for the good stuff?"

"Uh, well, I'm not a doctor, but I can go find out for you, okay?"

She nods, tears slipping down her face. "Yes. Yeah. Okay. Thank you."

"Everything alright in here?" Rory peeks through the door.

"Yeah, is Charlee alright?"

A shocked smile spreads across her face. "She's at six centimeters already! You were right, Kinsley. Those were definitely not Braxton Hicks contractions."

My phone dings. Digging it out of my pocket I read the text from Quinton.

QUINTON

Landed. In the car. On our way. Speeding.

"Okay, they're on their way." I turn back to Carissa. "Colby's on his way, okay? He'll be here within minutes, I'm sure."

"Thank fucking Christ." Carissa relaxes only a little before another contraction builds.

"Rory, will you stay with Carissa while I ask about an epidural for her?"

"Yeah absolutely."

"Great. I step into the hallway and head for the nurse's station when I see Charlee in her room with Tate who is being escorted by a nurse toward the door."

You have got to be kidding me.

"Tate? What's going on?"

Tate gives me a half frown, half smile. "This lovely nurse here saw my huge ankles and asked when I was due and then asked to take my blood pressure and it's through the roof."

"What? Oh shit. I'm sorry Tate. The guys are on their way. Dex is coming, okay?"

"I may need a C-section, Kinsley. Please can you keep Dex updated for me while I get this figured out?"

"Yeah. Absolutely."

"Oh, and have Rory call my sister. She's been staying at our house until the baby comes so she can help with Summer. Rory has her number."

"I'm on it. Don't worry," I tell her.

I watch the nurse get her to a room with a bed across the hall, my nerves freezing me in place as I try to wrap my head around what's happening right now and how I can best be of use to all my friends at the same time.

Drugs.

Drugs for Carissa.

Check on Charlee.

I peek my head back into Charlee's room. "Hey. You okay in here?"

She nods silently and I can tell she's trying to do some controlled breathing. "Yeah. I'm good. They have to break my water because it hasn't broken yet. Milo ETA?"

"Uh...minutes. Only minutes. They're on their way here right now."

She nods again and goes back to her breathing.

Whoa. It's like she's practiced for this.

Maybe it's all the yoga she does.

"I'll be right back to check on you. Gotta help Carissa for a minute."

I make it to the nurse's station and let them know Carissa would like an epidural, but when she screams from down the hall everyone goes running.

"Carissa? What is it?"

"Her contractions are only seconds apart now," Rory says. "This little one is not waiting."

Nurses check her vitals and the on-call doc comes back in to check her cervix, nodding to Carissa and the nurses around her. "Well, you're clearly an overachiever, Mrs. Nelson. You went from a seven to a ten and it's time to push."

"No," she cries. "I can't do it. I can't push without Colby."

"Yes you can," Rory tells her. "Kinsley and I are right here. You grab our hands and break us if you have to." Rory looks to me for confirmation and I nod in response. "You're not going through this alone, okay?"

"Mhmm." She sniffles and tries to breathe while the medical team works around her preparing for the birth of her baby.

"Isn't this exciting?" I give her hand a comforting squeeze. "You're about to have a baby, Carissa. A tiny little human bundle of joy."

Sniffle. "It would be so much better if Colby were here."

"I know babe. I promise he's almost here. He's coming."

"Alright, Carissa." The doctor stands at the foot of her bed. "One of these ladies is going to crawl up there behind you and help support you so you can push."

Rory looks at me and I tell her I'll do it. "In case Tatum needs you."

"Good thinking."

I crawl up behind Carissa and lean her body back against mine. The nurses help get her into position and pull her legs back. Rory holds one thigh while a nurse holds the other.

"Grab my hands," I whisper to her. "Squeeze as hard as you need."

"Okay when the next contraction starts you're going to take a deep breath and push for a good ten seconds. Ready?"

"Mhmm. Yeah. Okay." Carissa squeezes the absolute

fuck out of my hands and we haven't even started yet, but I don't dare tell her she has the grip of an Eagle.

"Alright here it comes, big breath in and push!"

The nurse beside her counts as Carissa groans like she's being ripped apart from the inside out. "One...two...three... four...five...six...seven...eight...nine...ten. Excellent job. Relax."

"Oh God," she sighs, falling back against me.

"Great job, Babe. You're doing great."

"SMALLS?"

Oh, thank God!

They're here.

Carissa cries out, "COLBY!" and he's in the room in a split second.

"Babe. Oh fuck, I'm so sorry I'm late."

She cries even harder. "It's okay. It's okay. You're here. Colby it's time. I need you."

"I'm here. What can I..." He gets one look at what's already started. "Oh shit. You're really...fuck. What do I do?"

"Come take my place, Colby. She needs you here."

He nods, his face ashen as he takes in everything. He helps lift me off the bed and takes my place, Carissa already sinking into him and preparing for the next contraction. I kiss the top of her head and knowing she's now in better hands than my own, I skip out of the room to check on Charlee and Tate.

"KINK!" Quinton's standing in the hallway with Hawken, neither one of them knowing where they should go until they see me.

"Quinton!" I run to him and he lifts me into his arms in

a bear hug so tight I almost lose my breath. When he puts me down he holds my face in his hands and kisses me hard. Claiming me. Telling me how much he missed me.

How much he loves me.

Hawken clears his throat. "Uh...hi. I'm still here too, lovebirds, and if you keep kissing Kinsley like that you may as well have her gown up and get her a bed because one of these tiny human things is gonna be popping out of her in no time too."

Quinton laughs but holds on to me and never lets go. "Hi."

I smile up at him. "Hi yourself."

"How are you?"

"I'm okay." I nod. "It's baby-palooza in here. How the hell is this even happening?" I shake out my hands that are still tingling from Carissa's vise-like grip.

He laughs. "I have no idea but thank God we all got here in time."

"Charlee! How's Charlee?"

Hawken gestures to his right. "She's in there with Milo right now and Dex was taken to the operating room. I guess Tate has some kind of complication?"

"Pre-eclampsia," I tell them. "Her blood pressure was too high and that can be bad for the baby so they must be doing a C-section. Hopefully Dex made it in there in time and everything is okay."

"Yeah. Now I guess all we do is wait."

More screaming comes from Carissa's room as Rory steps out and finds Hawken with us. "Phew!" She lifts her hand to give me a fist bump. "Go us, huh? Baby patrol. We should've had shirts made."

"You're so right."

"Well, do we just wait in the waiting room then?"

Rory nods. "Yeah. We can head there. The guys can come find us when there's news."

Rory and Hawken move toward the waiting room, but Quinton tugs my arm and holds me back. "Walk with me?"

"Yeah, sure."

He gestures to Hawken with his chin. "We'll catch up with you guys in a few minutes."

Hawken smirks. "Whatever you say Loverboy."

Rory slaps Hawken's arm. "Leave them alone."

Quinton and I walk down the hall and out of Labor and Delivery into another hallway empty of people. He pushes open a restroom door and pulls me inside with him.

Giggling, I nearly trip on the way in. "Quinton what are you—"

He kicks the door shut and turns the lock and then his lips are on mine and he's backing me up against the wall.

28

QUINTON

My body ignites into a frenzy of pure lust for the woman standing with me in this hospital bathroom. I need her. Want her. Love her. God, do I love her.

Her mouth parts for me and I stop myself for one damn second to take her in. The scent of her. The way her eyes penetrate mine. The way her body melds to mine no matter where we are. She never questions. She just...gives. She gives me anything I've ever asked her for and right now I'm begging for her.

She rubs her nose gently against mine, her lashes fluttering as she bites her lower lip. I pull at that lip with my thumb and then grip her jaw and try to restrain myself.

"Please, Quinton."

I press my mouth to hers, gripping her tightly around the waist, and pull her into me as hard as I can, her breasts pressed firmly against my chest.

"I missed you so fucking much, Kinsley," I explain in between sloppy, wet, hurried kisses. I smooth her hair back, holding her face so I can angle her head just right and dip my tongue in her mouth. "I love you."

She moans against my lips. "I love you too, Quinton." My cock stirs at the sound of her voice. Her lips are soft, supple but insistent. Her tongue swirling with mine with every stroke I make inside her.

I close any distance between us and lift her shirt from her body so she stands before me in a purple bra. Hooking my finger over the piece of material covering her breast, I yank it down, exposing her. Her breath catches and she whispers my name.

"Quinton."

I smooth a hand over her breast and her back arches, pushing it out further. I bend down and take her nipple into my mouth, my tongue circling the hardened peak as she runs her hand through my hair.

"God, yes, Quinton."

I lift her arms and pin them to the wall above her head, holding them there with one hand while the other explores her body. "Need you, Kinsley. Right fucking now."

She gives me a reassuring smile. "Then take me."

I turn her around so she's facing the sink and bend her over. She grips the porcelain basin as I tug down her leggings and panties and then feather my hand up the inside of her thigh until I reach the spot I'm dying to be inside of.

"Quinton!" She gasps when I trail my fingers through her arousal.

So, fucking wet for me.

I yank my own pants down and line myself up, my painfully hard cock needing to be inside her. With one hard thrust both of us moan out loud at the way her body welcomes me.

"Fucking hell Kinsley." I rest my forehead on her back, feeling the way her warm soft pussy stretches around my cock. "I can't be without you," I confide. "I don't want you to leave."

"I'm not going anywhere, Quinton."

"Promise me."

Her eyes find mine in the mirror in front of us. "I promise."

"Mother fucker, you're so goddamn tight light this. Look at us in the mirror, Kink. Watch me take you. Watch me touch you." I slide my hand up her torso and palm her breast, her mouth falling open in response.

"Tell me again, Kink. I need to hear you say it."

"I love you Quinton. And I'm not leaving. I promise."

Her words are my undoing and I let loose.

I grip her hip with one hand, the other moving between her breasts and her throat and I thrust inside her from behind hard with an untamed fervor I can't begin to control. I kiss her neck, her shoulder, her back all while thrusting in and out, in and out, claiming her sweet pussy as my own from this day forward.

There's no slowing down.

There's no perfected rhythm.

The only sound is our breathing, our grunts, and our groans as our bodies slap together until I feel the beginning of the end. My knees start to shake and my spine begins to tingle.

"Fuck, I'm right there, Kink. God, I'm so fucking crazy for you."

"Touch me, Quinton." She takes my hand from her breast and moves it down toward her pussy. She presses my finger to her clit and cries out. "Ooooh God, yeah. Don't stop."

Leaning forward I bite down on her skin and thrust inside her harder, faster, my balls tightening, my forehead sweating. I rub her clit in tiny circular motions until I feel her pussy clamp down over my cock.

"Quinton! Yes! I'm coming! I'm coming." She moans quietly through her climax and then I'm losing myself inside her. I come so hard I have to grip her to steady myself, my body shaking as my pulsing cock empties into her.

"You're mine now, Kinsley Kendrick," I whisper against her ear as we come down from our highs.

She smiles through her panting breath and says, "I was yours the moment you said hello."

The sun hasn't even come up yet, but already we've welcomed three brand new family members into the Chicago Red Tails family. Milo and Charlee gave birth to a baby girl, Amelia Charlene Landric. Colby and Carissa had a baby boy, Carter Alexander Nelson. And after a surgery with only minor yet still scary complications, Dex and Tatum are the proud parents of a son, Dexter Dennis Foster Junior.

"Dennis?" Zeke frowns. We're all together in Tatum's

room the following morning since she's a little less mobile after her surgery. "Your middle name is Dennis?"

"Yeah."

"Why have I never known that?" He looks around at the rest of us. "Dexter Dennis? We could've been calling him Double-D for all these years!"

We all burst into laughter at Dex's expense.

"Well, now this little guy really will be a Double D.," Hawken says as the first of us to get to hold his new nephew to be. "Double Dex." He holds Dex's tiny fingers in his strong hand. "Oh, we'll have so much fun with you little man. Uncle Hawk will teach you everything your daddy won't."

"Rory and Kinsley, we can't thank you enough," Colby says when there's a pause in conversation. "Knowing the girls were in good hands while we were in the air was at the very least a tiny bit of peace for those of us who may or may not have been ready to pull our hair out to get on the ground."

"We wouldn't have missed it for the world," Rory tells them. "That's what family is for."

"Truth." Kinsley nods with a sincere smile. "It was very much our pleasure to be able to help in any way. We'll always be here for you guys and your families."

"Speaking of family." All eyes are on me now as I hold Kinsley's hand in mine. "I think we should elope."

Gasps are heard all around but Kinsley's smile fades and she stares at me with confusion. "What?"

"Elope," I repeat. "You know...when two people run off and get married without having a big wedding?"

"Yeah, I know what it means. But why would you want—"

"Because I love you, Kinsley." I give her my best smile. "I'm so fucking in love with you I can't see straight half the time."

"Ain't that the truth," Zeke mumbles.

"I want to marry you, Kinsley, but I could give two shits about a big wedding, small wedding, no wedding, whatever. If we elope, you don't have to go through the stress of planning a wedding with your mother nagging you to do it her way."

Please say yes.

"That's true..."

"We could go to Hawaii. My sister's resort. Kamana Wanalaya."

Her eyes grow in excitement. "Oooh, I've always wanted to go to Hawaii!"

"I know."

"No fair!" Carissa pouts. "I want to go to Hawaii too!"

There's a sparkle in Kinsley's eyes. She's asking me the question without asking out loud and I give her all the approval she wants.

"Whatever you want, Kink."

She turns happily to her friends, her new family and squeals. "You guys can come too! Oh, my God! If we do this, will you all come? I know Quinton said you usually go to Key West but oh my God you guys, Hawaii!"

"Tell you what," Dex says, folding his arms over his chest. "You agree to marry Quinton and we'll absolutely change locations and come to Hawaii to help you celebrate."

She turns to me, her eyes glistening. "You really want this?"

"More than I've ever wanted anything in my life. Kinsley Ida Nippy Kendrick, I love you. Marry me in Hawaii."

"I love you too, Quinton. I love you so much!" She throws her arms around me squeezing me tightly.

"Wait," Dex interrupts with a furrowed brow. "Did he just call you Nippy?"

Kinsley throws her head back in a laugh. "Maaaybe."

Hawken nods. "Yeah I heard it too. Kinsley Ida? Nippy?"

"Oh fuck!" Dex tries to hold back his laugh. "Your initials spell KINK?"

"Maaaybe."

I wink and happily press my lips to hers. "Is that a yes, Kink?"

"Yes!" she squeals. "A thousand times, yes!"

The end

Want more Quinton and Kinsley?
Visit my website for their extended epilogue!
www.authorsusanrenee.com

Want more of the Chicago Red Tails?
Turn the page for an excerpt of
Zeke Miller's story.

BONUS GAME EXCERPT

Zeke

"A FLESHLIGHT? Are you serious, Landric?" I shout as I step out of Milo and Charlee's guest bathroom. "You have a fucking FLESHLIGHT sitting out in your guest shower?"

"What are you doing peeking in their shower, Miller?" Dex challenges from the dining room table where the rest of the group is seated for game night. Looks of surprise and snorts of laughter fill the room as I gesture inside the bathroom trying my best to rein in my own humored shock to no avail.

"Dude, the shower curtain was wide open when I went in there and Milo's got his fleshlight standing tall on the shower shelf like it's a statue on a goddamn living room mantle!"

Rory pulls an Uno card from the ones in her hand and places it on the discard pile. "Who keeps a flashlight in the shower?" She glances with a narrowed eye at a blushing tight-lipped Charlee. "Does Milo shower in the dark?"

Tatum leans over and whispers to her, "Not a flashlight, Ror. A *flesh*light."

Rory's brows pinch. "What's a—"

Hawken clears his throat, covering his mouth to hide his smirk as he performs a quick hand gesture for Rory.

She finally catches on and nearly chokes on a laugh. "Oooh. *Flesh*light..."

Colby shakes his head. "Poor Milo. Not even in the room to defend himself."

"Where'd he go?" I ask.

Charlee squeaks. "Changing Amelia's diaper."

Still horrified and amused I take my seat at the table next to Charlee. "My poor eyes. He could've fuckin' warned a man before leaving something like that around."

"Why? You want to give it a whirl, Zeke?" Dex laughs.

"Shut up, Asshole." I turn to Charlee. "What the hell does he even need that for? Do you not let the poor guy in or what?"

She bursts out a laugh, shaking her head as she plays a yellow SKIP card. "What can I say? That last trimester was a bitch so I bought it to keep him occupied while my baby factory was working overtime." She stands from her seat. "Plus, he showers in there when he gets home late at night and I'm already asleep, though I wasn't aware he had it on display. Sorry Zeke. I'll go get it. Oh, and you're skipped by the way."

"I got it, Goldilocks." Milo comes down the hall with a tiny bundle of joy clothed in pink footed pajamas on his shoulder, his large hand practically palming her entire body. "Don't get up." Charlee watches him lovingly as he holds their precious little girl against his body.

"It's perfectly normal for guys to have toys too." Kinsley pulls a yellow six from her hand and the play continues around the table. "Guys aren't exempt from having a little pleasured fun once in a while."

Charlee smirks. "Why do you think none of the other guys at this table have said a thing about Milo's fleshlight?"

Tatum snickers. "Because they all have their own flesh-lights just like that one in their own homes." She bumps Dex's shoulder with her own. "Dexter included."

"Oooh!" Kinsley sits back in her seat, glancing at Carissa, Charlee, and Tatum. "Did you three—"

"Yep." Carissa pops her P as she tosses a blue six onto the discard pile.

My brows furrow as I look around the table making the realization myself. "Wait. Hold up. You guys all got your own toys?" I gesture to the ladies. "From them?"

Colby and Dex try to hide their embarrassment much to Milo's amusement.

"We went shopping together and bought them at the same time," Carissa explains, playing a blue nine when it's her turn. "Sex is great and all, but when you're the size of a whale and your ankles are swollen larger than your forearms..."

"And all you want to do is sleep," Tatum adds, tossing a WILD card onto the pile. "Green."

Charlee adds, "Yeah. And you horny lot have a good game and need to fuck the energy and adrenaline away so you can sleep at night when you get home..."

Kinsley's jaw drops and she turns to Quinton. "So that's the secret! Sounds like I need to go shopping!"

"Wait." Quinton's eyes grow and his cheeks pinken.

"What's that supposed to mean? You trying to tell me you don't like when I—"

"Uht, duht, duht, duht, duht." Kinsley silences Quinton with a finger against his lips. "Let's stop you right there because yes I always love it but good Lord you guys are horny as hell at two in the morning and my body does not need to be bending that way between the hours of about midnight and six A.M."

Everyone at the table laughs, including me, though deep down I know I'm not nearly as happy for my friends as I am jealous. The guys all found their happy-ever-afters. They're all with the women of their dreams, and deservedly so, but me? I'm the loser whose wife left him—unexpectedly leaving me to raise Elsie on my own.

I should've been first. It should be me living a happy life. I was with Lori before Colby ever met Carissa. Before Charlee knocked on Milo's door several years ago. We were happy and starting our own family, but she was gone before our Key West trip that year. She was gone by the time Dex found Tatum. She was gone before Hawken and Rory finally fell in love. She was gone before Kinsley and Quinton got together. Now, instead of being a happily married man and world's best father I'm the guy who skips the hang outs at Pringle's after our home games so I can say good night to my kid who hasn't seen me in two or three days. I'm the guy who's waking up at the ass crack of dawn to get everything ready for the day before dropping Elsie off with my parents for God knows how long. I'm the guy who has to take his daughter to her grandparents several nights a week in order to do my job because there's no mom at home to help me.

I'm the guy who wonders if I'll ever get to be genuinely happy the way the rest of these guys are now. The one who wishes he had time to even consider meeting another woman let alone fall in love with her.

"Listen, I'm just going to say this once and then I promise I'll shut up and stop being a Debbie Downer. But you guys all have it incredibly lucky. You have each other to come home to. You have each other to help out with parenting woes." The play finally gets back around the table to me so I play a card and hold up the only other one in my hand. "Uno. Just...I don't know..." I shake my head. "When things get tough, and I promise they'll get tough, remember how blessed you all are. Talk to each other. Yell it out if you have to, though not in front of the kids, of course. Do whatever you have to do to keep the spark alive and remember why you love each other, because it's no fun when the spark snuffs out and you're alone."

Silence falls over the table.

"Uh...Miller?" Hawken cringes.

"Yeah?"

"You alright over there? You haven't said something that deep since...uh..."

"Ever." Quinton finishes Hawken's statement.

"Yeah." Hawk nods. "What he said."

Slouching in my chair, I look around the table at everyone's pitying and concerned faces. "Yeah. Sorry guys. I promise I'm fine. I really am."

"You know you're allowed to not be fine, right?" Colby throws a Draw Four card onto the pile and calls out, "Red."

"It's not that I'm not fine. I am. Truly. Elsie is fine. She's a happy kid who doesn't know any different than the life she has, but..." I sigh. "I'm not going to lie. It sucks having to take her to my parents all the time. It's like they're raising her and I'm the fun uncle that shows up from time to time. I love my parents. I do. And I very much appreciate that they've stepped up and been willing and able to help out, but let's be honest here, they should be enjoying retirement. They should be enjoying being the grandparents that get to come over and spoil their granddaughter from time to time. Not the ones putting her in time out or making sure she eats a balanced meal several times a day. That's my job."

"But you can't always be there." Charlee shrugs. "It's the nature of the career. Everybody knows that. Certainly, all of us. Nobody blames you at all for the way you parent your kid, Zeke. You're doing the absolute best you can. We love Elsie to pieces."

"Am I though? Am I really doing what's best for her? She barely lives in her own home for Pete's sake. How is that good for her? And she starts preschool. Someone has to be available to pick her up mid-day."

"What do you *want* to do?" Colby asks me. "What does the perfect life with Elsie look like to you right now?"

I scoff lightly. "I'm not sure the perfect life can exist for us right now. To her, the perfect life is one where both of her parents are around every moment of every day. I mean this summer has been magical because I've been home with her more often than not. We've spent so much time together these last couple of months, but the regular season is about to get into full swing and that means we're back to several days and nights a week away from each other. I just want to be able to come home at the end of the day and be a dad, you know?"

"And maybe date again?"

"Hmph." I roll my eyes. "That'll be the day. With our schedule? Who's going to want to date me when I can't commit to anything for a good nine to ten months out of the year?"

"There are good women out there, Zeke," Rory states. "Women who understand the business and would support it. I mean look at all of us."

"Is there a list out there or something?" I tease. "A list of promising hockey wives and girlfriends? That might make things a hell of a lot easier."

Rory smiles. "That's an innovative idea. I'll have to do some internet research."

"What about a nanny?" Carissa suggests. "Someone who could help with Elsie in your home so when your workday is done, you don't have to spend time traveling to the opposite side of town to pick her up only to bring her home and put her to bed and do it all again the next day? If you had someone at the house with her, you could be home in fifteen minutes and have more time to spend with her."

"I've thought about a nanny." I nod. "But you're talking like, a full-time live-in kind of deal?"

She shrugs. "Yeah."

"And that isn't weird? Asking some random person to pick up their lives and move into my house?"

"It's not like you don't have the space," Quinton reminds me. "You have more than enough bedrooms in your house. The nanny would have plenty of space so it's not like you would be on top of each other all the time."

"I mean...unless he wants to be on top of her," Dex jokes. Hawken shakes his head at the absurdity of Dex, but he laughs just the same.

I roll my eyes. "Dude, that's gross. I'm not going to fuck the goddamn nanny."

"You say that now," he smirks, "but have you met the nanny yet? I mean, maybe she'll be hot. You could add that as a requirement." He gestures up in the air as he calls out his headline. "Full time nanny for hire. Hot as fuck is a must."

"Fuck you, Dexter." I finally laugh. "I can only imagine the kind of people that would be lined up for that interview."

"Right? It's genius if you ask me. And they'd all be lucky as hell. Man or woman, cause you're a catch, Zeke." He winks.

"Thanks, I think."

"Think about it." Carissa smiles. "If you want some help coming up with a job posting or a list of responsibilities, we're happy to help any way we can. You deserve to be happy just as much as the rest of us."

"Yeah. Thanks." I nod. "I'll definitely give it some thought."

A full-time live-in nanny. I gave some thought to the idea of a part-time nanny as a glorified babysitter before, but never the idea of having someone in my home full-time. That could take some getting used to.

But if it's in Elsie's best interest...

There's nothing I wouldn't do for her.

She's my world.

"Missessss..." Dex looks down at the resume in front of him. "Fahrtinga? Did I pronounce that right?" He makes a guttural noise with his mouth trying not to laugh out loud at this poor woman's name. As annoyed as I might be at Dex's immaturity, I'd be lying if I said I was taking any part of this interview seriously. I should've just said thanks but no thanks, but Tatum and Carissa thought her resume looked good and that I should overlook the odd last name.

Seriously though, am I really going to live with a woman whose last name is Fahrtinga?

Please let someone else's interview be better than this.

For the love of God.

"Yes, that's correct." The stout older woman nods with a stern scowl.

I give her a polite smile and shake her hand, taking notice of her firm, confident handshake. "Thanks for coming in today, Mrs. Fahrtinga. It's lovely to meet you. Please allow me to introduce you to a few of my colleagues." I gesture down the table. "This is Dex Foster, Milo Landric, and Colby Nelson. They, like me, have children so they know the rigors of the job and what might be needed for my daughter, Elsie, so I asked them to help me out with the interview process."

"Fair enough," she answers.

I spend a few minutes explaining what I'm looking for from a full-time nanny and then give the guys a few moments to ask questions so that I can sit, listen, and watch. More than anything I really want to get a good feel of who these potential hires are and what their personalities might be like when they're around my kid all day.

"Mrs. Fahrtinga," Colby starts. "Do you have children of your own?"

"Four grown children, yes." She nods without as much as a smile. "Two of my daughters work at the Color Me Happy salon on the southeast side of town. And one of my sons works for the sanitation department."

That's three...she said four.

"And the fourth child?"

Her face remains neutral as she answers curtly. "Incarcerated."

Jesus.

What the hell for?

Drug possession?

Theft?

Murder?

Rather than ask further questions about it, Colby continues on. "And what was your parenting style as they were growing up? Did you have strict schedules for them to follow or were they free to do a lot of whatever they wanted?"

But more importantly, why the hell is your son in jail?

Mrs. Fahrtinga opens her mouth to answer Colby but I interrupt her because my gut won't let me not ask. "I'm sorry, Mrs. Fahrtinga. I don't mean to interrupt with such a personal question but would you be comfortable telling us why your son is incarcerated?"

She rolls her eyes slightly and I can't tell if she's annoyed with me for asking or her son for getting himself into trouble.

"They accused him of taking part in a child pornography ring online."

"Oookay." I stand with force almost knocking over my chair and step to the door. "Thank you for coming in Mrs. Fahrtinga but I won't be needing anymore of your time. I'm certain this job is not going to be the right fit."

She pops up from her chair, her eyes wide.

"But—"

"There are no buts, Ma'am."

Like hell if I'm going to let anything like that even remotely close to my child.

"We're done here, Mrs. Fahrtinga. Have a lovely day."

"So, you said you have kids of your own Ms. Silverman?"

"Yes," she answers with a smile. "Six kids. Three different fathers. Will they each be getting their own bedrooms when we move in? I'll especially need to make sure Nico and Nash are separated. They don't always get along and tend to end up fighting. And Jennica, she sleep-walks a lot so she'll need to be on the main floor so she doesn't fall down the stairs."

Next.

"Oh, I do have a list of allergies I should go over with you if I'm going to be in your home," our next interviewer adds after our round of questioning. She's a middle-aged woman, petite, with long brown hair and silver wire-rimmed glasses she pushes back from the bridge of her nose. So far, her interview has been great and her disposition completely opposite that of Mrs. Fahrtinga. Thank God. The more I get to know her, the more I think Elsie might like her.

"Absolutely. I want you to be as comfortable as possible in my home."

She hands me her list of allergies and I read down through the extensive file.

Carrots

Beets

Watermelon

Green grapes

Wheat bread

Flour

Milk

Feathers

Cats

Dogs

Goats

Gerbils

Hamsters

Grass

Maple trees

Pine trees

Oak trees

Ragweed

Marigolds

Dandelions

Garlic

Pesto

Rosemary

Cotton

Dust

Mold

Mildew

I'm also sensitive to most scented soaps, perfumes, and candles.

I hand the paper back to her and nod kindly. "Thank you for your time, but I don't think this will be the right fit."

"Ms. Bendit," Milo begins, glancing down at our next applicant. "Can you explain the three-year gap in your resume between your last job and now? Did you go back to school...or..."

"Uh..." Her face pinkens and she shifts in her seat. "No. I didn't go back to school. I've actually been gainfully employed these past three years making a very solid income."

"Oh, great." Milo clicks his pen. "Can I ask what you do for a living currently then?"

"I sell my panties."

What. The. Fuck?

All of us look up from the table, speechless.

Milo clears his throat, his brows furrowed. "I'm sorry?"

"My panties," she repeats. "I sell my panties online."

"Do you design underwear or something?" I ask her with morbid curiosity.

She shakes her head. "Oh no. I wear them for the day and then I package them up and send them out to the next buyer."

Dex leans forward in his chair. "You sell...used panties?"

She nods. "Yes."

He cocks his head. "How does that work exactly?"

Oh my God, I can't believe he's asking this.

What am I saying? It's Dex, of course I believe it.

"It just depends on what clients want. Sometimes they'll ask for one day of wear. Sometimes they'll ask me to wear them for two or three days. I've had a guy ask me to masturbate wearing a pair and I even had one who asked that I pee on them before sending."

She cannot be serious.

Dex smiles like a goofy teenager. "Fascinating. And what do they do with—"

"Thank you for your time, Ms. Bendit," Colby says for me as I'm still trying to pick my jaw off the floor. "But I think we're going to go in another direction."

"I apologize for my frankness here, Ms. Wiltzer, but before we get any further into this interview, I need to ask if you sell pictures of child pornography online or if you send out used panties to willing buyers?"

The young woman, who can't be a day over twenty, laughs. "Good Lord, no."

"Thank Christ." Dex sighs with relief. "It's been a day around here."

"But I do run a podcast called Orgasmic ASMR."

The fuck?

Milo chuckles, shaking his head. "Aaaand thank you for your time."

When the last applicant walks out of the room, Carissa and Kinsley walk in with our lunch delivery.

"Lunch time gentlemen." Carissa smiles, lifting several bags filled with pasta and breadsticks from one of our favorite Italian restaurants. Time to carb-load before afternoon practice. "Any luck? Did you find someone good for Elsie?"

"That's a huge negative." I scoff, exhausted already and it's just barely noon. "Are there seriously no good people in Chicago who love kids and are, I don't know, normal?"

"Uh oh." Kinsley cringes. "That doesn't sound good."

Colby chuckles, his face half cringing, half smiling. "I would've never believed it myself if I hadn't been here listening to some of these whack jobs."

I slump down in my seat, opening my container of pasta. "Something tells me this is going to be harder than I thought. I won't let just anybody around my daughter twenty-four-seven. I have to find the right person, or I have to figure out a plan B...and C...and D."

Kinsley tips her head to the side, chewing on the inside of her mouth. "You know, I might know someone."

"Really?"

I would trust Kinsley's taste in people. She's fun. Energetic. Nice. Friendly. She's been a great fit for Quinton.

She nods. "Yeah. Great girl. She works at the animal

shelter. She's the one who introduced me to Nutsack, and we kind of clicked right away. Her story is...well, I should let her tell it. But I know she's been looking for something a little more full-time than what she's currently doing. And she actually used to be an elementary school teacher."

"Well that sounds promising," Milo says, taking in a huge mouthful of his spaghetti.

"Yeah. Maybe."

"I'll call her and see what she thinks. If she's interested, is it okay if I pass along your contact information?"

"She doesn't sell feet pictures online does she?"

Kinsley smirks. "Not unless they're the boudoir pictures I took of her last year."

"So, she's married?"

"Uh, no." Kinsley shakes her head. "Not married. Again, I should let her tell her story. It's not mine to tell. But trust me, she's as normal as normal can be and has a great personality. Aaaaand she's hot."

Dex sits up, his brows peaked in interest. "Oh yeah? How hot are we talking?"

"Uh, like I'd do her if she swung that way. Her boudoir shoot was fire."

Dex claps me on the shoulder. "Just what our man Zeke needs! A hot nanny! Let's bring her in."

I roll my eyes at Dex but give a nod to Kinsley. "Alright. I trust you. Thanks Kinsley."

"Sure. Anything I can do to help."

ACKNOWLEDGMENTS

Special Thanks to my Patreon subscribers for sticking with me in so many aspects of my writing process!

Katie Powell

Dawn Bryant

Betsy Chapman

Lindsay Brewer

Interested in joining my Patreon
or learning more about it?
Visit my website:
Authorsusanrenee.com

BOOKS BY SUSAN RENEE

All books are available in Kindle Unlimited

The Chicago Red Tails Series

Off Your Game – Colby Nelson

Unfair Game – Milo Landric

Beyond the Game – Dex Foster

Forbidden Game – Hawken Malone

Saving the Game – Quinton Shay

Bonus Game – Zeke Miller

Remember Colby's brother, Elias Nelson? Here's his story! A spinoff of my Bardstown Series of small town interconnected romances!

NO ONE NEEDS TO KNOW: Accidental Pregnancy

(Elias and Whitney's story)

(Bardstown Series Prequel – Previously entitled SEVEN)

I LOVED YOU THEN

The Bardstown Series

I LIKE ME BETTER: Enemies to Lovers

YOU ARE THE REASON: Second Chance

BEAUTIFUL CRAZY: Friends to Lovers

TAKE YOU HOME: Boss's Daughter

ROMANTIC COMEDIES

Smooch: Arya's Story

Smooches: Hannah's Story

Smooched: Kim's Story

Hole Punched

You Don't Know Jack Schmidt

(The Schmidt Load Novella Book 1)

Schmidt Happens

(The Schmidt Load Novella Book 2)

My Schmidt Smells Like Roses

(The Schmidt Load Novella Book 3)

CONTEMPORARY ROMANCE

The Village series

I'm Fine (The Village Duet #1)

Save Me (The Village Duet #2)

*The Village Duet comes with a content warning.

Please be sure to check out this book's Amazon page before downloading.

Solving Us

(Big City New Adult Romance)

Surprising Us (a Solving Us novella)

ABOUT THE AUTHOR

Susan Renee wants to live in a world where paint doesn't smell, Hogwarts is open twenty-four/seven, and everything is covered in glitter. An indie romance author, Susan has written about everything from tacos to tow-trucks, loves writing romantic comedies but also enjoys creating an emotional angsty story from time to time. She lives in Ohio with her husband, kids, two dogs and a cat. Susan holds a Bachelor and Master's degree in Sass and Sarcasm and enjoys laughing at memes, speaking in GIFs and spending an entire day jumping down the TikTok rabbit hole. When she's not writing or playing the role of Mom, her favorite activity is doing the Care Bear stare with her closest friends.

facebook.com/authorsusanrenee

x.com/indiesusanrenee

instagram.com/authorsusanrenee

tiktok.com/@authorsusanrenee

amazon.com/author/susanrenee

goodreads.com/susanrenee

bookbub.com/authors/susan-renee

patreon.com/RomanceReadersandWishfulWriters

Made in United States
North Haven, CT
15 June 2024

53684887R00174